AN UNRULY LITTLE ANIMAL

A NOVEL

SCOTT RANDALL

AN UNRULY LITTLE ANIMAL

A NOVEL

LIVRES DC BOOKS

Cover design by Leaven Agency.
Author photographs by Molly Wei-Randall.
Book designed and typeset by Leaven Agency.
Edited by Keith Henderson.

Legal Deposit, Bibliothèque et Archives nationales du Québec
and Library and Archives Canada, 3rd trimester, 2023.

Library and Archives Canada Cataloguing in Publication
Title: An unruly little animal : a novel / Scott Randall.
Names: Randall, Scott, 1970- author.
Description: First Canadian edition
Identifiers: Canadiana 2023045268X | ISBN 9781927599600 (softcover)
Classification: LCC PS8585.A5454 U57 2023 | DDC C813/.54—dc23

This is a work of fiction. Names, characters, places, and events are either products of the author's imagination or are employed fictitiously. Any resemblance to actual events or locales or persons, living or dead, is entirely coincidental.

For our publishing activities, DC Books gratefully acknowledges the financial support of SODEC and of the Government of Canada through Canadian Heritage and the Canada Book Fund. Nous reconnaissons l'aide financière du gouvernement du Canada.

Société de développement des entreprises culturelles Québec

Canada

Printed and bound in Canada.
Interior pages printed on Enviro Book, an environmentally responsible paper containing 100% post-consumer recycled fibre, processed chlorine-free and manufactured using biogas energy.
Distributed by LitDistCo.

DC Books
5 Fenwick Ave., Montreal West
Quebec H4X 1P3
www.dcbooks.ca

for Molly Wei-Randall, whom we adore

CHAPTER 1

On the morning of Richmond East Elementary's Career Day, Darby Tamm sits alone in the kitchenette of his townhome, picks at a dry bowl of Toasted Bran Nut Clusters, and worries. What he worries about, however, does not really represent what he is worried about. Darby's using sublimation, which Darby's mom has told him can be a useful way to refocus his mind when it gets stuck on an unproductive thought. The trick works by distracting his mind with a whole entirely different and more productive thought, and this morning, Darby has chosen to worry about his Toasted Bran Nut Clusters – or more specifically, why the milk carton contains only a slosh of milk and why he has to eat his cereal dry.

When school day mornings go as scheduled, Darby comes downstairs to the galley kitchenette before his mom, and he pours his own cereal, filling the bowl almost-but-not-quite to the brim. Too close to the brim is a mistake because the clusters are buoyant and – cause and effect – they will rise until they tumble out over the top. With time, Darby has learned that a good four centimetres from the brim is the ideal. This morning, though, when he lifted the Beatrice 1% milk carton from the fridge and felt its weight, he right away knew that something was amiss. No more than a single slosh of milk remained. While he could have emptied out the last of the 1% and at least moistened the bottommost clusters, Darby opted for dry cereal instead. A slosh of milk is not enough for a bowl of cereal, but it is enough for the morning mug of orange pekoe his mother will make when she comes downstairs. Dry cereal isn't ideal, of course, but Darby's larger question is why his mom forgot to buy more milk in the first place.

Since his mom writes out both a weekend and a midweek shopping list – one major and one minor – and she posts them in plain sight on the refrigerator door next to the four-month calendar page detailing school trips, dental appointments, and the prearranged weekend visitation schedule with Darby's dad, the chances of running out of either staples and sundries are quite low. In fact, Darby cannot recall ever running out of mint toothpaste, multigrain bread, cheddar cheese, or milk, and chewing on a single dry Toasted Bran Nut Cluster, Darby puzzles over this puzzle. He doesn't want to choke, so he chews slowly. Even though this will certainly make breakfast longer, he doesn't think it'll throw off his and his mom's morning schedule.

Upstairs, the shower water runs, and when the sound stops – if all goes according to schedule – Darby's mom will call downstairs.

"Are you dressed and eating?" she calls down.

"Yes."

Next, he will hear the hair dryer, and shortly after that, his mom will come into the galley kitchenette where they will eat together and prepare their pack lunches. As with most routines, Darby finds their school day schedule reassuring.

"Down in a few minutes," she calls.

Because she works as an elementary school teacher, Darby's mom tends to be all upbeat and chipper – she rustles his hair and kisses his head and tells him she loves being his mom when she drops him off in the Richmond East Elementary drop-off lane – but oftentimes lately, Darby has wondered if her upbeat and chipper exterior isn't a fake ruse. He's wondered if perhaps her crooked smile and contented expression drop away just as soon as he exits out the car and walks away off to the schoolyard. Perhaps she flips the radio from *CBC Ottawa This Morning* to CRFB Contemporary Folk and Adult Alternative and listens to sad and wistful acoustic music. Perhaps she stops pretending that she is slowly-and-surely adjusting to Darby's dad leaving the executive townhome and moving into a low-rise apartment complex.

Or maybe not. Maybe she goes on pretending. Maybe the fake ruse isn't just for Darby's sake, but for her own as well because she's trying to trick herself. Her own bit of sublimation.

On the kitchen counter radio, *CBC Ottawa This Morning* says that the time has come for the half-hour news update, which means that Darby and his mother are still on schedule. When he was younger in grades Kindergarten through Four and they lived in Calgary, Darby's parents allowed only music or chapter book audiobooks on the kitchen counter radio and in the car because not all news stories are appropriate for all ages. Last November, however, Darby's mom decided that he'd reached an age at which he could sometimes decide appropriate and inappropriate by himself for himself. As a recognition of his increasing maturity, Darby appreciates the local, national, and international news of the day, and some days, the stories give him and his mom unexpected topics of conversation. Other days, though, a particular news story is less welcome.

This morning, for example, the lead story that begins the half-hour news update tells of an incident in the Ottawa suburb of Kanata, where two evenings earlier, a detached single home caught fire and burned. A thirty-nine-year-old real estate broker and a thirty-seven-year-old personal care worker along with their two teenaged daughters perished in the incident, which the fire marshal says originated in the garage of the family home. Names of the deceased are being withheld from the public because trace elements of accelerant have been found in the master bedroom and the children's bedroom located above the garage. Police are treating the deaths as suspicious, and the investigation is ongoing.

Exactly what is appropriate and what is inappropriate can be hard to know, but Darby suspects that neither he nor his mom really needs to hear more about this news story. He leans across the breakfast nook and flips the radio to the compact disc function, pressing play on Irving Berlin and "Oh, How I Hate to Get Up in the Morning." The music is a remainder-bin-compilation collection of American Songbook songs by Gershwin and Porter and Berlin that Darby bought for his mom at a Calgary mall three birthdays ago.

Because she teaches primary-junior music, many of the gifts Darby has gotten his mom for her birthdays, Christmases, and Mother's Days have been thematically connected to her career and main hobby-interest. Compact music discs and iTunes cards, but also a gold-coloured violin brooch, a treble clef tea cozy, and a set of decorative woodwind Christmas tree ornaments in the shape of a bassoon, oboe, and piccolo. Darby's dad says that when someone has a hobby or a real strong interest, it makes buying meaningful and personalized presents much easier. Darby's mom says the Gershwin, Porter, and Berlin compilation CD has a special place in her heart of hearts because it was the first gift Darby ever picked out on his own and paid for on his own with chore money. The music never fails to put her in a good mood, and Darby thinks it'll make her happy this morning.

It does. After a few nut clusters more, Darby's mom skip-walks in between the kitchenette counters, puts the kettle on, and swings open the fridge singing along to "Oh, How I Hate to Get Up in the Morning," dah-dah-dahhing the parts where she has forgotten or never really knew the song's lyrics. From the cupboard, she removes the sleepy bear mug and the tea canister.

"Red Rose," she says.

"Only in Canada, hmmmm?" Darby says.

This is an old commercial that his mom told him about and they watched together on YouTube, and it has become a running joke between them. She says running jokes with your kid are a good thing and one of the best parts about parenthood.

"Only in Canada, hmmmm? Pity," she says, which was the end of the commercial and has become the repeated punchline in the running joke.

A slosh of milk will be good enough for one mug of tea, but once she pours it and empties the carton, Darby tenses. He imagines her emptying the used carton and flattening it for the recycling basket under the sink in a socially responsible manner, and then – cause and effect – she will realize that she forgot to buy milk. She'll wonder how she forgot, and she'll think about how she has too, too much on her mind since moving to a whole new city and starting a new job and watching her marriage fall apart. In Darby's opinion, this is why sublimation doesn't really work. Sublimation doesn't really work because too often the worry he uses to hide another worry grows into a whole entire new worry in itself.

After his mom empties the carton of 1% skim, though, nothing at all happens. Well, not nothing. She turns to him to say good morning with a quick kiss on the top of his hair, which he still likes even though he has to pretend he doesn't.

"We are excited about Career Day?" she asks.

"We are," he answers.

To project a chipper and upbeat mood, she will sometimes talk in an exaggerated chipper and upbeat manner.

"Looking sharp." She points to his cobalt blue button-down shirt and tan slacks.

"Thank you. Freshly ironed by my mom."

"You're welcome," she says. "Are you worried about your presentation?"

This is another reason sublimation does not work. No matter how Darby focuses on one thought to avoid another thought, and no matter how well his mind is able to replace one worry with another, the world outside of his mind does not cooperate. The world outside of his mind too often reminds him that he's just only sublimating, which is the case this morning because he's also been trying not to worry and think about the Career Fair Pair Presentation.

"I guess I am," he says.

When Darby first arrived to Ottawa and enrolled in Richmond East Elementary in October, his original teacher Mr. Henderson was just then dividing up the enriched grade five class and setting up presentation partners for February. Everyone was allowed to request partners but since Darby was brand new to the class, one partner seemed pretty much the same as the next, and Mr. Henderson wound up assigning him to Jennie Phelps-Christianson, whom nobody else at all wanted to work with.

Then, Jennie talked Darby into Veterinary Dentistry as their Career Fair Pair Presentation topic. Not ideal, but she did turn out to be a hard worker. Back in December, she performed solo in front of the whole entire school plus parents and grandparents at the Winter Holiday Concert Celebration, so Darby knew she had public speaking skills too. For him, the idea of presenting in front of his classmates made his mouth dry all the way to the back of his throat, which didn't make eating his cereal any easier.

"What is Jennifer wearing?"

"She prefers Jennie."

"*Ah, bien sur*. What is Jennie wearing?"

Darby shrugs again. "*Je ne sais pas*."

He and his mom sometimes slip into French because at some point after the move to bilingual Ottawa, they agreed that everything is kind of funnier in French. Another running joke.

"*Quel dommage.*"

Though she was the one to insist upon business and office professional clothing for their presentation, Darby cannot quite imagine Jennie Phelps-Christianson dressed up. In class, she tends to wear golf shirts in unlikely solid colours like lime green and pastel yellow. Their classmates Alexander and Them make fun of her for her absence-of-style style, but Jennie doesn't seem to notice, which is just as well. Alexander and Them will also most probably make fun of Darby's cobalt blue button-down shirt and tan slacks, which kind of make him look like one of the mall kiosk guys who try to get people to buy a new cellphone plan every time they pass by on the way to Booster Juice.

"We don't even have to dress up," Darby says. "Mr. Henderson would have cared, but Monsieur won't care at all."

Monsieur Substitute took over the grade five class after Mr. Henderson had an unfortunate car accident and drove himself off a bridge and into a coma back in November. Whatever Mr. Henderson is thinking or not thinking about in his coma, Darby's pretty sure it isn't business casual clothing.

"Well, I think Mr. Henderson was right." With her mug of tea and a banana from the banana hanger, Darby's mom slides in across from him in the breakfast nook. It seems like maybe she won't even notice the absence of milk after all.

"There's no need for a top hat and fancy schmancy tuxedo, and it's important to be comfortable," she says, "but you'd be surprised what a difference nice clothing can make. It can affect your mood and your confidence, and it can make all the difference in the world."

Darby doesn't say she's told him this before, but she has told him this before. In teachers' college, his mom learned that shabby or uncomfortable clothing will only distract students from what the teacher is saying, but overly formal clothing with a sleek, expensive tie or extra ostentatious jewelry will also draw too much attention to itself. Business and office professional clothing is just the right middle ground.

"And you're ready for the weekend as well?" his mother asks.

"Yes, also ready for the weekend."

"Don't forget to bring your *New Horizons* reader and a pair of long johns. Your father is taking you to the ice sculptures in Gatineau."

Sometimes, Ottawa grows so cold that it is too cold to snow, which is something the city has in common with Calgary. Good for ice sculpture exhibits, but not for much else, and long underwear is often necessary. This colder-than-snow weekend is supposed to be a mom weekend, but because it's Friday and because Darby's dad is coming to Richmond East Elementary's Career Day to talk to the enriched grade-five class about the career of a mechanical engineer this afternoon, plans have changed, and it's going to be a weekend visitation weekend.

Darby would have preferred his mom coming to class to talk about her career as an elementary music educator, but since she needs to be at Woodfield Elementary all day and her contract is only temporary and personal days are unpaid leave days, such a preference is unrealistic. Also, everybody who's ever been to school knows what a teacher does, so there'd be no point at all. With his dad coming near the end of the day for the Career Parent presentations, it only makes sense that he'll drive Darby home and it only makes sense to switch weekends. The visit to his dad's low-rise apartment and the mechanical engineering presentation are two more topics Darby has been trying to unfocus on, so sublimation has again failed him. Twice.

"Nervous?" his mom asks.

Since he's not all too good hiding his feelings from his mom, Darby has learned that changing the topic can be an effective strategy at such moments.

"What are you teaching today?" he asks.

"You're nervous?" She looks at him with up-turned eyebrows that mean she wants him to talk about things he should talk about, but then she smiles instead. This is kind of her way of telling Darby that both-you-and-I-knew-full-well-we-need-to-pursue-this-matter-but-I-love-you-so-I-won't-make-you-uncomfortable.

"I will be teaching musical notation. First to the grade fives and then to the fours after morning recess. I'm using the xylophone and a kind of game. *Write That Riff.* My own variation on *Name That Tune* but the students are in pairs trying to write out notes."

"I can name that tune in eight notes," Darby says.

"I can name that tune in seven notes," his mom says.

"Five notes."

"I challenge. Name that tune." His mother grins.

"It's dah, dah, dah, something something, something." Another running joke.

"Most of the students like the lesson well enough."

Darby and his parents played *Name That Tune* for the first time when he was in Kindergarten and they drove to Calgary Zoo, but that time was mostly "Old MacDonald's Farm," "Bingo Was His Name-O," and "Stay Awake." They played it in a more serious and challenging manner later on during a trip to Fort McMurray where his mom spoke at the Northern Access Curriculum Development Conference and then again on another car trip to Winnipeg where his dad networked for long-term employment opportunities at an Alternative Energy Symposium.

Darby's mom did best at *Name That Tune*, of course, because she teaches music and knows many instruments. Her big joke to new classes is that she teaches students to play but she also teaches guitars to strum, cellos to hum, drums to beat, and recorders to bleat. Before his degree and professional designation, Darby's dad was in a university band called *Sea Monkey See, Sea Monkey Do*, which was a big part of the reason his parents once-upon-a-time fell in love and became a family. For whatever reason, though, Darby's dad wasn't all too adept at naming tunes during long car trips, and he was usually the first one to grow tired of the game.

"So what are you nervous about?" his mom asks.

After the downturn, when they went to Brandon and Surrey, where his dad had follow-up job interview opportunities, they played the game again, but after that, they stopped going on too many trips. Their longest family drive was Calgary to Ottawa last year because Iogen Enterprises offered his dad a permanent position with pension and benefits, but no one was in the mood to play *Name That Tune* on that drive.

"Everyone feels nervous about public speaking," Darby's mom says.

It's rude not to answer, so Darby nods. His nervousness comes from Career Fair Pair Presentations worries and from his father's mechanical engineer Career Parent Presentation and from weekend visitation worries, of course, but all three worries combine together also. If the presentation does not go well, Darby's dad will know right away, and the disappointment will be a whole entire weekend disappointment. What he is nervous about feels like too much to talk about.

"We can change the topic?" he asks.

His mom waits a beat, and he knows she's waiting to give him a safe and comfortable and judgement-free space to enter into and discuss what is on his mind and what might be troubling him. It's a long beat.

"Yes," she says, "we can change the topic."

The November weekend that his father moved into a low-rise apartment complex exactly coincided with the weekend that Mr. Henderson drove off a bridge and into a coma, and Darby has connected the two in his mind even though he rationally knows that two events closely connected to one another in time are not necessarily cause-and-effect linked to one another. That kind of thinking is a fallacy of causation and untrue – but it's also hard to shake. The move from Calgary to Ottawa, the teacher's unfortunate accident, and weekend visitations – all of these events have become connected, and Darby wishes he could sublimate all of them but he can't.

He can't not think about how depressing his dad's apartment is. And he can't not think about how his dad makes a big deal about cooking healthy homemade meals and not buying restaurant takeout food, but his dad's idea of healthy is a wholegrain meatless meatloaf. And he can't not think about how his dad usually only takes him to places like the History Museum, the War Museum and the Royal Canadian Mint – which was believe-it-or-not even more sad than the War Museum. Back before, when they both lived together in the same place, Darby and his dad used to build Lego together for whole afternoons and it was something they both liked, so Darby doesn't at all understand why they don't just do that during the weekend visitation weekends instead of outing after outing.

"That cereal doesn't look very appetizing," his mom says.

"It's good this way."

Once, just before he moved out, Darby's dad took him to Le Parc Safari, a combination petting-zoo-water-and-amusement-park-drive-through-safari in Quebec. The outing should have been a good outing, but the fatal flaw in that plan was the two-hour drive. Without his mom there to play entertainment and social coordinator, the car was filled with nothing but awkward conversation, and it turned out the whole entire father-son trip was a fake-out prelude to the trial separation announcement.

"It's good that way? It isn't too dry?" His mom points to his cereal bowl.

"It's good this way," he repeats, and to prove his point, he spoons a whole entire spoonful of Toasted Bran Nut Clusters into his mouth.

"Yogurt. Have you ever tried cereal with yogurt?"

At the thought, his mom gets up and retrieves two fruit bottoms from a snack-pack in the fridge. Blueberry and wildberry. She separates the two yogurt cups with a satisfying snap crack, a sound and sensation that Darby and his mom long ago agreed was a most pleasing audible and tactile experience, and they both grin and nod in silent acknowledgement of this shared pleasure.

"Wildberry," Darby says. "Please."

He scoops out the white yogurt onto his clusters of bran and nut, letting the wildberry syrup pour down on top.

"You should mix it first." She demonstrates with her own blueberry syrup.

Darby shrugs. "It's good this way."

"It's better mixed up first."

"I do know how to eat yogurt."

"Fair enough."

The worst part of the Le Parc Safari trip came afterwards when Darby realized that his dad didn't just all-of-a-sudden-and-out-of-the-blue come up with the idea of a father-son getaway. His mom and dad must have talked about it because they both knew they were arguing too often and too intensely and they knew what was coming. Though he didn't want to, Darby could imagine their conversation.

MOTHER:

Harold, we need to set aside some time to discuss how to best make the separation less intrusive in Darby's day-to-day life.

FATHER:

I think we've agreed to call this a temporary trial separation, Doreen.

MOTHER:

Yes, fine, Harold. We need to set aside some time to discuss how to best make what we're calling a temporary trial separation less intrusive in Darby's day-to-day life.

FATHER:

Thank you, Doreen. I do believe using the proper terms will keep matters clearer for both of us in the long term.

MOTHER:

Not at all Harold, but I'm afraid word choice isn't the issue at present, and what is at issue at present is what kind of weekend excursions will both engage an eleven-year-old boy and distract him from the fact that he has been uprooted from the only home he has ever known and relocated to a whole new city only to learn that after thirteen years of a relatively happy and somewhat stable marriage, his darling father has up and decided to abandon all responsibilities and strike out on his own.

FATHER:

Doreen, I think perhaps now you are the one to drift from the issue at hand.

Darby's throat lumps thinking about the conversation, and he chooses to think about the better moments of the Le Parc Safari trip. As they drove highway 40 south of Montreal toward Hemmingford where Parc Safari was, they passed over the St Lawrence River and his father took the moment as an opportunity to explain the difference between suspension bridges and cantilever bridges. This talk led to his father's thoughts on the relative importance of chemical, civil, and electrical engineering compared to mechanical engineering – and specifically, how civil, electrical, and chemical engineering often rely upon the foundational machinery developed by mechanical engineers – and the topic wasn't exhausted until they were nearly in the petting-zoo-water-and-amusement-park-drive-through-safari parking lot.

Now reconsidering the conversation his mom and dad might or might not have had, Darby crunches on a yogurt-covered cluster and the throat lump threatens to return until he once again forces his mind to change the topic. The topic that comes to his mind is the music floating about the galley kitchen.

"The man who lives for only making money," he sing-says.

"Lives a life that isn't necessarily sunny."

"Good song."

"Yes."

"How sad do you think Ira Gershwin was when George died?"

"Very sad. I suspect he was very sad." His mom nods.

"Yes."

"Jennifer is excited about the presentation?"

"She prefers Jennie."

"Jennie then."

"Veterinary Dentists. National Occupation Classification Code 3114." Darby nods. "She is very excited."

"It's an odd choice to present on."

Darby shrugs. "Jennie chose it."

"You divvied up the speaking equally? It's important for group and pair presentations."

"Yes. Pretty much. Maybe she's talking a bit more, but I'm explaining our visual aids."

"The PowerPoints?"

"We're sharing the PowerPoints, and I'm setting up the video."

"Good. You've practiced together and alone?" Darby's mom leans forward as she talks, as if she's excited about every little thing and every little thing is exciting, which is either a specific kind of encouraging and cheerful mom trait or a specific kind of cheerful and encouraging teacher trait.

"Yes. More alone, though, but together too."

"Jennie-not-Jennifer did a wonderful job during the Winter Holiday Concert Celebration. Comfortable. She's quite at ease in front of an audience."

"She is, yes."

"Yes." Yogurt spoon in hand, she points to Darby's cereal bowl. "You should have something to drink with that."

"Juice?" he asks.

At the fridge door, she removes two pitchers, but then the upstairs telephone rings and interrupts her, so she just has to stand there waiting, juice in hand. Darby stops chewing his Toasted Bran Nut Clusters, though he doesn't imagine they make that much noise. It just feels more polite waiting for the phone to finish its ringing.

They wait for the second, third, and fourth ring until voicemail picks up, which is a habit they've fallen into for the past couple of months. When they first moved into the executive townhome back in October, Darby's dad said that they'd been paying Ma Bell too much for too long and nearly everyone has internet telephone, so they'd installed the telephone in the upstairs office with the office desktop computer. The plan was to install extensions in the galley kitchen and the family room walkout basement area, but then who really used their landlines all that much anymore? According to Darby's dad, ninety-five-point nine percent of their calls came in through their cellular mobile telephones, and so why toss money away through an open window? Darby thought his dad presented a solid argument, but then he moved out to a low-rise apartment complex.

The upstairs phone rings its last ring, which echoes in a kind of hollow way down the stairs. To Darby's way of thinking, there is something kind of sad about the sound, and his mom probably agrees, but she's never said so. What she has said is that the term landline telephone is a kind of retroactive name given only after the invention and popularization of the mobile cellular telephone. Before cellphones, landline telephones were just telephones. It's like acoustic guitars after the invention of electric guitars. Darby nods a lot and tries to demonstrate interest and attention when she talks excitedly in such a way because he can tell that she wishes she could still share these kinds of thoughts with his dad.

When the ringing upstairs stops, Darby's mother nods. "We have orange juice and pomegranate-pineapple," she says. "Two extremes of juice."

"Orange?"

She's passing him a glass and the orange juice pitcher when her cellphone rings a muffled ring out somewhere in the dining room.

"It's in my shoulder bag," she says.

This oftentimes happens after the telephone upstairs rings. If a caller can't reach Darby's mom on the landline telephone and the call is necessary and important, the mobile cellular telephone rings a few minutes after. Cause and effect. Events have unfolded in this pattern often enough that without his mom even asking,

Darby reaches to turn down Cole Porter. A trip to the moon on gossamer wings is just one of those things.

"Hello, yes, this is Doreen Tamm."

Darby watches her on the telephone, which she clamps under her shoulder so she can start their pack lunches, which is the next part of their morning schedule. She removes bread and cheddar slices from the refrigerator so she can simultaneously listen, talk and assemble a nutritious lunch meal, but then she stops.

"Yes, I understand."

From her tone of voice, Darby can tell that the call is a potential new worry. Well, he can actually tell from her tone of voice and from the fact that this call came first thing in the morning because good news seldom arrives this early. Good news is more of a late riser, roll-out-of-bed-at-eleven kind of phone call.

"I will talk to Darby," she says, but as she says this, she looks at Darby and places a hand over the bottom of her phone. "It's all right," she whisper-speaks. "Help me with the lunches."

It doesn't sound all right, but helping with the pack lunches will be a distraction, so Darby helps. His lunch bag, her lunch bag, and the Tupperware are all kept in the same drawer by the dishwasher. The executive townhouse kitchenette allows only small movements, but even though there's only a narrow strip of floor between the limited counter space, they rarely-to-never bump into each other, which Darby finds kind of amazing. She pulls out the margarine tub while he pulls out a butter knife, and she removes cellophane from the second drawer while he opens the whole wheat from the breadbox on the opposite counter. The routine grows even more complicated with apples to quarter, celery sticks to chop, and red peppers to slice. These coordinated kitchenette movements feel kind of like a choreographed movie musical dance routine like from *An American in Paris,* and Darby sometimes imagines he and his mom twirling about as if from high up above from an overhead camera angle.

"Yes, I understand," his mother says. "This was last night?"

With the dance of the pack lunches complete, Darby has no choice but to turn to his mother, but all she does is smile and raise a finger. It is the index pointer finger, and the gesture means *please be patient and wait please.*

"Yes, I understand," his mom says.

They are usually out the door and going by 7:45. Running late can induce stress and is no good way to start the day, so Darby checks the red digital clock on Mr. Coffee, which says 7:28. The blue light clock on the microwave says 7:29, but the green digital clock on the stovetop disagrees with both the microwave and Mr. Coffee, and it says 7:27. The three clocks never agree, and the problem isn't a new one. Darby's dad used to try to fix it every spring and every autumn for daylight savings time when they lived in Calgary, and trying to synchronize the clocks used to make him impatient because he never did succeed. Time is slippery. His dad usually wound up saying that close enough was good enough, and then he'd add that daylight savings time was an outdated concept that no one really needed anyway.

"All right." Darby's mom nods at the phone. "Yes."

It never occurred to anyone while they lived in Calgary, but Darby now realizes that he and his mom and his dad maybe could have synchronized the microwave, Mr. Coffee, and the stovetop all together as a family. With each of them on a different appliance, they might have gotten the timing of all three digital clocks just right.

"Yes, thank you."

Darby's mom switches off her phone and checks her watch.

"I'm afraid it's about Mr. Henderson," she says to Darby.

It turns out that after four months in a coma in the ICU at the Ottawa and Capital Region Healthcare Centre, Mr. Henderson has died. Right before the start of Career Day, he died without ever waking up.

ON UNLIMITED DUCKS AND THE UNFORTUNATE ACCIDENT

In the early years of Richmond East Elementary's participation in the Ducks Unlimited program, the duck species that came to the school courtyard to pass the long slow days of nesting and breeding and brooding varied. Dabbling ducks as diverse as American wigeons, cinnamon teals, and northern pintails called the enclosed courtyard their home. Over time, though, the waterfowl families that came most and endured best were the mallards, and each and every spring, they gratefully settled into the homes and habitats that greeted them. The Ottawa-Carleton District School Board tended to splurge for luxurious cottage boxes with hay piles and rooms with a view, raised off the ground for increased warmth and fronted with a slow incline ramp entrance. In consultation with a local landscape artist, the ground space was converted into a convincing marsh environment with not only a water feature in which the ducks might teach their daughter and son ducklings to take their first tentative paddles into the world, but also a tumbling waterfall – a fake babbling brook over fake rolling rocks that was well worth the school's extra investment because it both drew the eye of the beholder and circulated the pond's water to ensure against stagnation and foul bacteria.

Here, pairings of enamored drake and hen mallards came, their minds filled with romance and passion, and because wisdom in this earthly world is best and most often passed down from generation to generation, the ducks that came later were the direct descendants of the original mallard family. They knew the enclosed courtyard would protect their kith and their kin from the worst of the ground predators and the worst of the world, and the drake and hen mallards that came home to roost in this safe habitat enjoyed a security and peace of mind unknown to most edible animals. Thus, these courtyard courtships and the fertilization of the eggs within those four windowed walls represented some of the greatest of their salad days, producing generations of offspring and satisfaction.

There existed the threat of school children, of course – the bullying and the mean-hearted who enjoyed nothing more than suddenly and loudly banging on the courtyard windowpanes – but the generations of ducks had learned just how empty these empty threats were. Older adults and kindlier children invariably nudged the aggressive offenders – *cut it out already* – and in truth, none but the gentle janitor who daily replenished their feed possessed a key to open the heavy door of glass and metal into the courtyard.

One particular year, upon arriving at Richmond East Elementary and while stretching his legs in the artificial pond, a drake mallard surveyed the faces behind the glass walls and noticed an especially upset teacher reprimanding the more unruly boys at the window. Though the drake had come to the school courtyard for several years running, he had never before seen this young teacher. An oddity in odd tortoiseshell eyeglasses, the man seemed genuinely uncomfortable with his authority over the hooligans, and in the duck's experience, such discomfort was not the norm for an elementary school teacher. The norm for an elementary school teacher was strict and severe, and so perhaps this young man had just recently begun his teaching career, and perhaps he had just recently begun to understand the aggression of grade five boys. Across the young man's face, the duck saw the teacher was not only saddened by them, but also befuddled.

Mr. Mallard felt no such confusion. He had seen the behaviour of boys before, and he had seen their innate hostility toward the vulnerable grow into irrational anger. It was an anger that only intensified once eggs hatched hatchlings and newborns broke through their shells to waddle unknowing into the world. In fact, it seemed to the drake mallard as if the ducklings' degree of helplessness increased the boys' degree of viciousness proportionally by some sort of calculable measure that might be writ out in a formula. Why would that be? There was no way to know, but Mr. Mallard saw that the young teacher was just then understanding that he did not understand. No matter how rewarding a teaching career might be – the comprehension of cross multiplication breaking across a young person's face, the symmetry of a class of twenty-one student desks in clustered groups of three, the beautiful self-awareness of a child moving through cognitive development and into empathy – none of these joys could counterbalance the cruel calculus of bullying. It was at that moment that the duck and the teacher made eye contact and shared a moment of mutual recognition.

The drake blinked first, and he looked away embarrassed, turning his attention to the other side of the kidney-shaped pond where his partner hen was plunging her head straight down and lifting her backend straight up. The unexpected eye contact with the teacher had left him unsettled, but in truth, he'd already felt unsettled on this particular spring day. While the courtyard was safe and secure and a good part of him was looking forward to his fertilizing responsibilities, he was also second-guessing his commitment. Mallard ducks are by nature neither monogamous nor duplicitous, and thus whether or not a male breeding partner acts honourably and does right by his hen for the full twenty-three to thirty-one days of incubation to fulfil his parental responsibilities to the eight to twelve eggs is very much up to chance and individual character. This particular drake's character was divided. Yes, he foraged for the twigs and sticks and hay left in the courtyard, and yes, he helped line the nest with all that he found, but as with many fathers of a certain age, his mind drifted toward other flightpaths as well. Too often, he and his hen whisper-argued about nothing in particular, and too often he did not feel good about himself.

To his credit, the drake stayed after fertilization, but with too many long hours, days, and weeks to sit his turn on the nest, this particular mallard had too much time to brood whilst brooding. Nest, molt, migrate, and repeat. Repeat for fifteen to twenty years. Certainly there was more to a life cycle than this? But even with such dissatisfaction weighing upon him, he stayed until the school year at Richmond East Elementary came to a close. He stayed until his flight feathers returned to him. He stayed until the very eve that the eggs began to crack. And then he stayed no longer, but left.

In the summer that followed, Mr. Mallard enjoyed dipping his beak into more than one pond around the capital region, passing whole mornings at Dow's Lake feeding on food-truck French fries from tourists gathered for the tulip and dragon-boat and Renaissance reenactment festivals and passing whole afternoons floating down the Ottawa River past Parliament where tourists snapped shots of his pretty plumage. And yet, when summer ended and fall fell, he often turned his head to the sky to see flocks flying in formation, and he too often wondered which of those Vs might contain his family. The dissatisfaction that held him then was regret and guilt both – he remembered the way his hen waddled when particularly proud and he thought of all those eggs to whom he never gave his love – and as often happens when regret and guilt comingle with isolation, the drake drifted toward depression and into darker thoughts.

Thus, on a Friday evening in November when he found himself flying especially low, he dipped down and flew deliberately toward the windscreen of a Nissan Leaf just as it was crossing a bridge. Drawing nearer, the drake looked through the glass and once again made eye contact with the sensitive young teacher Gerald Gerard

Henderson. Though many months had passed since their courtyard encounter, they once again shared a moment of recognition before colliding. He might not have died upon impact, but then, the compact car veered from its lane, off the bridge, and into the water below.

CHAPTER 2

Without any exceptions that he can think of, all of the portable classrooms Darby Tamm has anywhere ever seen in any schoolyard have always been covered with textured siding in a kind of mustard taupe, and their outside perimeter bottoms have always been skirted with plywood in a kind of chocolate brown, and while the two colours do kind of complement each other, it's not really in a good way.

Richmond East Elementary has six such portables. On the mornings when they arrive early before most everyone else, Darby and Jennie Phelps-Christianson sit on wooden steps of the portable farthest from the school building. Because she wears a hearing aid in her left ear, Darby always makes sure he sits to Jennie's right, but maybe they're so close that it doesn't matter which side he sits on.

"So they were the same exact colour in Calgary?" Jennie asks.

"Yes," Darby says. "The mustard is a brownish yellow."

"Like Dijon."

"I suppose."

Because Darby's mother has to drop him off at Richmond East Elementary early so she can get to work at Woodfield Elementary and set up the music room and because Jennie's mother is a vice-principal at Richmond East Elementary who gets in early so she can tend to administrative matters and managerial responsibilities, Darby and Jennie often arrive before most everyone else. On days when the temperature is bitter dangerous cold with a risk of frostbite, the school administration allows students into the building to sit at their desks for independent and quiet work until second morning bell, but on the days when it's only regular cold, students are prohibited inside the school building. This morning is only regular cold, but regular cold in Ottawa is still uncomfortable. Darby and Jennie sit close enough together that their sides are pressing up against one another, and though he might have once drawn back from such contact, he lets it happen – for warmth against the Ottawa cold, but also because it feels all right.

"The portable windows were all the same too," Darby says. "With steel grates painted brown."

"To protect the windows, I'd guess" Jennie says. "So stray basketballs and soccer balls don't break the glass."

Darby hadn't thought of that, so he tells her. "Makes sense."

The Richmond East Elementary schoolyard contains few places to sit, so the portable steps are a good place to wait in the morning, but in addition to this advantage, they also offer an expansive perspective. Sitting on the steps, Darby need only turn left and look over the paved basketball and four corners courts or turn right and survey the length of the whole entire playing field. Beyond the hopscotch courts, the darkened windows look into Mr. Henderson's decorated classroom, and beyond the staff and faculty parking lot, the school drop-off loop lane will soon bring a steady stream of students.

Thus, the view from the steps offers much, but this morning, the location has distracted Darby and he's talking about the portables more than he wants to. What he actually wants to talk about is about Mr. Henderson and the teacher's unfortunate accident and his fresh-from-the-headlines comatose death, but broaching such a sensitive topic may well be problematic, so he's talking about mustard and brown portables instead.

"Must be a reason for the uniformity," Jennie says.

Together, they conclude that such a level of uniform consistency can only really be attributed to two causes: 1) either mustard taupe and chocolate brown and a set of two-step stairs is the ideal and perfect design for a portable classroom and every architect and exterior designer has reached this same conclusion independently or 2) the layout and colour scheme and production of portable classrooms is overseen by a central control facility that ensures all materials and component parts are sourced using strict guidelines – similar to how fast food franchise restaurants have to make sure every chicken nugget taken from the same bit of genetically enlarged chicken breast of white meat or every six-by-two rectangular prism submarine sandwich unit looks and tastes pretty much the exact same whether in Calgary or Ottawa or anywhere.

"My dad says fast food will make you die faster," Darby says.

"Carcinogenic," Jennie says.

"Yes."

"When I was little," Jennie says, "whenever my father went away for Ministry of Agriculture conferences and meetings, he would return with small gifts. Most often souvenirs like fridge magnets or Christmas tree ornaments with names of different cities. Sometimes, though, the small gift was a toy, one of those movie tie-in toys. The kind that come with fast food. And this was odd because my mother and father both said fast food wasn't allowed. I didn't tell them, but I put two and two together. He must have been eating the kind of food that he should not have been eating while he was away on business."

"I'm not allowed fast food either," Darby says.

Since Jennie's mom Vice-Principal Phelps-Christianson made the morning calls to all the pupils in the grade five class, Jennie for certain knows about Mr. Henderson's death. Though Jennie sometimes disagreed with their original teacher and he sometimes said she was trying his patience, Jennie has more than once said that Henderson's classroom pedagogy was sound, which isn't something she said about Monsieur Substitute in any way whatsoever at all.

It's hard to tell whether or not Jennie actually admired the deceased teacher, but she might have, and if that is the case, broaching the sensitive topic of his death might be insensitive.

"Getting all four of your recommended food groups can be hard when you travel," Jennie says.

"Perhaps he has to eat fast food even when he doesn't want to." Though he has never met Jennie's father, Darby feels he should stick up for him for Jennie's sake, and it feels good to be kind.

"He doesn't bring the toys home for me anymore. I don't know if that's because he's stopped eating fast food or because I stopped being little."

"Perhaps he tries to use the hotel pool and exercise room whenever he can," Darby says.

"Maybe. He speed-walks on a treadmill at home."

"And perhaps he passes on all sorts of continental breakfast Danish and bagels, even though they usually come free of charge for business travelers."

"Probably. One bagel equals five pieces of bread. Did you know that?"

Though the portable steps are wide enough for the two of them to sit side by side, the extra addition of bulky winter clothes make the tight fit even tighter. Over his business office professional khaki trousers and a cobalt blue button-down, Darby wears his puffy ski jacket and snow pants, and he feels at once cold and sweaty. He's not sure what Jennie has chosen to wear for their Career Fair Pair Presentation, but she has on an arctic ice parka and snowpants, so she's dressed all bulky like he is, and now that he thinks about how close they're sitting to one another, he also thinks about how they might appear to the students who have started to arrive in the schoolyard. Darby realizes that from their perspective, he and

Jennie might appear not only huddled together for warmth but cuddled together.

He wonders if he should scooch away from Jennie to avoid this perception, but then he decides not to. The move would seem unkind, and it would maybe undo the good he did complimenting her father, but also when he thinks of how the sight of them sitting together might appear to other students in the schoolyard, well – it feels all right.

Jennie does not seem to have thought of any of this because she is paying all her attention to the basketball and four corners courts where the snow sculptures left over from Outdoor Winter Carnival still stand.

"Everyone is scared to touch them," Darby says.

"Scared of my mom, I'd guess."

The snow sculpture animals on the basketball court and the snow sculpture buildings on the four corners courts are all arranged by grade level, and even though the Outdoor Winter Carnival ended over a week ago, the temperature hasn't risen or fallen all that much so the statues still all stand. During first morning announcements, Vice-Principal Phelps-Christianson has made it clear that any student found tampering with or destroying a snow sculpture would face a two-day in-school suspension and a prohibition from all extracurricular activities for the remainder of the semester.

"Which is your favourite building sculpture," Jennie asks, "and which is your favourite animal?"

"The kitten is the most detailed," Darby says, "but you have to look too close to really see that it's detailed."

Most of the classes and grades opted to add snow paint to the sculptures, and even though the colours look a bit fake, Darby can see why. The primary reds, blues, yellows, and mixed secondary colours make the snow statues stand out from the background of snow, and only the white kitten on its back playing with a white ball of yarn is unpainted. With both the foreground and the background white, Darby thinks the white effect was a poor choice and far too subtle, but then the kitten was designed and constructed by the creative arts stream of grade eights and maybe they chose to be subtle for some creative arts stream reason.

"For me, the Parliament is the best building," Jennie says.

"I do like the way the Peace Tower stands up all on its own," Darby says.

Darby's dad took him to visit the Canadian Parliament Building during their very first weekend visitation weekend, and they rode an elevator up inside the clock tower and had to speak in whispers out of respect for the nation's capital and dead soldiers, which was when Darby learned the name of the Peace Tower. He sometimes holds onto unique information like the name and carries it around for a while looking for where he might put it down, and he's always pleased when just such an opportunity presents itself.

"They used water on the snow for the tower, I'd guess," Jennie says, "so the sculpture would ice up and not fall over."

"I suppose my second favourite is the Roman Coliseum and third is the Shanghai Pearl Tower."

"They used to have people killing people in the Roman Coliseum and lions killing people, but they also sometimes used to fill the stadium up with water and had shark and octopi killing people. Did you know that?"

Jennie has a habit of producing facts like this, which is probably the kind of habit Mr. Henderson meant when he said she tried his patience.

Of the animal snow sculptures, Jennie and Darby both agree upon the grade seven goldfish as the clear favourite. With three different hues of orange, the floating goldfish not only has textured scales and a flowing tail that swoops down and supports the whole weight of the structure, but it also seems to be really swimming in place there in a way, like real-life goldfish sometimes do when they just stay in place drifting and looking out from within the bowl or aquarium.

"It's more creative than the creative arts kitten in my opinion," Darby says.

"The creative arts kids try too hard."

"Goldfish do not have bad memories, did you know that?" Jennie asks. "People say they forget everything every fifteen seconds as if their brains reboot all over again and they're like a newborn, but it's a myth that isn't true. If goldfish didn't remember stuff, they wouldn't swim to the top of the bowl when you dropped flakes on the surface of the water and they'd bump stupidly against the inside of their fishbowl all the time. They can actually remember stuff like two or three months."

Darby feels himself shrugging off her trivia, but then remembers that it feels good to be kind, so he nods.

"And two or three months is really long," Jennie says, "when you think that most goldfish are usually dead before their first birthday."

"That's a decade to us."

"Yes."

"Goldfish die too soon."

The sad and brief lifespan of goldfish would perhaps provide a natural opening to bring up Mr. Henderson, Darby realizes, but at the same moment that he thinks of the connection, he looks over to the school drop-off loop lane, and he spots a forest green Dodge Caravan minivan among the congesting line of vehicles.

On some days, the sedans and sport utility vehicles congest and back up when a new parent or guardian doesn't realize the lane flows and circulates only one-way. On other days, a parent or guardian treats the lane like an airport kiss-and-ride and draws a quick peck on the cheek way out into a fond farewell of lingering wistful waves. It's surprising how quickly the angry horns of parent drivers honk.

This morning, the sedans and sport utility vehicles seem to stream along slow-but-steady, and the forest green Dodge Caravan stands out. Alexander's father left long ago, but he left behind the early model minivan with rust on the bottom of the side-sliding door. Alexander's mom and his older sister Hannah share the eyesore vehicle, and it's pretty easy to spot. Hannah is easy to spot too. At eighteen, she studies at university and wears her hair dyed with a magenta streak. Sometimes she wears a short metal rod through her pierced cheek but other times wears a tiny metal loop through her pierced eyebrow or nostril. From the portable steps, Darby's too far away to see which she's wearing today. Perhaps all three or a combination of two. He hasn't seen her since they met during her work break at Southgate Bayview Mews Mall when Alexander found them chatting and kind of freaked out, but Darby can't remember what jewelry she was wearing then.

In the drop-off lane now, she waves a happy bye to Alexander, and Alexander tosses back an obligatory wave bye to her in return, and the sight almost makes Darby wish he were part of their family. The sight makes him wish he could go to Alexander and talk about Mr. Henderson's all-of-a-sudden-and-out-of-the-blue death in his sleep. Darby can't, though, because Alexander and Them are still angry at him. Well, more than angry really. After the surprise meeting at the Southgate Bayview Mews Mall, Alexander and Them found Darby during first morning nutrition break and promised that first bloody chance they got they were going to beat the sense out of him, and since then, they've muttered threats to him in the hall and passed him threatening notes in class. Sometimes they've claimed they'd beat the sense out of him, and other times, their language has been less appropriate, and they promise to beat the piss out of him or beat the snot out of him or beat the shit out of him. It's all pretty scatological.

So Darby just watches Hannah drive her lovely self out of the drop-off loop lane and away from Richmond East Elementary, and he just has to resist the stupid urge to rush over and talk to Alexander with a bunch of questions. What time did Vice-Principal Phelps-Christianson call his place? Did Alexander's mother sit him down to break the news in a tactful manner? What was Alexander doing when he found out? Does Alexander think this means they'll never ever find out how the unfortunate accident happened?

How and why Mr. Henderson drove off the bridge and went into a coma in the ICU became a topic of conversation immediately after the incident. To himself, Darby wondered if the bridge was a cantilever bridge or a suspension bridge or an arch bridge and he imagined different variations. Without really meaning to, he started inventing different accident scenarios to explain the details of the unfortunate accident to himself. Then, when he became friends with Alexander and Them, they made a kind of game of the scenarios, adding to each others' ideas and exaggerating more and more. Kind of fun, even though Darby knew the fun was a mean-spirited sort of fun. Not a topic of conversation he can mention to Jennie, which is a shame because as the Vice-Principal's daughter, she might have all sorts of insider information about the funeral memorial service and visitations.

Jennie might even know about how many Richmond East Elementary faculty and staff members will have to give respects, and she might accompany her mother along to the funeral memorial service and visitation. The funeral might even be open casket, Darby realizes, and that'd be very uncomfortable.

"What business office professional did you wear for our presentation?" he asks.

"Slacks and a blouse. I thought about a skirt, but that would be a hassle with snow pants. The slacks are pinstriped, though."

"Good for public speaking," Darby says.

"Almost as important as eye contact," Jennie says.

Although he knows that no one can entirely help or control what they think, Darby also knows that thinking about the Career Fair Pair Presentation will lead to thoughts of his dad's visit and Career Parent Presentation. Cause and effect, those thoughts will lead to weekend visitations and the inevitable consequences of trial separations, and Darby doesn't want to think any of those thoughts.

"You had good eye contact," Darby says, "at Winter Holiday Concert Celebration."

"Thank you."

"My mom said your comfort in front of an audience was impressive," he adds.

Jennie performed "Have a Holly Jolly Christmas" at the school concert, which isn't really as non-denominational as it should be for the public school system, but then again, it isn't exactly nativity-play or weepy-pieta intense either like they do in Catholic school. After watching the performance, Darby realized he was lucky to have her for the Career Fair Pair Presentation, even though she wasn't his choice and Mr. Henderson just only put them together. He was lucky because it was clear she was good at public speaking.

Exactly why she's good at public speaking is less clear. In front of an audience, Darby feels his stomach tighten and sometimes he gets an unsteady sick feeling that affects his balance. Then, sometimes, he feels his lip quivering and worries that it might lead to a throat lump that'll turn to red eyes or outright tears if he doesn't stop thinking about it. His mom said everyone felt this way, and his dad said it was an evolutionary response called *fight or flight*, which was physiological and near impossible to control consciously. So what gives with Jennie?

"Poised and confident. That was what my mother said."

Poised and confident might be going far overboard, and Darby doesn't actually remember his mom saying those exact same words, but then again, the kindness feels good even if he's exaggerating. Also, passing along compliments from his mom is much more easy than giving a compliment straight outright, and to Darby's way of thinking, Jennie probably needs the compliments. On top of being the vice-principal's daughter and on top of standing a good hand shorter than most of the grade five pupils, she seems unaware of her own oddity. She parts her hair too sharply in the middle with a tight little-kid ponytail at the back in a way that's very different from the current grade five fashion of carefully combed but freely flowing.

Then there's her hearing aid. To think about or remark upon matters of physical, mental, and personal disability is unkind and wrong, of course, but it's also hard to control where one's mind goes sometimes, and Jennie's hearing aid is one of those peachy beige curvy plastic ones that really looks too pale in colour and too glossy to be realistic or not noticed. It rides overtop of her left ear like a tumour, and Darby can't really believe there isn't a better invention to help people hear. When they're sitting across from each other, Darby has to work not to stare, but fortunately for him, she prefers to sit with her good ear facing the person she's talking to, so the hearing aid is mostly out of sight. Fortunately for her, she is wholly and entirely unaware of potential shortcomings that she really should be aware of.

"Have you ever been to a funeral?" Jennie asks.

The question is an odd question. Not Jennie's usual oddness, but that's all right because Darby knows why she is thinking what she's thinking, and he has, indeed, attended a funeral.

"My granddad," he says. "Dad's dad."

"Opened casket or a closed casket? Do you remember?"

"Closed. My dad says open casket funerals are morbid and only for people who like to indulge themselves in their grief. The closed casket is sad enough."

"Yeah, I guess so," she says.

"My dad says some funerals even have receiving lines like weddings. And the deceased person's wife or daughters or husband and sons stand by the exit and shake everyone's hands as they go out, which is really ridiculous and melodramatic like tearing at your hair and rending your garments in the centre of the city square."

"That's kind of a long opinion," Jennie says.

"My dad has lots of long opinions," Darby says.

"Yes?"

One of his dad's longest opinions was about Mr. Henderson's enriched class because he said that the standardized admission testing used for enriched, gifted, and talented programs are by design biased and unreliable, and the programs themselves are sometimes justified and sometimes not. Once schools and school boards have established and funded and staffed such streamed programs, however, enriched or gifted and talented students are needed to fill seats every fall. These students are most often the children of pushy and/or well-off parents applying pressure and influence upon school administrators. The conclusion to his dad's opinion is that whether or not such preferential streaming programs should exist is debatable, but as long as they do exist, the question is moot, and it is better to be in an enriched or gifted program than not.

"Yeah," Jennie says. "I can see why Alexander or Kamil or Kayla got into the enriched class, but some of our classmates? Sarah? Stewart? I don't get that."

Darby agrees but doesn't want to say he agrees because in truth he often wonders just how he got into the enriched class. Once after Mr. Henderson's unfortunate accident, Monsieur Substitute teacher gave a surprise pop quiz in cross multiplication, and Darby did not do well. Upset, he suggested to his mom and dad that perhaps he should switch to the regular stream because he wasn't like Jennie or Alexander and Them or any of the other pupils. Darby's mom made a sympathetic face, and said he should be more confident, which really didn't reassure Darby at all. His dad explained his long opinion about enriched and gifted programs and said Darby's worries were valid but immaterial, which also wasn't any help.

Because Darby's mom couldn't help but be chipper and upbeat, she added that of course he belonged in the enriched program. She reminded him of his Stanford-Binet scores and his Wechsler scores, emphasizing his percentile standing in the verbal comprehension and working memory indices, but Darby wasn't convinced. For one thing, exactly how percentiles differ from percentages is one of those slippery facts that Darby sometimes thinks he understands but then later can't put together how he previously understood. For another thing, there was a Ms. Benet who worked in the school cafeteria in Calgary, and for all of second grade, Darby somehow confused her for the Binet of Stanford-Binet, and later, when he realized his previous error, he just kind of felt embarrassed and humiliated. Even thinking about it now still kind of makes him feel ashamed. A lot of mistakes are like that.

"I think my dad is right about funerals," Darby says.

"Yeah," Jennie says, "Closed casket is better."

"Don't you think pop quizzes are unfair?"

"Very unfair."

"Death too," Darby says.

"Yeah."

First morning bell rings, and over Jennie's shoulder, Darby sees Alexander has moved closer to the basketball courts. He's with Billy Pace and Stewart Holgermonsson huddled all together in their heavy boots and coats, and they're giving Alexander some of their pocket money in exchange for some of his sister Hannah's cigarettes. All three of them are glancing and scanning back left and right and over their shoulders towards the school for teachers. Dumb – because all they're really doing is calling attention to themselves. If anyone good were on morning yard duty, the teacher would notice right out and walk right over to see what's going on.

"Smoking is ridiculous," Jennie says. She's figured out what Alexander and Them are doing, it seems.

"Yes. Ridiculous." Darby tries to lower his voice to add a tone of sad disbelief to his words. "Carcinogenic," he adds.

Since he smoked pretty much every time he hung out with Alexander and with Hannah, he feels he needs to sell his disapproval, and he considers adding a sad shake of his head, but then doesn't. Best not to overdo it.

"You're not friends with Alexander and Them anymore?"

"I guess not really, no."

"Did something happen?"

Darby shrugs. Explaining why he's no longer friends with them would be a lot to get into, and plus there are actually two reasons.

1. *The first reason why Darby has stopped being friends with Alexander and Them.* During a weekend visitation weekend to his dad's low-rise apartment, Darby discovered a collection of over five dozen *Oui* and *Club* magazines stacked in the back of the double closet behind an unpacked box of summer clothes

and a milk crate of unsold eps from his dad's old university band. Surprised by the novelty of print pornography, Darby flipped through the table of contents looking for publication dates even before he flipped to any of the pictorial essay portfolios, and as he suspected, the periodicals were issued in the late nineteen seventies and early nineteen eighties. 1976 to 1983. Subtracting in his head, Darby calculated that the earliest magazines dated from around the time that his dad had been his own age, and since it was unlikely that his dad had been carting around over five dozen pornographic magazines for over three decades, a mystery was afoot. Of course, in addition to the mystery, the magazines presented a greater danger: once discovered, the nude pictorial essays demanded attention, and Darby found himself paging through them late at night, which led to lots of confused feelings and regret. At the end of every weekend visitation weekend, he promised himself he would never again look at the magazines, but then, by the time his next weekend visitation came, his resolve pretty much dropped away, and Darby even found himself inventing rationalizations to justify his curiosity. One must learn about anatomies and better to investigate here than on the open internet where all sorts of complications and varied sexual predilections might interfere with learning; further, any investigation online opened computers up to the possibility of all strains and variations of viruses and malware programs that would slow down the operating system significantly. In addition to the mystery presented by the collection and the naked women in the collection, the discovery also complicated weekend visitations with his dad because after many late hours studying the photographs in *Oui* and *Club*, Darby was usually tired from a lack of sleep, which made daytime walks through the Nature Museum, History Museum, War Museum and the

Royal Canadian Mint much less engaging. Once, he paused to wonder if how his dad felt toward the wonderfully naked women might complicate his dad's relationship with his mom, but the thought was confusing and he pushed it from his mind. Fortunately, the mystery of the magazines proved much easier to solve. Used bookstores. It was obvious once Alexander said it. Vintage pornography from used bookstores. Of course. The Southgate Bayview Mews Mall just right across the street from Darby's dad's low-rise apartment complex, in fact, had a used bookstore called Plot's End that sold old pornographic magazines. Darby had seen and pretended not to see the boxes full of such magazines underneath the rack of contemporary literature trade paperbacks when he and his dad were book browsing. Mystery solved. Telling Alexander and Them about the magazines was probably a misstep because the information snowballed into a mistake. He wasn't exactly bragging when he talked about the collection, but he may have been bragging a little bit, and then Billy Pace kind of insisted Darby share with them. Billy said Darby could sneak one or two magazines out of his dad's place, and no one would be the wiser. Darby could use the big duffel he took for weekend visitations, and he could even bring the one or two magazines back and switch them out every couple of weeks. Billy worked out a plan in no time, and Darby's opportunity to take exception just sort of passed away. It was peer pressure of the kind Darby's mom warned against, but he went along with it because Billy could be frightening. When the magazines were returned wrinkled and ripped or with entire pages torn out and Darby couldn't believe his dad would never at all not notice, peer pressure switched to intimidation. Then, after Alexander stopped talking to Darby, Darby just refused to continue with such a ridiculous plan, and the intimidation became threats.

2. *The second reason why Darby stopped being friends with Alexander and Them.* Darby became secret friends with Alexander's older sister Hannah. Alexander found out.

While either one or both of these reasons explain why they might wish to beat the sense, piss, snot, and shit out of Darby, neither reason can be explained to Jennie without leading to more and more complicated conversation, so Darby shrugs at her questions.

"It's complicated, I'd guess" Jennie says, which is kind.

From the basketball court, Darby hears Stewart Holgermonsson claim that v-neck t-shirts are for douche sacs, and Billy Pace punches him on the side shoulder. Stewart is a Methodist or Lutheran or somesuch, and he doesn't really know how to swear. He also kind of lacks common sense, which is why Billy often punches him on the side of the shoulder, which he does with a twisted knuckle fist so it leaves a sharp bruise. Billy does this because Billy is mean.

"You're better off," Jennie says. "Alexander and Them are more trouble than they're worth."

Darby nods. "Perhaps."

"What could they be laughing about so much?" she asks.

Probably they are talking and laughing about Mr. Henderson and the hypothetical accident scenarios, but like pornography and like Hannah, the scenarios aren't good topics of conversation with Jennie, so Darby stays silent and feels bad.

When the second morning bell rings, Darby reminds himself that his mom says it's always better to get up and move and get busy than to think too much and feel too bad, so he does. Shrugging on their backpack knapsacks, he and Jennie leave the portable steps, and since neither of them wants to get too close to the basketball court and Alexander and Them, they walk in an arc toward the side doors of the school. Glancing to the side, though, he sees that Alexander and Them are lingering, and then he sees why.

They're lingering because of the creative arts snow sculpture. Standing on the sculpture and walking in place and tramping the snow down, Alexander and Them are erasing the white ball of yarn and the white kitten entirely, not even worried about Vice-Principal Phelps-Christianson's two-day suspension warning and a prohibition from all extracurricular activities. Passing by, Darby tries not to stare at the destruction just in case they see him, but Alexander and Them have noticed him anyway.

"We're going to beat the ass out of you," Stewart says, which doesn't make sense, but seems to be a threat.

ON THE ARITHMETIC OF COMMON GROUND

If viewed as the overlap between two individual circles of experience, common ground can be seen as the darkened area of the Venn diagram in which all differences are set aside and all similarities come together. A couple first meets. Born within six months of one another, within the same medium-sized city of Calgary and of comparable socioeconomic class, they automatically overlap somewhere between 33 to 35 percent. Make them both only children who – as a consequence of their solitudes – have both grown up somewhat unsociable and somewhat bookish and who both dutifully attended music lessons in guitar and piano to complement their school work, and their common ground might go as high as 40 to 55 percent. The 45 to 60 percentage points of difference in their nature or nurture might place them in separate post-secondary programs – her excess empathy and caring predisposes her to the liberal arts and a career in education and his pedantic obsessiveness predisposes him to the physical sciences and a career in mechanical engineering – but their extra-curricular interest in music persists. He forms a band with some other over-achiever schoolmates, and she attends one of their under-attended shows. With such common ground, the two have a fair chance of falling into conversation at the mostly-empty downstairs tavern performance space after the show. She nurses her one-beer-limit beer, and he orders his alcohol-is-a-slippery-slope coffee, and later, when they fall together and become a couple, they will likely use the money they save with a city-hall wedding for a detached home within walking distance of a school and with three bedrooms. One bedroom for them, one for a child, and one for a home office. Later still, when that one child is born as tangible, living proof of their common ground, the couple will, for a short while, overlap more than they ever have or ever will again.

For group dynamics, a diagram of paired circles insufficiently conveys the common ground shared by each separate individual, and for complicated configurations such as three, four or five, the trippy twisted geometry of a whirling and twirling Spirograph doodle might better illustrate pockets of similarities and differences. A boy seeks out new friends. Make him the son of the music teacher and the mechanical engineer, involuntarily relocated from the medium-sized city of Calgary to the medium-sized city of Ottawa. Make him the new kid in the class who stumbles into a preexisting group of three mathlete friends with whom he shares only slivers of common ground. In a new city in a new province, enrolled in a new school a full month into the fall term, and victim to his parents' out-of-the-blue and all-of-a-sudden trial separation, he shares only slivers and thin crescents of common ground with any one of the new friends. In the chubby follower sheep of a friend whose swears are often illogical, the boy sees a fawning need to be liked, but also recognizes his own helpless yearning for safety. In the mean-streak nasty piece of work of a friend whose violence is barely contained, the boy sees an unpredictable danger, but also recognizes his own helpless rage. In the weary and tired philosopher king of a friend whose bemused laughs are worth working for, the boy sees an easy and careless cynicism, but also recognizes his own helpless sadness. Counted separately, perhaps the common ground he shares with any one of his new friends accounts for little more than 15 to 20 percent, but as a full sum total of 45 to 60 percent, he is welcomed into their darkened overlapping areas. As a late addition, he does not share the rich history his new friends share – a storied past of misadventures and triumphs stretching from junior kindergarten to the fifth grade – and in addition, he does not share their gifts for arithmetic – gifts that have found them on the math team years ahead of their time. Studious by nature and nurture, the boy has almost just about gotten the hang of cross multiplication as long as it isn't sprung on him entirely unannounced in an unkind surprise pop quiz, but he cannot at all keep up when the three friends try to trip up one another with Cartesian practice test questions at recess, shove properties of integers at one another in the playing field during daily physical activity, or mock one another's lack of precision with a protractor and compass in the gymnasium-auditorium at lunch hour.

Common ground is not static, however, but inevitably expands its borders over time through shared experience, and 45 to 60 percent may well beget 48 to 63 in a matter of school weeks. A boy spends nearly every lunch hour with three new friends for almost a whole month in November and December. Make their activity an illicit activity as the boy is welcomed into the fold with lunch hours passed blocks and blocks off school property behind the Good and Quick Gas and Sip, and the percentage of common ground can become a groundswell, ballooning with each of their shared trespasses. Welcomed along to their retreat behind the convenience-store-gas-station-snack-bar for grumble-and-grouse-and-shoot-the-shit sessions far from the workaday world, the boy shares in the respite of salted language and tobacco cigarettes, the shared secrets of their prohibited endeavors opening new grounds, and while the boy cannot calculate calculus and may never become secretary treasurer of the coding club, he learns that his attention and memory have served him well enough. He shares an anecdote about his father's university band *Sea Monkey See, Sea Monkey Do*, the box of unsold ep cds that now inhabits a closet, and the jewel case's hand-drawn cover art depicting an ape playing with its own feces. He shares an anecdote about Le Parc Safari, the waterpark-community-zoo-drive-through-safari in Quebec that his father took him to back in October when they first moved to Ottawa and the deer enclosure they walked through called *le sentier des cerfs* where they saw an unwise squirrel hunting and gathering deer droppings for the coming winter. He shares a story about the Customs and Conservation Canada glassed-case exhibit he examined at the Calgary airport on his way to Ottawa and the displayed collection of illegal animal byproducts forbidden for import and export, including cosmetic compacts made from the front paws of tigers, keychains of infant elephants carved from the ivory of adult elephants, and packets of finely ground powder made from rhinoceros tusk to be sold *for love or medicine*. Integrating through ingratiating, the boy becomes less and less an interloper, and over time, and much to his astonishment, he grows to understand that he can actually and actively construct common ground, pushing himself past the halfway mark into a 51 to 54 percent range.

While groups of four may be easily divisible, common ground amongst individual factions and fractions of the whole may be harder to discern because similarities and differences may not be proportioned evenly or consistently. Over time, however, as the fall term progresses into first snow and many excursions to the Good and Quick Gas and Sip have passed, hidden parallels and connections between pairings will emerge. For example, though unalike outwardly, the chubby follower friend and the nasty piece of work friend have both internalized and inherited their parents' socially and politically orthodox world views and deep inside will carry this influence all their days. As well, both collect and trade the Scandinavian fantasy-themed collectible trading card series *The Broadswords of Gungnir* with a passion that borders on mania, and on weekends, the two visit one another's homes to discuss and debate the comparative strength and constitution scores of vile lindworms and honorable boatmen.

Similarly, similarities heretofore unseen between the boy and the philosopher king of a friend emerge as well, the biggest of which are the broken homes in which they live. Such a similarity is not one to be discussed, for such common ground should never be acknowledged aloud. The boy cannot say that the forgotten box of unsold ep cds has moved from the executive townhome closet to a closet in a low-rise apartment complex, cannot say that the trip to *Parc Safari* was prelude to a family meeting to announce the break in their home, cannot say that his father laugh-sneered and nodded at the ground-down rhinoceros tusk in the Calgary airport.

One Thursday before the upcoming holiday school break, though, after the second nutrition break bell rings and the group of four friends are scurrying back to school property, exchanging peppermint chewing gum to hide the tobacco cigarettes on their breath, the boy receives an out-of-the-blue and all-of-a-sudden invitation to come on over during the holiday. With a nod to downplay the invitation's import, he mutters *yeah*, not at all revealing that the moment is a moment of mutual recognition and certainly not admitting that his thoughts have turned to his mother. How glad she will be to learn he has made such a close friend; how glad she will be to hear of the invitation, and how glad she will be to drive him over to the home of her son's new friend and watch from through the car window as her only child enters inside. She will be reassured that he is settling in all right in his new class in the new school in the new city, and all will grow better given time. Time – with its restorative nature and curative properties – will heal the wounds wrought by family.

There is a small snag, though, because in medium-sized cities like Ottawa that hover around a million people, small coincidences and small connections hide around every corner, and as it turns out, the philosopher king resides in the same low-rise apartment complex of yellow brick buildings as the boy's father – two yellow buildings down and on the other side of the emptied-out outdoor pool that seems to have sat for some years emptied and in disuse. An unhappy happenstance, and it only reminds the boy that his parents' temporary separation will likely be not at all temporary. Though his parents once shared much between them, time and circumstance have undone many of their connections. After university, her teaching career advanced from two one-year mat leave contract teaching positions to a permanent unionized spot with medical and dental benefits and a pension, but after university, his engineering career was stillborn with a precarious series of short-term contracts, stretches of sporadic unemployment insurance, and occasional bouts of self-loathing. While active love, marriage, and a child increased their common ground in the short term, unemployment, underemployment, and learned helplessness ground it down in the long term.

The boy worries that the low-rise does not bode well for the visit, and he is right to be concerned. In the car outside of the apartment complex, as his mother waves him off from the front seat and tells him to have a good time, she smiles to betray neither worry nor concern, but the boy has learned to calculate losses well. He can subtract all that has been taken from both of them within a few short months – city, home, friends, acquaintances, and all and sundry. He estimates their shared losses at 60 to 75 percent or perhaps as high as 70 to 85 percent.

Peering into the dimly-lit foyer hall of the shabby low-rise where a stack of Pennysaver flyers and an orphaned tennis shoe lie on the scuffed tile floor, he is not at all sure that this is common ground he wants to enter, but he struggles against his uncertainty and he walks in and up the littered stairwell to the third-floor apartment where his friend waits to open the door in greeting. In the hallway outside the threshold, the boy looks in over his friend's shoulder and spots a make-shift room in the living-room-dining-room alcove with a pastel blue bedsheet strung from one wall to another wall, and through a gap in the imperfect partition, he sees an unmade bed tangled with thrown-off clothing, and his uncertainty grows to outright reluctance. Walking down the low-ceiling hall to his friend's bedroom, the boy realizes that though he and his new friend are of the same age and they live in the same city, they may not be of comparable socioeconomic backgrounds, which he knows should not make him feel awkward because all people are equal in rights and dignity – but which makes him feel a little awkward anyway. For a snack, they open a box of Ritz and two ginger sodas, and as they sit on a throw rug of questionable cleanliness on the floor of the crowded and cluttered bedroom, the friend explains that the empty top bunk of his bunkbed was once his older sister's when they shared a room, but now his mother said they were getting too old to share, so his sister took the second bedroom, and his mother set up her belongings in the apartment's living-room-dining-room area. His mother is out today because she's a social services worker who sometimes has to do weekend outreach, so the sister is supposed to be the sitter, but since she works weekends at the Chez Animaux at the Southgate Bayview Mews Mall, she is out as well. Nodding, the boy feels his sense of order offended by the disorder around him, but he suppresses his reluctance and his urge to leave.

There's something he should see, his friend says, because it's something he will maybe appreciate, and the friend drags a box out from underneath the bottom bunk of the bunkbeds. It's a box left by the friend's absent father, he says and pauses, and in the pause, the boy realizes they are speaking of things they haven't spoken of before. Their darkest of common grounds, the broken homes they share. What's in the box? The boy right away thinks of pornography – his friend's father has left behind a box of pornography. Confusing pictorial essays with progressive images that illustrate ladies in increasing states of undress. Confusing double-page spreads of soft-focus photography in fancy-and-also-schmanzy bedroom and hotel room locales. Confusing cartoons punning on private parts.

But the boy is wrong. It is not a box of pornography, but a box of dead animal parts. Well, not really dead animal parts – but a collection of lucky rabbit's feet – so yeah, a box of dead animal parts. Again, the boy suppresses the urge to exit and instead leans forward to look inside where there's mostly key chains of rabbit's feet but also a couple of pendants attached to what look like necklace chains and one foot that has been grafted to a novelty pocket flashlight though the light part doesn't light up anymore at all. Many of the feet are dyed unnatural colours not found in rabbits and hares found in nature – greens and blues and a magenta – so the dark dyes not only cover the fur but also have worked their way down into the flesh of the under pads under the animal paws and into the cracked grain of the nail fragments peeking out from the furred finger digits. As a youth, the friend's father hunted and gathered these charms of good luck for years and years at carnivals, midways, and funfairs, and even once a year at the annual Canadian National Exhibition down in Toronto.

The part of the boy that wants to run from the apartment mess also wants to decry and revolt at the collection. He wants to tell his friend that it's a nightmare box. A box of nightmare horror experiments – except for the flashlight, which is maybe more like a nightmare science-fiction cyborg experiment – but another part of the boy understands. The unwanted empathy part of the boy sees that in opening the box to him, his new friend is opening up to him, and with a nod to downplay the moment's import, the boy mutters *yeah* and with reluctance accepts 5 to 10 percent more of this unwanted common ground.

Too young to discuss the matter at length, they instead spend the next three hours on the floor of the friend's crowded bedroom with game controllers in hand as they explore an alternative post-apocalyptic world, covering the awkwardness with round after round of *Killcraft WarMachine*, a first-person shooter player game the boy has heard tell of but has never before seen. They live as split-screen first-person soldiers battling undead hordes and insectoid armies, where mutant dogs chew on the faces of the human dead and where most everyone must certainly suffer from some form of post-traumatic stress disorder and any number of psychological injuries. Tearing ass through the trenches past fallen comrades crying out in terror at their lost limbs, they ignore carcasses of the dead and decaying, and they ignore scurrying alien rodents hungry for offal, but then, the boy's hand slips on the game controller, his first-person soldier slipping in the fetid mud of the battlefield as a mammalian mutant mass closes in above, everywhere, and all around. Up ahead, his friend's first-person soldier comes to a halt and glances over his shoulder, his face an internal debate of conflicted struggle until at last, panting in exhaustion, he lumbers back and reaches out a gloved hand.

The moment of sacrifice lasts for no more than a moment, and as both screens of the split screen image fill with an attacking multitude of mongrel ferrets, weasels, and martens and their first-persons suffer painful deaths, both the boy and his friend jolt back, laughing and letting loose a string of unseemly swears and appropriate expletives. A hoot and a half, another 5 to 10 percent is gained.

CHAPTER 3

Monsieur Substitute is a crap teacher.

Although *crap* is not truly a full-on profanity, Darby understands that it is much closer to the neighborhood of inappropriate than appropriate, so even while he wouldn't ever say the word out aloud and risk other people overhearing, he feels all right about letting it pass through his mind if it's justified. In addition, sometimes when use of the word is very much justified, Darby will allow himself to breathe the word soundlessly, which is what he does when Monsieur strolls past his desk during Silent Reading Period. *Crap*. It feels right.

A few other words hover between appropriate and inappropriate.

a. bloody
b. hell
c. damn
d. asinine
e. areola

Crap aptly describes Monsieur for a number of reasons.

Monsieur Substitute is a crap teacher because he starts each and every school day with a silent reading time, which includes a fictional reading from the *New Horizons* anthology, a comprehension question set, an integrated vocabulary exercise, and an autobiographical expansion composition. A full period during which Monsieur does little more than his daily morning word search. Seventy-five minutes. Maybe he tells himself the daily routine builds organizational skills and reinforces individual responsibility, but Darby suspects it's just a lazy lesson plan shortcut to pass the block of time in between morning announcements and first morning nutrition break.

Monsieur Substitute is a crap teacher because he has not at all altered or attended to the classroom decoration since Mr. Henderson's unfortunate accident last November, and maybe Monsieur Substitute tells himself that the Dominion of Canada Historical Timeline over the board and Planets of the Solar System Galaxy display above the door are necessary lessons to be not only learned but relearned and such visual repetition does have pedagogical justification, but there's really no reason not to replace the construction paper menorah and manger on the Seasonal Display Board from December with hearts and flowers and cupids for February.

Monsieur Substitute is a crap teacher because he pays too little attention to Alexander and Them and too much attention to Jennie. Maybe the teacher tells himself that he needs to pick his battles, and that's why Alexander Andrews and Billy Pace and Stewart Holgermonsson are allowed to hand in silent reading reports that are entirely superficial and slapdash in every way. Maybe Monsieur tells himself that it's best to keep his head down until the end of his open-ended contract position, and maybe that's why Alexander and Them are not even called out when they sneak their forbidden cellular mobile telephones to send and receive text messages and barely bother to hide what they're doing under their lift-top desks. There is no excuse, however, for spending so much time lingering at Jennie's desk, which is where Darby sees Monsieur now.

"Good morning, Mademoiselle Jennifer," Monsieur says.

The only reason Monsieur does this is to curry his favour with Vice-Principal Phelps-Christianson, and none of his intents and purposes are honorable. No matter how many times he stops by Jennie's desk and no matter how many times he speaks to her in his all-interested voice to ask how her work is coming along, he always without fail forgets to speak into her good ear, and he always consistently calls her Jennifer no matter how many times she corrects him.

"I prefer Jennie," she says.

"Ah, *oui*, yes," says Monsieur. "I remember."

"That's all right." Jennie shrugs.

Darby watches the crap teacher lean casually and cheerily against the side white board while he chats the morning away with Jennie. Over the teacher's shoulder, the names of the four career parent presenters coming to the class later in the afternoon after second nutrition break are written in white board green marker.

a. Financial Advisor and Asset Manager Terence Gendry
b. Dental Hygienist Cintia Holgermonsson
c. Mechanical Engineer Harold Tamm
d. Social Services Outreach Facilitator Olivia Beecham-Andrews

Trying not to look at or even at all think about his father's name on the board, Darby wonders if Kamil and Stewart and Alexander are trying not to think about their parents' names on the board. Darby's mom says such feelings of discomfort are natural in social settings with one's parents present, but the knowing does not change the discomfort, so instead Darby turns his attention back to Monsieur, who is standing there in an all relaxed and lofty manner. The sight irritates and distracts Darby, but irritation and distraction both feel better than discomfort, and besides that, he needs to be distracted because he already finished his silent reading work from *New Horizons*, which took him only forty-five minutes.

His reading this morning was from the Man vs. Society conflict chapter of the *New Horizons* reader, which came after the Man vs. Nature and Man vs. Himself conflict chapters. In November before his unfortunate accident, Mr. Henderson pointed out that the classroom textbooks were outdated and the students shouldn't use the terms *Man* to stand in for all of humanity. He added that pronouns like *himself* could also be a problem, which made sense to Darby because social justice is a fundamental right worth fighting for. When Darby told his mom what Mr. Henderson said, she agreed but sighed and then said it could be tiring to worry about everything all the time, which Darby also agreed with. After a moment, his mom said that the world was not perfect, which Darby also agreed with but seemed a bit off topic.

"Should I water the plants?" Jennie asks Monsieur. "Or feed Gauss? Or something?"

Darby thinks Jennie's voice sounds a little impatient, which makes sense because she's probably noticed how much Monsieur is lingering but she doesn't quite understand the reason why.

"You can," Monsieur says.

The teacher either doesn't notice Jennie's impatient tone, or more likely, he's just chosen not to mention it.

"Have you completed the silent reading assignment?" Monsieur asks.

"Almost. I'm on my composition," Jennie says. "I'm trying to finish my composition."

Darby grins because the implied message that she wants Monsieur to infer is *if you would leave me alone, then I could finish my composition*, but again, Monsieur either doesn't notice the tone or he chooses not to infer the implication.

"*C'est bien*," he says. "You can water the plants then. After you finish, you can water the plants."

Watering the classroom plants and feeding the class's remaining hamster are usually privileges that Monsieur Substitute bestows only upon deserving students. He seems to think the privilege is the opportunity to help the teacher, but the real privilege is the opportunity to leave the classroom to fill up the drinking bottle for the hamsters and fill up the watering can for the plants. The trip to the hall drinking fountain is only a few minutes, but it's a good break from first morning period.

"All right then." Jennie's eyebrows crinkle in a kind of surprise.

Aside from morning attendance and filing up and down between the desks, assigning the privileges are kind of the teacher's only activities during first morning period, and no one has really just outright asked for the privileges.

"Maybe," Jennie adds. "Maybe Darby can feed Gauss?"

Monsieur pauses before replying, and though it's only a seconds-long pause, Darby comes to understand that Jennie knows she is asking for too much and Monsieur knows that Jennie knows, but by pausing, the teacher can agree and still keep his teacherly authority.

"Of course." Monsieur turns toward Darby to include him in the exchange. "When the two of you have both finished, you can together take care of the plants and hamster."

"*Bien sur*," Darby says and then feels dumb. "Yes, of course."

From his left, Darby hears someone who is probably one or more of Alexander and Them snort a laugh. Probably they've been watching Darby and watching Jennie talking with Monsieur, but Darby isn't about to turn and look and risk any kind of eye contact.

"Once you have both finished your silent reading assignment," Monsieur says again, "you may both go get the water."

The teacher nods to bring the matter to a satisfactory close and returns to filing up and down the rows of desks, looking over students' shoulders but also reading over his Dell word search puzzle book. He kind of paces in measured steps like he's policing the class to make sure no one is off task, as if morning silent reading is an important cumulative end-of-the-year assessment, which it isn't at all.

Jennie's head is turned back to her work, and she's writing more of her autobiographical expansion composition. Darby knows she likes to recheck her work for grammar and spelling and clarity of thought, and the chances are good she'll be at it another ten minutes at least, so Darby sneaks his PowerPoint slides from inside his lift-top desk. Technically, reviewing for the presentation is off task work because the presentation won't come until after first nutrition break, but Darby doesn't want to sit and do nothing and wonder if Alexander and Them are still staring at him. His mom says it's better to be productive and useful instead of thinking, stewing in one's own worry, so he lifts his *New Horizons* reader and slips his notes on Veterinary Dentistry (National Occupation Code 3114) underneath. The move feels stealthy.

At his mom's recommendation, Darby printed out the presentation three slides per page so as not to waste paper but still have space to hand write his speaking notes, and he's pretty sure this was a good idea. At Jennie's recommendation, Darby also printed the notes double-sided to waste even less paper, which was also sound advice. The two recommendations together have created a potential problem, Darby now realizes, because his hands sometimes shake during public speaking. Even though he's dressed in business office professional clothing and he's practiced his scan pause to distribute eye contact, he's not sure he can do anything to stop his hands shaking, and double-sided page notes will just make matters worse.

Following the assignment page that Mr. Henderson gave to the class before his unfortunate accident, Darby and Jennie wrote fifteen PowerPoint slides. Though Darby's mom knows lots about public speaking, she didn't have much specific advice about making PowerPoint slides for the presentation, but luckily, Jennie did.

a. Ensure conciseness with bullets
b. Organize bullets logically
c. Include no less than three bullets and no more than five
d. Revise bullets to follow correct parallel structure
e. Use a sans-serif font

What Darby likes best about the Veterinary Dentistry slides and the bulleted content is how they make order out of disorder. All the random information he and Jennie collected about mammalian bicuspids, reptilian gum diseases, and the Ontario Ministry of Training, Colleges, and Universities labour market projections for Doctors of Veterinary Medicine – all of it, neatly distilled to concise lists. The unruly made ruly. It's a good, calm feeling, and even just reviewing the printouts relaxes Darby.

It is a shame that Mr. Henderson will not be about to see how carefully he and Jennie followed the assignment criteria because they definitely tried to make the slides involving and stimulating in the way that the teacher liked. Maybe he would even have printed out some of their presentation slides and put them on the Wall of Successes in between the Current Events board and the Ducks Unlimited fundraising thermometer. Darby's own Music in Society report on George and Ira Gershwin is still on the Wall of Successes, but the sight of the report feels less like success and more like ambivalence.

When he did the Music in Society assignment, Darby found too, too much information, and according to his mom, the best way to control and contain an excess of information was to focus on one particular element of the brothers' music, which is what Darby did. The focus he chose was the Gershwins' influence on other musicians in later generations, which is why the front of the report cover shows a genealogical family tree with the Gershwin brothers as great, great grandfathers and dozens and dozens of musicians' faces from later generations branching out below.

Darby's first and original idea for the Music in Society report was a paper about his dad's band *Sea Monkey See, Sea Monkey Do*, but he never told his mom or dad about the idea. The switch to Gershwin was because even though his dad's band's live shows had a good reputation and were well reviewed in the *Calgary Arts* weekly, they only ever released three independently produced compact disc eps, and the entire musical endeavor is kind of a touchy subject for his dad. In the end, Darby thinks George and Ira Gershwin was a better choice because, well, his dad's music never influenced generations of musicians or anyone at all, but now whenever he looks at the report on the Wall of Successes, it feels like less of a success. The drawing of the family tree is well done, but whenever Darby looks at it, he can't just think about how catchy "I Got Rhythm" is and how wonderful "'S Wonderful" is. He also has to think about his dad's unsold eps. The Wall of Ambivalences.

In a way, Mr. Henderson's whole entire room brings on mixed feelings like this. The over-decoration is too much, so while it's sort of good that the teacher cared so much to make the room a stimulating environment, in a whole other different way, it makes focusing hard for Darby. Ideally, the classroom could balance stimulation and distraction in a 50:50 ratio, but Darby isn't sure how such a balance might be achieved. Is there maybe a way to control and organize one's thoughts and a way to condense and tame the classroom into nicely contained balanced parallel lists of bullets? Maybe all the decorative elements in the room could be categorized and grouped together – mnemonic learning tricks with other mnemonic learning tricks, student-centered-and-generated works with other student-centered-and-generated works, and authentic-real-world-materials with other authentic-real-world-materials – so everything could fit into a nice round number of PowerPoint slides?

Darby notices that at some point while his mind has been wandering around the room, Alexander's eyes have turned to him, and all-of-a-sudden-out-of-the-blue, the two of them have eye contact. It doesn't feel like the threatening stare-down variety of eye contact, however, so Darby doesn't look away. Instead, he looks at his former friend's face, where he sees something low and sad, which isn't an entirely unusual expression for Alexander. His former friend's face has held something low and sad for as long as Darby has known him. According to his mom, some people are simply born more inward and introspective than other people, and maybe little can be done to make them less low and sad, but that doesn't mean Darby can't try. He gives Alexander a quick wave, but the wave isn't returned.

"I'm done," Jennie says.

She says this too loudly, and when Darby looks up at her, he sees nearly everyone in the classroom is also looking up at her. Monsieur has a frown because he's maybe wondering if he should point out that she is disruptive when she speaks so loudly, but he does not, which is good because sometimes Jennie speaks too loudly because hard-of-hearing people sometimes have difficulty negotiating volume, and so reminding Jennie to speak softly would be inappropriate and insensitive.

"*C'est bien,*" Monsieur says. "Darby, you are finished?"

Sliding his PowerPoint slides into his *New Horizons*, Darby nods and walks over to unhook the drinking bottle from the hamster cage. The watering can for the classroom plants is kept by the door, so Jennie's already in the hallway a bit ahead, and he has to scurry to catch up.

"Thank you," Darby whisper-speaks to Jennie, "for getting Monsieur to pick me."

Jennie shrugs and doesn't say you're welcome, but Darby thinks that's all right.

"Did you see the way Monsieur was hanging out at my desk," she asks instead.

Darby says he did.

"I wonder why."

Darby shrugs, and says he has no idea, but his lie is a benevolent lie. According to his mom, a benevolent lie can save someone from a malevolent truth that the person does not necessarily need to know, and the malevolent truth of the matter is that Darby does have some idea why Monsieur Substitute might want to spend extra time around Jennie's desk: because Jennie's mom Vice-Principal Phelps-Christianson and Monsieur Substitute are having a secret sexual affair while Jennie's unsuspecting cuckold father travels out of town for business conference meetings and indulges himself with fast food.

"I have an idea," Jennie says.

"Oh?" he asks.

Darby looks at the floor because benevolent lying is easier without eye contact than with. At the drinking fountain, Darby unscrews the lid of the hamster water bottle and hopes his hand doesn't tremble. Keeping secrets about secret sexual affairs requires focus.

"It's about my mom," Jennie says. "I think Monsieur wants to get on my good side because of my mom."

Staring at the floor, Darby notices that the tile in the hallway resembles tiles he's seen in other schools – a cream white background mostly covered by flecks and specks of dark grey. Whoever designed the tile probably wanted a light bright pattern that hid scuffs and dirt, making it ideal for schools. The sight of the tile makes Darby think about the uniform consistency of school portables, and he could mention the connection to Jennie in order to change the topic, but he doubts such a strategy would work at the moment.

"With Mr. Henderson gone," Jennie says, "Monsieur's short-term open-ended teaching contract will probably go until the end of the year in June. It's my mom who will make that decision. Also, the school will need someone to take over the grade five enrichment class next year when we're in grade six? My mom'll be part of that decision too, I'd guess."

"Hmm," Darby says. "I think you are right." He doesn't think she's right, but a second benevolent lie can't hurt.

"House plants should be watered with lukewarm instead of cold water because the cold can stress their roots. Did you know that?" Jennie asks. "Room temperature water is best. The watering can really shouldn't be filled up at the drinking fountain."

"Do you want to go get some from the girl's bathroom instead?" Darby says.

The nearest girl's bathroom is around the other side of Richmond East Elementary's central courtyard, so that's where they go. Strictly speaking, plant and hamster privileges extend only as far as the drinking fountain, but Jennie has a point about room temperature water and Monsieur will never even notice.

Waiting outside the girls' bathroom, Darby peers into the central courtyard, an open area created by two walls of classroom windows and two walls of corridor windows. The square space is an outdoor space, but since it touches the outside world only from above, it also kind of feels like a cozy and contained indoors space, and the sight of the courtyard always makes Darby wish he could enter and spend time there. At the moment, snow covers the inside-outside courtyard – deeper than the snow is in the school yard because no one shovels inside the locked-and-out-of-bounds-to-all-students-and-faculty space. The Ducks Unlimited ducks supposedly come here to nest in the late spring, but Darby hasn't spent a spring at Richmond East Elementary yet, so he can only imagine the sight.

Jennie returns with the watering can full of lukewarm water and smiles at Darby.

"That '*bien sur*' you said to Monsieur was odd," she says.

She must have been thinking about it while she was in the girls' washroom.

"Yeah," Darby says. "Not sure where it came from."

"Did you know that tortoiseshell is made of plastic, but once a long time ago, it was made from actual tortoises?

"That's cruel."

"Yeah. Now it's only fake cruel, I guess."

"You're thinking about Mr. Henderson's glasses?" Darby asks.

Jennie nods but doesn't say more about it.

Back in the classroom, Monsieur is still strolling up and down the rows of student desks, but he pauses and looks at his watch when Jennie and Darby enter. The gesture either means that he thinks their trip to the drinking fountain took too long and their detour may hurt their chances at future plants and hamster privileges, or it might mean that Monsieur is checking the time because he's anxious for the first morning nutrition break bell and his retreat to the teacher's lounge. It could also mean nothing at all, Darby supposes. Monsieur can be hard to read.

His real name is Monsieur P. Desjardins. Since no one in the class has found out what the P stands for, the students behind his back refer to him alternately as Pierre and Patrice and Phillipe and Pascal. Darby's imagined preference is Pascal, and when he pronounces the name in his mind, he gives the first syllable an extra flourish of an extra exaggerated Paris accent, which he knows might be culturally insensitive, but since no one else can hear the voice in his head, it's probably also all right. All teachers deserve a certain amount of esteem and deference, according to Darby's mom, and outwardly, Darby does try to fake respect, but there's a reason the students call him Monsieur Substitute behind his back. He's a crap teacher, and the biggest reason he's a crap teacher is that he let one of the two class pets die over the December school holiday break. In the hamster cage, there used to be a Gauss and a Euclid, but Monsieur just dumped a bunch of pellets into their bowl and left them to their own devices for nearly three weeks. Cause and effect, Euclid died, which kind of makes Darby feel ambivalent about hamster privileges. He'd rather water the classroom plants.

Nonetheless, he hooks the bottle on the outside of the cage upside-down and watches Gauss scurry over for a sip. The lid of the bottle contains a cleverly angled metal tube, which is kind of a marvel of mechanical engineering because it curves in the middle to bend inside the cage. The end of the metal tube contains a small metal ball bearing inside, which gravity and the weight of the water hold in place until Gauss presses her small hamster snout against it and drinks.

"There you go," Darby whisper-speaks.

Unlike plants, hamsters seem to like cold water. Jennie says at best hamsters don't get more than twenty-four to thirty months of health and happiness and cedar chips, so they need care. Common sense and the better angels of our nature say you don't just abandon them for nearly three weeks, but since it's best to focus on the future, Darby unlatches the cage door and removes the hamster's ceramic bowl to feed Gauss. The bowl is the size of a condiment-sized bowl from a restaurant, which is called a ramekin, which is a good word, and Darby plans to use it in conversation the first chance he gets.

In his travels up and down the rows of desks, Monsieur has stopped by the Current Events board, and he has paused in a way that looks especially reflective to Darby. Swaying in a speculative and meditative kind of way, the teacher clasps his hands behind his back while he scans the posted newspaper clippings. The display hasn't been added to by anyone in over two months, not since Sarah Underhill posted a magazine news article about a genocidal war crime perpetrated by one subculture against another subculture within the same city somewhere between Eastern Europe and Western Asia. Darby can't remember the details because he read only the first two paragraphs and stopped because he remembered news items of local, national, and international interest all tend to be depressing. The lack of newer and up-to-date news on the Current Events board is kind of a shame because, well, the whole point of current events is that they're supposed to be current.

It occurs to Darby that perhaps Monsieur is thinking this same thought, and perhaps he wants to add a clipping, but doesn't feel it's his place. Perhaps Monsieur's haughtiness has nothing at all to do with his essential nature, and he only acts the way he does because he feels bad about Euclid. Maybe the substitute teacher knows that the whole class thinks he's a poor substitute, and maybe he's deliberately trying not to engage with the students as a pre-emptive measure against rejection. Perhaps.

"Eat up," Darby says to Gauss.

Sometimes when his mind wanders, Darby winds up feeling mixed emotions that may or may not be based on what he's imagining, so he can't really trust what he's feeling at the moment. His thoughts about Euclid and genocide seem to be all mixed in with his sympathy for Monsieur. His dad says it's an excess of empathy, but now in the midst of the excess, Darby has an urge to add to the Current Events board. If he spent first nutrition break in the library resource centre, he could find a news story that might work. Not an article of local, national, or international importance, but a human-interest story that would reaffirm the rightness of and need for current events. If Darby looked for a while, he could maybe get a recent *Ottawa Magazine* profile about a retired civil services widower who has converted his home into a sanctuary for cats the humane society couldn't find homes for, and if Darby photocopied the story and put it up on the Current Events board – cause and effect – his gesture could inspire other students in the class to follow suit. Together, their actions would revitalize the display and make it once again vibrant and relevant, which would not only cheer up Monsieur, but also act as a fitting tribute to the recently deceased Mr. Henderson.

Inside the cage, Gauss leaves the feed pellets untouched in their ramekin, and she returns to sleep in the corner under cedar chips. Though he has the urge to pet the hamster, Darby suspects he'd just be bothering her, so he closes the top latch of the cage.

At the ferns, Jennie is still finishing up her plant privileges, watering the side window plant that has impossibly survived winter and has now outlived Mr. Henderson. Billy Pace and Stewart Holgermonsson are watching Jennie, Darby notices, and their attention is no good at all. They know about Vice-Principal Phelps-Christianson and Monsieur's sexual affair secret, and since Billy is the kind of guy who likes to knuckle his finger before he punches someone on the shoulder so the punch will leave a darker purple bruise in the middle of the larger blue bruise, he's probably watching Jennie and wondering how he can hurt Jennie with the secret. Stewart is the kind of guy who can't even figure out how to swear, so he's watching Jennie and probably wondering something like *Jesus Christing* or *Ass Mother* or some such asinine nonsense. Really, it's kind of surprising he is even still in the enriched program at all.

He must have gotten in just based on his math skills and quantitative test scores.

Watching Billy and Stewart watch Jennie won't lead to anywhere good, so Darby returns to his desk with his head down. The same flecked and specked white tile covers the floor in the classroom, and Darby wonders if it's everywhere throughout the school. From within his lift-top desk, he removes his PowerPoint notes and pretends to read, nodding slightly as if mulling an idea that has just occurred to him. When Darby does chance a look up again, he sees Stewart and Billy are no longer staring at Jennie, but have in fact turned their attention on him.

"*Bien sur*," Stewart and Billy whisper-speak together.

Which is kind of unpleasant. Without wanting to at all, Darby somehow makes eye contact with both of them, but he knows not to hold the eye contact too long and turns right away back down to his PowerPoints. Feeling threatened, he thinks *you're nothing but a fat ass and a violent unbalanced asshole*, and he lets the unsaid words cross his lips breathlessly. The words come so suddenly to him that they feel like fight or flight, but on second thought, they also feel unkind because maybe Stewart will outgrow his unfortunate metabolism and maybe Billy's aggressive nature is nothing more than a preadolescent phase he will later look back upon with regret. Then again, on third thought, Darby refuses to let his mind apologize. Maybe their *bien sur* was only just mocking, but in a way, the words felt like a threat too, and he wishes he didn't see them at all.

"*Cinq minutes,*" Monsieur says.

Above the classroom door, the wall clock disagrees with Monsieur's wristwatch and actually says four more minutes, but time is slippery. However much time remains, Darby decides to fill it by organizing his thoughts, and he recalls memories that he doesn't want.

a. Although Darby told Jennie Phelps-Christianson the truth about his granddad's closed casket funeral in Calgary and he happily didn't have to see his grandad's dead body at rest during any of the three visitation evenings or on the day of the final nondenominational memorial service, Darby did see a dead body, which is something he wishes he'd never seen. The Kelly funeral home franchise in Calgary where his grandfather's body was moved after an extended stay in the Royal Alexandra Hospital contained three visitation halls and three memorial service parlours that all looked pretty much the same with sparse decoration and dim light to allow mourners to reflect in calm. The home's restrooms were located downstairs, and Darby would rather not have gone down by himself, but his mom and dad needed each other for emotional support, so he did. After, when he climbed back up the stairs, he turned left instead of right, and he wandered into the wrong visitation hall at the wrong time and saw a complete stranger's dead body at rest. It was an accident that could have happened to anyone, and he did not mean to see the pale middle-aged woman who was wearing a headscarf in the casket, and he did not mean to see the surprised faces of any of the complete stranger mourners who turned to look at him all at the exact same time.

b. Although Darby's mom and dad have always limited and monitored his screen time and online internet use and he usually avoids inappropriate images and disturbing material, Darby did see an article of national importance about a twelve-year-old girl's suicide, which is something he wishes he'd never seen. Mr. Henderson believed authentic-real-world-material should be part of the learning process and required students to contact real-world professionals for the Career Fair Pair Presentations. Since they could not find anyone in Ottawa to discuss Veterinary Dentistry (NOC 3114), Darby and Jennie reached out through email to the Calgary Zoo where a very enthusiastic Veterinary Dentist sent them wonderful information. After reading one message from Calgary, Darby signed out of Jennie's email and was taken directly to MSN News, and the page contained a current events story about the arrest of a retired police officer in Brandon, Manitoba. It was an accident, and Darby should not have clicked on the story because the retiree-turned-online-predator was impersonating a twelve-year-old girl online and wound up blackmailing an actual twelve-year-old girl in Sault Ste. Marie, Ontario, who later committed suicide.

c. Although Alexander's older sister Hannah took it in stride and did not mock him at all when he showed up at the Southgate Bayview Mews Mall after the two of them met only a couple of times at Alexander's apartment over December Break and she seemed actually to enjoy his company when they sat together during her work breaks from Chez Animaux and he was able not to stare at how beautiful she was, Darby once stared right at her bare shoulder, which is something he wishes he'd never seen. Making eye contact is important to demonstrate sincerity and interest, but is especially difficult when someone is beautiful, and Darby knew his tendency to look at the floor might be seen as bad manners. He decided a good alternate eye contact strategy with beautiful Hannah was to look at the beautiful pierced nose in which she most times wore a golden stud but sometimes wore a golden loop ring. Hannah noticed but didn't at all mind his staring at her pierced nose and actually was happy to tell him the story behind it as well as the stories behind her tattoos, most of which were located on forearms and ankles and not at all difficult to show. Her favourite tattoo, however – a small, multi-coloured image of Froot Loops mascot Toucan Sam – was located on her left shoulder just by her clavicle. When she tugged down the shoulder of her Chez Animaux golf shirt uniform to show Darby, he tried not to stare but his eye was caught by a confusing thin strip of gleaming beige material. Had it been a brassiere strap, Darby would have known to avert his eyes, but the delicate strip of material made no sense, and he stared longer than he should have. He stared until Hannah let out a laugh and told him it was a camisole, which is a good word.

d. Although Darby's dad's new employers at Iogen Technologies paid for the family to relocate from the fully detached with a backyard house in Calgary to a tall narrow executive townhome in Ottawa, Interprovincial Movers Inc recommended that customers move belongings of a private or irreplaceable nature, including confidential documents and papers, themselves, and Darby stumbled across his mother's new teaching contract, which is something he wishes he hadn't seen. Busy settling into Ottawa, the family did not unpack their boxes of family photo albums and papers for a good few weeks, a delay that stretched even longer once his dad moved out of the executive townhome and into a low-rise apartment complex. It wasn't until Boxing Day after the crappiest Christmas ever that the boxes were opened. Home and bored, Darby decided to help his mom avoid the potential pain of family photo albums and stumbled across her employment contract with the Ottawa-Carleton District School Board. Though he wasn't about to read through all seven pages of clauses and subsections, Darby glanced at the conditions at the top of the contract and saw that the position was temporary and ended at the end of June, which meant that his mom gave up a permanent job she'd had for all of Darby's life so his dad could take a permanent job in another city, which wasn't right. On top of that, after relocating in the other city, his dad shortly afterwards left, which really wasn't right.

e. Although his mom has explained the dangers of carcinogenic tobacco and his dad has told him that accepting a cigarette in order to lower social barriers demonstrates a weakness of personal character, Darby went along with Alexander and Them off school property to smoke behind the Good and Quick Gas and Sip, and near the end of lunch period they all saw Monsieur and Vice-Principal Phelps-Christianson together, which is something Darby wishes he'd never seen. Walking back to Richmond East Elementary together, they were listening to Billy Pace telling them a story about how he watched a pornographic video on his father's laptop and the password was super easy to break because his father just always uses his little sister's middle name for a password. Because Stewart Holgermonsson was not smart about what he should say and what he should keep to himself, he stopped Billy midsentence to ask him what an areola was, and once it was explained, Stewart said the word sounded Spanish or Italian or something like that. Alexander laughed and elbowed Darby in a friendly way, and then they all spotted Monsieur Substitute's Volvo station wagon parked in the emptied-out parking lot of First Unitarian of Ottawa. It was an accident, but they crept closer to see why the car was rocking and shimmying back and forth and immediately saw

Vice-Principal Phelps-Christianson sitting on the Frenchman's lap with her face buried in his hair and his face buried in the stylish scarf still knotted stylishly around her neck.

When finally, the first nutrition break bell rings, Darby picks up his PowerPoint slides and his *New Horizons* and returns them inside his lift-top desk. Packed up and ready to head to the library resource centre, he notices a change on the side white board.

a. Financial Advisor and Asset Manager Terence Gendry

b. Dental Hygienist Cintia Holgermonsson

c. Mechanical Engineer Harold Tamm

d. ~~Social Services Outreach Facilitator Olivia Beecham-Andrews~~

Monsieur must have most probably crossed out Alexander's mom's name while Darby and Jennie filled the drinking bottle and watering can, and most probably the change means that Alexander's mom has cancelled. In the nearly dozen-some times Darby went over to Alexander and Hannah's apartment in December and January, work had always kept their mom away and Darby never did get to meet her.

His former friend's low and sad face makes sense now.

ON COMPETITION AND COLLABORATION AT THE GOOD AND QUICK GAS AND SIP

Located four blocks away from Richmond East Elementary, off the main arterial road, and past two four-way stop intersections, the Good and Quick Gas and Sip provides isolation and quiet for elementary students venturing boldly beyond school property. Far from the prying eyes of faculty and staff, the independent gas-station-snack-counter-convenience store housed inside a low slab cinderblock construction of chipped painting discourages most casual shoppers. Two rusted barrel drums bank the four fuel pumps, but these garbage cans go unused, and predictable rubbish litters the front lot: emptied bags of off-brand potato chips, half-crushed cans of caffeine energy drinks, and used scratch tickets. Taken altogether, the locale gives off such an unapologetic air of failure that most potential patrons drive past, and even passersby in need of a public toilet will hold off and wait for the more reliable restrooms of Mac's Milk just three blocks down.

Behind the building, however, the chaotic clutter offers something more. Scavenged but forgotten shelving units lie on their sides in a random arrangement to create a small clearing amongst the clutter. It is an accidental alcove with milk crate seating for four, a secret garden idyll offering quiet and solitude to a group of four young friends learning to smoke cigarettes and socialize. Here, the intimate privacy of the place offers a safe environment and trusting atmosphere in which four boys might share with one another their stories.

On one cold lunch hour in December, upon arriving behind the Good and Quick Gas and Sip, the least clever of the four might launch into a bravado-filled tale about smoking at his house and outwitting his babysitter. As a dental hygienist and a dentist, the boy's mother and father both adamantly oppose smoking for health and aesthetic reasons, but their career successes mean that their son's room in their suburban home comes with its very own ensuite bath, and it is in this private place that their son has taught himself to smoke.

"They go in there only once in a long while to make sure I've got enough toilet paper and toothpaste and stuff, but not too often, yeah? The only real dangerous danger is that my mom or dad might somehow sniff out second-hand smoke drifting into the hallway or maybe third-hand smoke that could stick on my clothes. But the solution I came up with was smoking right in the shower. No bragging, but it was a smartacool strategy. What I did was I waited for their Tuesday night movie date night when tickets are half-off and the sitter comes over. Once mom and dad were good and gone, I rolled up a hand towel to stuff up under the bathroom door and seal the room so I could smoke and nothing at all would seep out? Then, I ran the shower on hot for a minute so there'd be steam all in the air, and I got in the shower and lit up a cigarette. To protect the burning ember part, what I did was I smoked it like one of those dockworkers do when it's all windy down by the waterfront docks, and I cupped my palm around the cigarette. So then, I do that, and I'm almost done the entire king size extra light without the babysitter once suspecting, and I'm about to do a quick lavender body wash all over so as no one's the wiser, but then I start to feel dizzy? It's the cigarette making my head fuzzy, but also, I'm too hot because of all the shower and the steam in the air means maybe I'm not getting enough oxygen. I could have gone ass-end over and bonked my head on the side of the tub, and the sitter would have had to come in and I would have been naked, which would have been real embarrassing. What I did, though, was I steadied myself against the wall? So I wouldn't fall down? So the only thing that happened was I dropped the cigarette butt, which fell onto the shower curtain and melted it. So now there's a circular cigarette burn in the shower curtain? But no one's noticed yet."

With his anecdote at an end, the least clever boy will look to his audience for approval and appreciation, looking from face to face to face at the three seated around him on milk crates. Two of the three friends grin. Though they might rightly question the truth of the entire tale and though they might wonder at its greater point, they can intuit the need for validation in the unclever boy's eyes. Approval and a couple of grins cost them nothing at all, but beyond that, the two boys innately understand how everyone everywhere needs appreciation, and so they smile, and they nod to honour the anecdote.

"I hope your parents never find the cigarette burn."

"Yes, a clever strategy."

The fourth boy does not offer such well-intentioned feedback because he is not well intentioned, and he sneers instead. Although they have been classmates since Junior Kindergarten, the least kind boy chooses to sneer and belittle the least clever boy because he can. Too often, such is the spirit of boys and men, and while the safe environment and trusting atmosphere behind the Good and Quick Gas and Sip might inspire anecdotes told in the spirit of camaraderie, they might also inspire competitiveness.

"That's nothing," the cruel boy says contentiously. "I locked my sitter in the bathroom so I could smoke. She's supposed to spend time with me, and that's what she gets paid for, but all she does is text on her phone or look at Instagram pages. One time, she promised we'd play at least two levels of KillCraft WarMachine, but then she goes to the bathroom for ten minutes and doesn't come out, and I can hear her fingers tapping on the screen. The bathroom door faces the upstairs bannisters, so I figured I could tie a rope around the door handle and loop it through one of the bannister rungs, but then I remember the luggage bungee cords we have in the kitchen junk drawer, and they work even better. Then I decided I might as well smoke on the patio since she's not going to know the difference, and I do. Ten minutes later, I come back upstairs expecting she will be banging on the door and will have learned a lesson, but it turns out she doesn't even notice. She hasn't even tried to open the door, and I could have just quietly unhooked the bungee cord and all's well ending well. But then, I thought no. No, let her think about what's she's done for a while, and I went back downstairs and turned up the television so I didn't have to hear her knocking and calling out to me and yelling for help. I guess I knew she'd text my parents right in the middle of their couples counselling, and they'd have to pick up and they'd be pissed when they got home, and I'd lose a week of screen time and my allowance would be reduced, but that didn't matter as much as the principle. Anything worth doing is worth doing well, you know?"

With his one-upmanship thus ended, the least kind boy grins and looks to the other three. His expression expects approval for the anecdote, but none of his friends' faces responds as he wishes. One face bites its bottom lip in confusion, and one face puffs its cheeks in astonishment. The last one bunches his brow in worry, and for a moment, the cruel boy doesn't seem to understand. Do they not believe his anecdote? Has he so badly breached Good and Quick Gas and Sip etiquette? Should he shrug off this moment of discomfort, or should he curse with great profanity for their lack of appreciation? In the end, he chooses anger, but it is a silent anger.

In the quiet moments that follow, the newest boy in this group of four thinks variously about Calgary, his mom, and the discomfort of a milk crate. He drifts from unhappy thought to unhappy thought until his unsettled mind settles upon the true topic that is most bothering him – the nasty and brutish nature of competitiveness. Though new to excursions off school property, he has already too often witnessed discussions devolve as they have done today, and it seems to him that perhaps competition will always progress in a destructive direction. Camaraderie quickly sours in such a situation, and even enterprises as unifying as sharing cigarettes and anecdotes cannot succeed. Perhaps putting four young boys together will always lead to such a dilemma, but then the boy thinks about their absent teacher.

"What do you think happened to Mr. Henderson?" he asks.

"He drove his Nissan Leaf off a bridge."

"He's in a coma."

"Yes, but do you think perhaps something happened on the bridge? Do you think perhaps a bird flying overhead distracted him?"

"A graceful and swooping overhead hawk caught Henderson's attention and distracted him."

"What? No, a chicken hawk flew overhead and shat-pooped on his windscreen."

"A chicken hawk with irritable bowel syndrome."

"Who had overindulged in fast food left over in the mall garbage bins."

"Mr. Henderson automatically clicked the windshield wipers but they just smeared the shat back and forth."

"He collided with the bridge guardrail."

"Balanced all precarious-like and teetering over the rushing rapids below."

"His airbags deployed but they rammed his spectacles into his eye sockets."

"Those stylish tortoiseshell frames that he's so proud of wound up blinding him."

"And he would have survived but he couldn't see."

"Cause and effect, he opens the car door not realizing the danger he is in."

"Bassackwards, he and the car go tumbling off the bridge."

Conversation has turned more callous than the boy might have predicted, and in truth, all four friends speak heartlessly in order to hide their fear. All four wish their teacher would wake and once again fill their days with well-planned lesson plans, and all four boys have suffered sleeplessness and dark dreams because of the unfortunate accident. Behind the Good and Quick Gas and Sip, though, the cruel tone of their collaboration not only feels right and reassuring, it also allows them to leave competitiveness behind them.

CHAPTER 4

At temperatures below 20 degrees with a contributing wind chill, the Ottawa Carleton District School Board guidelines mandate indoor nutrition breaks in the school gymnasium-auditorium. Since the window thermometer outside of the grade five classroom hovers at negative 19 this morning, the grade five students have two options: out to the schoolyard or off to the library resource centre. Monsieur Substitute is halfway out of the classroom door and heading to the teacher's lounge when he makes this announcement, and it's a bit obvious to Darby that the guy isn't much concerned with which choice the students pick. He could've at least faked caring a bit better for politeness, though.

"Library?" Jennie asks.

Since the library is what he was thinking, he tells her that it was what he was thinking.

"Library it is then." Her voice is a bit low and flat. She must still be trying to puzzle out why Monsieur lingered by her desk this morning and/or dwelling on the fact that Mr. Henderson will not return. Either way, something has her out of sorts. Jennie is usually quite good about modulating her pitch and tone, which according to Darby's mom is another essential presentation skill and a vitally important one. Even if a speaker's business office casual is ironed neat and tidy and even if the speaker makes natural and non-threatening eye contact, a flat tone will come across as off-putting and will bit by bit alienate an audience.

"Do you want to find something new for the Current Events Board?" he asks.

"No, why?"

Jennie's voice turns from low and flat to peevish, and Darby doesn't think he can explain why he might want to cheer up Monsieur, and talking about Monsieur might get too close to the secret about Jennie's mom and the parking lot of First Unitarian of Ottawa, which is a secret Darby wants to steer wide of. He kind of wishes he didn't mention the Current Events Board at all, but before he has the opportunity to apologize, she does.

"Sorry," she says. "Touchy subject for me."

On the Current Events Board, back in October just after Darby arrived at the school, Alexander and Them taped up a news item about a retired public service widower in Ottawa South who in anger had killed his own golden retriever with a garden shovel to the dog's head. Alexander said Mr. Henderson took the clipping down the same morning and explained to the class that such stories were not news at all but rubbish that lazy journalists use to fill meaningless columns of text, and his jaw muscles tensed tight. Everyone should have known the matter was not up for debate, but Jennie put up her hand anyway, and she pointed out that while distasteful, the news item qualified as local and the story was, in its own way, of morbid interest. Then, she asked whether or not what was news and what was not news was a kind of subjective decision. Darby watched Mr. Henderson's face contort as he tried to make the moment a teachable moment and come up with a response that was both educational and kind, but he couldn't. Mr. Henderson just kind of nodded as he crumpled the paper and threw it in the waste bin.

"I do want to use the library computers, though," Jennie says. "Maybe we can find out more about Mr. Henderson."

"You mean whether his funeral will be open or closed casket?"

"What? No, that won't be online. But maybe there'll be some announcement of his death or an obituary or something."

"Oh."

She wants to make sense of the unfortunate accident and death, which is just trying to make sense of something else that probably makes no sense, but Darby thinks it's an all-right idea. The chances of them finding a useable-and-not-depressing human interest story for the Current Events Board weren't good anyway.

"We should hurry," Jennie says.

She nods to confirm the goodness of her own the good idea and tells him to step lively *vite, vite, vite* because students can only sign up for up-to-two fifteen-minute time slots on the desktop computers on a first come, first served basis.

"If we don't get there right off, the multimedia stations will be full," Jennie says. "We won't get on any computers at all."

Her enthusiasm sounds genuine and quite keen, which is better than low and flat, and Darby thinks to compliment her on her pitch and tone modulation. His mom says that while a low and flat tone can alienate an audience, a lively and modulated tone can act as an emotional contagion that spreads to the audience. Darby, in fact, feels certain that Jennie's improving mood improves his too, but then over his shoulder, he hears Alexander and Them walking down the hallway. One of them who is probably Billy bangs on the glass as he walks past the tall courtyard windows, and one of them who is again probably Billy laughs low like what he's laughing at is too inappropriate to repeat. Darby peeks back to see them pass the courtyard and turn, which means they're heading out to the schoolyard, which is a piece of good fortune. Darby would have liked to talk to Alexander and express his sympathetic empathy about Alexander's mom not coming for the Career Parent Presentation, but since Alexander probably still feels angry about Hannah, the idea is a bad one.

At the library resource centre, there's more good fortune because the multimedia station indeed is nearly filled to full – mostly a bunch of grade eights whose teacher must have cut corners and let them out of class early and also some English as a Foreign Language immersion students from the portables – but Darby and Jennie get the very last two fifteen-minute sign-up slots. Their two desktop computers are side by side adjacent too, and Darby thinks to make sure Jennie gets the seat on the right so he can talk into her good ear and not to her hearing-aid ear.

On his left, he notices one of the EFL immersion students playing a sorting game in which she sorts through a rubbish pile of verbs and phrases and separates them into separate blue recycling bins marked *gerund* and *infinitive*. Each correct deposit is followed by a recorded clip of applause, which Darby thinks is a nice touch. Gerunds and infinitives are not a grammar lesson he has ever learned about, but watching, he sort of understands, so though he knows looking at someone else's computer monitor without permission is rude, he watches for just a moment more. Whoever designed the game thought to include a secondary lesson on environmental responsibility to go along with the primary verbals lesson, so even though neither the graphics nor the gameplay can compete with *Killcraft WarMachine* or any of the kind of immersive experiences he played with Alexander, Darby imagines it'd be fun to try the sorting game.

"Signed on?" Jennie asks.

"Not yet."

Jennie may or may not have caught him rudely staring at the EFL immersion student's screen, but she either does not hold the indiscretion against him or her mind is elsewhere.

"My computer's taking forever to boot up," Jennie says.

She turns her finger in a circle motion like a pinwheel while she waits for the computer to consider and accept her Ottawa-Carleton District School Board username and password.

"Mine too," Darby says.

Beside him, the verbals game applauds again. Neither Darby's mom nor his dad approves of video games, but they disapprove for different reasons. While his mother doesn't approve of games like *KillCraft WarMachine* because of the age-inappropriate material, his dad doesn't approve because he once read that becoming proficient at such an immersive game takes somewhere between 600 and 800 hours, and the time spent in such an endeavour could be better spent mastering cross multiplication and/or memorizing the lyrics of the great American songbook – half of Cole Porter at the very least. Disapproving for different reasons isn't the same as disagreeing, but it's not exactly like agreeing either.

"One of the most commonly-used passwords around the world is *password.* Did you know that?" Jennie asks.

The fact sounds credible and is interesting trivia. Darby decides to remember it and maybe share it with his mom at the dinner table Sunday after weekend visitation when she needs cheering up. Sometimes when he wants to remember such items for later use, he forgets them until he is alone and falling asleep in bed at night and the opportunity has passed. His memory is more reliable, however, when he repeats the trivia to himself five times. Password, password, password, password, and password.

"But does that mean p-a-s-s-w-o-r-d is one of the most commonly-used passwords around the world," Darby asks, "or does that mean that the word *password* translated into the many languages of the world is the most commonly-used password in the world?"

Jennie stops spinning her pinwheel finger like she thinks his question is a good one and she will respond with an answer, but she doesn't.

"I'm on," she says instead. Darby watches her open her internet browser home page to the search engine window. There may never be an answer to his question.

Because they are working together and both pursuing the same information about Mr. Henderson, Darby figures looking at her computer screen is all right and not at all rude. She types in "*Gerald Gerard Henderson" AND accident*, and the statement brings up 938 results.

"News," he says, "Up-to-the-minute and up-to-the-moment."

Of these results, 428 are duplicates and 57 have been inexplicably blocked by the parental control filter settings set by Richmond East Elementary. With what remains, Jennie begins her search, clicking through each result with such speed that Darby thinks he might compliment her on it, but he does not. The sites unfortunately turn out to be older news items about the car accident that came out last year in November when the accident happened, but Jennie clicks on and back, on and back, on and back for each one.

Once he too is signed on, Darby tries "*Gerald Gerard Henderson" AND "cause of death*." The search uncovers no complete hits, but the auto-modified "*~~Gerald Gerard~~ Henderson" AND "~~cause of~~ death*" results in 234,308 results. Of these, the parental control filter settings block 231,496, but it doesn't really matter. Darby can right away tell that the available links mostly go to news stories and coroner's reports and cold cases and medical information sites about unrelated Hendersons. Most are in the United States too.

Clicking back, Darby adds AND *Ottawa* to his search, which auto-modifies to *"~~Gerald Gerard~~ Henderson"* AND "*~~cause of~~ death*" AND *Ottawa*, which kind of frustrates him and makes him wish there were some way to get rid of the auto-modification feature altogether, but instead of dwelling on that which he cannot change, he surveys the results. Lots of forgotten obituaries and duplicates of forgotten obituaries of people who've died or been buried in and around Ottawa. Clicking on any of them would probably lead to ruminations on the nature of death and would not be helpful to his mood or his search, so Darby only scrolls down lower.

At the bottom of the screen, he learns that there is another whole other place called Ottawa in Illinois in the United States of America where several Hendersons have also died. Ottawa in Illinois, Ottawa in Illinois, Ottawa in Illinois, Ottawa in Illinois, and Ottawa in Illinois.

"Anything?" Jennie asks.

"Not anything. You?"

"No." Jennie makes the pinwheel gesture again, but quickly this time – not like she is impatient for the computer to catch up with her, but like she's trying to hurry up her thinking. The strategy does seem to work because she has new search statements almost right off. "I'll try traffic deaths or traffic fatalities in Ottawa," she says. "You try the hospital."

The search "*Capital Hospital and Community Healthcare Centre*" *AND "Henderson"* produces few fruitful leads, but it does bring Darby to the hospital's website homepage, which is laid out in a clear orderly fashion for user-friendliness. From the drop-down menu of departments and units, Darby selects the ICU and learns that an efficiency and healthcare design team has recently reimagined and renovated the layout of the unit. The ICU's own sub-drop-down menu includes an introductory summary of the unit's innovations, a list of permanent staff health care professionals, and a 360-degree virtual tour feature, which Darby clicks on and which is kind of amazing.

Inside the immersive 360-degree feature, Darby is surrounded by the circular layout of the unit, which forms a circle with a central hub containing nursing stations, storage areas, and testing facilities surrounded by a round corridor. The patient rooms run along all around the outside of the circle's circumference with glass walls, which the website proclaims as an intuitive design for around-the-clock monitoring and ongoing health care. An ideal synthesis of form and function. With the mouse, Darby walks through the virtual version of the circular hallway and loops the unit twice to poke around.

As in *KillCraft WarMachine*, the point of view is first-person perspective, but the images in the ICU aren't nearly as clear and crisp. The post-apocalyptic background of the game was designed by teams of artists and computer engineers, but the ICU's 360-degree-virtual-tour feature uses a kind of photographic technology like Google Earth that blurs and bends perception when Darby turns too quickly. Still, the tour is interesting and impressive in its own way.

"Did traffic deaths lead anywhere?" he asks Jennie.

She's still clicking back and forth, but her head shakes no while she does so.

"Too much stuff. And some of the results are about human trafficking. Did you know that human trafficking has increased in Ottawa? How can that be right? Listen." Jennie clicks back, back, back and reads to him from her screen. "Victims in the national capital region are most often youth or females under the age of thirty, and the overall number of arrests for human trafficking and related crimes stemming from human trafficking has increased by over 7% in the past decade."

The information isn't helpful to Darby's mood or the search, and it's perhaps even more detrimental than random memorials and obituaries of Henderson ancestry. Maybe trying to make sense of death is too much to expect in one nutrition break.

"Shouldn't the parental control-setting block human trafficking stories?" he asks. "I mean, isn't that exactly what they're for?"

Jennie clicks off the article, and forward, forward, forward to where she was previously.

Though admitting defeat never helped anyone anywhere, Darby doesn't truly think that searching for more information will lead to more information. It could very well lead to more inappropriate articles that won't be helpful to his mood, so instead he wanders back to the ICU, taking two and then three steps before he realizes that he could probably do the same thing in Calgary.

The 360-degree Earth map of Calgary is remarkably easy to locate, and Darby crosses two time zones in no time at all. Within three clicks, he and his first-person perspective are standing on the sidewalk outside of Windermere Ridge Elementary, the school where he completed his first years of school. Like the ICU, the corners of his neighborhood blur when he turns and walks, which isn't great, but unlike how the real Calgary would be, the city presently onscreen is sunny and snow-free, so the source photographs for the site must have been taken during the spring or summer. Darby tries walking over the green lawn and into his old school, but the Earth map stops him at every entrance. He can, however, circle the building and enter the schoolyard from the back, and from there, he sees the windows of the school library and his long-ago kindergarten classroom.

On the inside window sill of his kindergarten room sit a dozen Dixie cups holding bean shoots sprouting seedlings stretching many centimetres upward toward the sun. Darby remembers he once placed his own kindergarten Dixie cup on that same windowsill, and at the library windows, he remembers the poster collage of

Alberta writers of lasting significance that was once tacked up on the back wall. In early primary years, he stared at the collage so much during story circle time that he sometimes lost the thread of the picture book plot that the school librarian was reading. Darby clicks around the school more, but no matter what he does with his computer mouse, he and his first-person perspective can't see all the way inside, leaving him little more than a passive protagonist.

Defiant, Darby turns about-face with a left mouse click and exits the schoolyard, following the Wintervale-boulevard-Washburn-crescent-Whittleton-road route that he and his mom once upon a better time followed daily. Walking along, he notes that little of his old neighborhood has changed in his absence, and then he arrives at 265 Whittleton to stand at the bottom of the driveway of the fully detached single home that he and his mom and dad lived in before they moved to Ottawa and had to settle for the compromise of the executive townhome from which his dad left them to go and live in a low-rise apartment complex. Onscreen, from where he and his first-person stand, he can look up at the wide windows above the double car garage at his old bedroom, but because most of the blinds in the photographs are closed shut, it is impossible to look inside even by zooming up close. When he drags the mouse down and zooms in at the front door, Darby notices a detail that is noteworthy.

The mailbox. There beside the front door to the left is the green wooden mailbox onto which his mother painted a flowing cluster of red, yellow, and brown autumnal leaves. The sight of the mailbox means that the fully detached single house he is now looking at was photographed when he and his mom and dad still lived there. The onscreen house is his house when it was his home because the real-world off-screen green wooden mailbox is not right now mounted beside the front door in Calgary. The green mailbox now lives in Ottawa at the executive townhome.

Darby moves the mouse up above the front entryway patio porch and zooms in on the windows of the home office. Inside he sees a greyish brownish silhouette contrasted against the side of the white bookcases, and the silhouette is his dad. His dad must have been working on the computer in the office when the photograph for the 360-degree Earth map was taken. Before his dad moved out.

Once again, Darby is reminded that this afternoon after his Career Fair Pair Presentation on Veterinary Dentistry, Darby's dad will give a Career Parent Presentation on mechanical engineering. Though he's fortunate his dad can come and knows he would feel low if his dad had to cancel like Alexander's mom, Darby once again worries. He worries about seeing his dad all the time now, but more than that, Darby worries his Veterinary Dentistry presentation won't go well and his dad will find out.

Staring at the computer screen and trying not to think thoughts about his dad, Darby realizes something even more noteworthy than the mailbox. The 360-degree tour works as a time machine. He clicks back. Back, back, back, twenty-five times, back to the ICU.

"Jennie, look at this."

"Just a moment."

Even though he knows interrupting her again would be poor manners, Darby feels he wants to do so, and so instead, he looks to his left where the EFL immersion student has moved to the next level of the grammar game, gathering biodegradable food scraps of past and present participles and dropping them in regular and irregular compost bins. It's a pretty good game.

"Did you find something?" Jennie asks.

Turning back to Jennie, Darby points at his screen.

"Kind of. Maybe. Look at this. It's the ICU at the Capital Hospital and Community Healthcare Centre."

Jennie leans over to look at his screen, and he demonstrates how he can walk the circular hallway of the unit.

"All the walls are glass with rolling curtains so the nurses and medical professionals can watch over the patients, but it also means you can see inside the rooms and at patient beds when you walk through the halls during the tour. And there's a zoom," he says, "and when I zoom, you can see that the hospital beds have patients."

Darby demonstrates. Some of the faces of the ICU patients face away from the camera, and some others are obscured by blankets or pillows or the unidentified medical machinery keeping them alive. The few faces that might be made out because they're facing the first-person perspective are pixelated – blurred to hide their identities out of respect for their privacy.

"But," Jennie says, "that doesn't entirely hide their identities, does it?" Her voice, Darby notices, is not only modulated, but up and down animated and all over the place. "Because there's still their hair colour."

"That's what I'm thinking too," Darby says. "And from the shape of the head, you can also sometimes kind of tell man or woman. And also, you can kind of see how tall they are in relation to the length of the bed."

Jennie scooches closer to him and his Dell electronic desktop and leans in close to his screen, which isn't rude because he wants her to do so. She's pushed up against him like she was at the portable earlier in the morning, and their sides are touching again, and like before, Darby thinks it's all right.

"Yes, but that doesn't mean we'll find Mr. Henderson." She nods and turns to look at him. "These photos could have been taken any-time. They could've been taken a long time ago. Before his accident.

"But, no." Darby nods and looks at her with eye contact. "Because look – the newly redesigned and renovated ICU only opened in December, which means the pictures were taken after then, which means he's probably here."

Jennie nods slowly like she definitely understands now. "Now I understand," she says. "Show me how you got there?" she asks.

Darby does, and the speed at which she travels to the Capital Hospital and Community Health Centre website, locates the ICU drop down, enters into the 360-degree tour, and situates her first-person point of view on her screen is kind of amazing. This time, he decides it's worth complimenting her aloud.

"You're fast," he says.

It would be maybe strange for her to thank him for the compliment or just even acknowledge it as a compliment, so she doesn't. What she does do, though, is stare at her screen and smirk without even turning to look at him, which is kind of an acknowledgement of the compliment without the awkwardness and way better than a thank you.

"There's two ways we can do this, I'd guess. You can walk one way past all the patient rooms," she says, "and I can walk the other way, and we'll eventually meet together on the other side of the hub."

"At the nurse's station?"

"Yes." Jennie nods. "Or we can walk together in the same direction. The first way is more time efficient, but I don't know if it is best because the second way is probably more thorough? Wait. Now that I think about it, the second option is better because the entire point is to be thorough."

And so they walk their first-person perspectives together side-by-side in the same direction down the hall, and it occurs to Darby that they're walking so close to one another that Jennie might almost reach out and take his hand or he might almost reach out and take her hand, and they could walk the ICU corridor together hand in hand without anyone in the library resource centre seeing or suspecting. And even if someone did somehow know, that'd be all right too.

Even with their pixilated faces and the indirect angles provided by the 360-degree virtual tour, the patients resting in the first four patient rooms of the ICU are easy to dismiss as definitely not Mr. Henderson for clear and objective reasons: 1) the first patient wears long scarlet burgundy hair that seems to be turning a blue-grey from within and the dyed hair indicates a stylish and culturally savvy older woman who has been a patient for an extended stay whose dyed hair is growing out, 2) the second patient sits up in a reclining position and faces in the direction of two seated hospital visitors who are probably friends or family and their slightly bent forward posture seems to indicate the kind of superficial casual hospital visitor chitchat that vainly attempts to mask genuine concern and worry, which would only be possible and feasible if the patient was conscious, 3) the third patient has breasts, and 4) the fourth patient is shaved bald and attached to a respirator and two tubing lines that connect up to two hanging IV bags, but the patient is so short that he or she must be a child who is perhaps about Darby's and Jennie's age and should be in a pediatric ICU, and there's probably a really upsetting story why this poor child is alone here, but this is a scenario that neither Darby nor Jennie wish to imagine or dwell upon at any length at all.

In the fifth room lies a fellow of approximately Mr. Henderson's height with chestnut brown hair just like Mr. Henderson. The problem is that Mr. Henderson is of a pretty average height and stature, and chestnut brown is common, so there's no way of being sure.

"Very well might be him," Darby says.

"But no way of knowing for certain."

On top of the lonely bald child a few doors down, the idea of not finding anything at all and wasting their entire first morning nutrition break makes Darby sad. While he knows he and Jennie won't make sense of the unfortunate accident and they won't make sense of death because such things probably don't make sense, the idea that nothing makes sense feels overwhelming.

"Try again?" he asks.

He suggests they first look at all the patients and then retrace their steps once they've narrowed down the possibilities.

"Like process of elimination," Jennie says.

"Yes."

The next two rooms are entirely empty, which either means that the ICU had more hospital space than necessary, which in the overall scheme of things would be good news, or it could mean that the ICU recently cleared out two spaces because the patients went downhill and did not recover at all but died. Not good news.

"This is it," Jennie says.

Clicking to catch up, Darby and his first-person perspective look through the glass and into the patient room that Jennie and her first-person perspective are looking in. The room is occupied by a patient, and indeed the patient seems roughly the same height as Mr. Henderson, but there is no way of making out any hair or hair colour because the patient lies completely flat and blocked from the shoulders up by a rolling hospital table.

"How can you tell?" Darby asks.

"You don't see?" Jennie asks, and she's not modulating her voice.

Darby doesn't see, and he doesn't understand, but then he does. There on the side table and not at all blurred out are Mr. Henderson's tortoiseshell eyeglasses, the ones he wore each and every day all through the first part of last semester before his unfortunate accident. Darby remembers the teacher leaning against the front of his desk pushing the glasses up his nose bridge as he addressed the whole entire classroom. It's definitely him. Some nurse or medical professional must have placed the glasses there so they'd be there close at hand when he woke up, but he never did wake up.

"Yes, I see."

ON SELF-CONSCIOUSNESS

As any child who has passed a seventh birthday and moved beyond the preoperational stage of mental development can attest, the growth of a mind from concrete perception to symbolic abstraction automatically brings with it the growth of self-awareness, and the all-too-common consequence of this growth is self-consciousness. All but the youngest of the young are by their own mind hobbled, for the more a mind can think, the more it can think of itself and be paralyzed.

To observe and fully appreciate the marvel of such self-inflicted torment, there may be no better environment for field study than a public elementary school during an open-invite assembly performance. Here, a wide range of preteens, tweens, and teens are placed on stage and on display. In a controlled setting such as the Richmond East Elementary gymnasium-auditorium during a gathering such as the Winter Holiday Celebration Concert, proud grandparents, parents, and all and sundry are invited in to shed their winter mittens, scarves, and toques and to gather together in rows and columns of metal stacking chairs to bear witness to the songs and skits of contemporary holiday classics and traditional holiday chestnuts. Onstage humiliation. What better ritual might there be for not only studying, but also edging on self-consciousness?

Ill-conceived and poorly-executed wool and felt costumes of dreidels, *bonhommes de neige*, and good gingerbread folk. Ukulele club members mumble-mouthing their way through a down-down-up-up-down-up Swiss Army strum pattern and fully forgetting all of the poetical lyrics of "When You Wake Up with Tinsel in Your Hair," "Hedgehog in the Hedgerow underneath the Snow," and "As If You'd Never Hung Your Stocking on My Fireplace at All." A daisy chain of homeroom class representatives from JK to grade eight hand-in-hand leading a follow-the-bouncing snowball singalong projected on the far wall by the away team's basketball net as a slideshow dissolve-fades through a highlight reel of still-life photo image memories with happy students, staff, and faculty in the corridors, classrooms, and schoolyard of Richmond East Elementary throughout the fall term. With prodigious and public self-consciousness suffer these children.

On stage and with all eyes thus upon them, these children of elementary years cannot help but cringe at their own participation in such a spectacle and cannot help but dread the .jpeg images snapped and .mov clips recorded by the phones and the devices of the parents and grandparents below on the gymnasium floor. These children can only dream ahead to a future after the school stacking chairs have been once again stacked and wheeled back into storage in the underworld under the stage, can only gaze forward in wonder to years beyond those school days of telling tales and biting nails, and can only imagine far afield into a yet-to-come adulthood free of such self-consciousness.

Their hope in the future is wrong, of course. Like children, these children falsely trust that once through the awkwardness of their concrete operational stage and well into the bloom of formal operational, they will be good and done with self-consciousness and the shames of childhood, but no. As all who have passed into their thirtieth, fortieth, fiftieth, and sixtieth year to heaven can attest, such logic is faulty logic, and as one young boy peeks out to the audience, he learns this truth.

New to the school and generally uncomfortable around others, this boy looks at the faces of the audience and begins to understand that adults suffer self-consciousness as well. Many who are seated in the chairs fidget uncomfortably, and surveying the audience, he understands everyone's discomfort, but he is looking for someone in particular.

Two someones. He spots his own parents, who are sitting together in the audience even though they no longer live together in the same home. They sit silent. Silent because they have agreed not to bicker, and even small talk leads to bickering. Silent because neither has the energy to be angry anymore, but they both still are. Mouthing the carol that he has studied with his class for the past month, the new boy sees his parents together but not together, and he imagines the three of them will go out for coffee, cocoa, and crullers after the Winter Holiday Celebration Concert has come to a close, and he imagines them all gamely creating conversation about the holidays. *Do you remember the way the rabbit droppings stood out against the bright white snow of our Calgary backyard? Do you remember when you figured out the truth of the Santa lie in kindergarten and couldn't say "Claus" without air quotes? Do you remember the City Lego advent calendar with the Salvation Army minifig and her little collection kettle?* The new boy sees himself going along with the conversation and does not like what he sees in himself. Watching his mother and father sit, he understands that they too suffer.

From her stacking chair on the gymnasium-auditorium floor, his mother might sit stiff beside the husband she now sees twice a week at the beginning and end of every weekend visitation, but she repeatedly rolls and unrolls the woolen scarf in her lap, just so she has something to do and doesn't have to think about how she and her husband once held hands while waiting through interminable student performances. Scrunching her brow and setting her jaw, she endures as "The Dance of the Flowers," "The Dance of the Sugarplum Fairy," and "The Battle against the Mouse King Army" play from the gymnasium-auditorium PA speakers during set changes, and she tries not to acknowledge that her family will never again travel to the Arts Commons for their family *Nutcracker* tradition and her family may never again be a family. Although she sees herself as the kind of woman who does not dwell on the past when dwelling does not one bit of good to anyone at all and it is better to keep busy and move forward, she does not like what she sees in herself tonight.

With his stacking chair scooted a bit away from his wife and the mother of his only child, the new boy's father might tap his toe and admire the senior music teacher's twenty-piece arrangement and orchestration and performance of *A Charlie Brown Christmas* for the grade seven-eight band, and enjoying the song, he might realize that his young son has probably never seen the television special. They can probably find the whole entire program on YouTube to watch together come next weekend visitation, he thinks, and maybe if the boy enjoys it, they can track down the soundtrack together, and the music will become a tradition the boy will later someday remember forgivingly as a fond memory. Of course, as he taps his toe, the boy's father knows that even if the idea is a good one, it will not be enough. Grinning and bearing the off-key vocalization through the song's refrain, the man thinks of years before – back to a time when his estranged wife was not yet his wife but a music student looking forward to teachers' college and he was not an estranged husband but a student in a band finishing up his engineering program – and he sees himself in their first apartment as they together trimmed their tabletop tree from Value Village. Unable to afford gift-wrapped gifts, they decided to arrange and orchestrate and record one another's holiday favourites for one another. Berlin's "White Christmas" for her and Porter's "All Through the Night" for him. It was a time when they worked harder at love, but he now sees he has soured that memory for them both, and he cannot like what he sees in himself tonight.

Thus and so, as the gymnasium-auditorium lights dim on the Winter Holiday Celebration Concert, it may well seem as if no one is immune from the symptoms and side-effects of self-consciousness, and the mandatory merriment of the open-invite assembly performance has served only to remind everyone of their shared failings. Before the curtain and such conclusions might be drawn, however, a fifth-grade girl steps forward for a voluntary solo. She isn't a particularly pretty girl. In fact, she looks peculiar – as if her physical development has not kept up with her age. Too short for grade five. Standing too formally for a young child. And she's dressed in a denim dress over a ruffled red blouse – clothes for not only an older person, but for a distinctly unfashionable older person.

Her voice when she speaks possesses that slight squawking undertone often heard from the hearing impaired, which all audience members notice and regret noticing. When she announces that she would like to say a few words about the history of American Sign Language, the audience members undergo a series of simultaneous and silent reactions. All are in secret relieved that the girl will not be singing a carol; all are somewhat shamed by their secret relief, and all are a bit confused. Still, they have sat patient and smiled through the drama club's ghosts of Richmond East Elementary skit, the basketball team's Harlem Globetrotter Holiday routine, and the flakey-but-fetching school nurse's mandolin solo, and they will certainly sit patient and smile as this girl explains that Thomas Hopkins Gallaudet popularized sign language in North America and began what would turn into the American School for the Deaf in 1817. A few chuckle at the girl's self-seriousness – they cannot help themselves – but she only pauses, waits for the quiet, and supplies them with something of a non sequitur.

Have a holly jolly Christmas. She sing-speaks the line in discordant chords, but her hands move in a fluid motion, her arms sweeping and dipping. *It's the best time of the year.* The sight surprises the audience. *I don't know.* The sight surprises the audience in its loveliness. *If there'll be snow.* There is a grace to her movements, all the more unexpected because she seems such an awkward girl. *But have a cup of cheer.* When she stops, the audience members return to themselves, shake their heads with a grin – some emitting audible harrumphs and sighs at their own enchantment and what a funny old world it can be – until the girl's expression turns peevish and she explains that proper posture is a basic fundamental of proper sign language.

They all need to stand up, she tells them – which they do, for there is something cute and adorable in a bossy girl who does not know she is not cute and adorable. By all rights this girl should be self-conscious, but she is not at all.

Have a holly jolly Christmas. The song isn't difficult, she reassures them, and plenty of people probably already know all the words. *And when you walk down the street.* She's going to teach them how to sign the words, and what they're going to do is have a sign-along-sing-along in ASL. *Say hello to friends you know.* All the students and teachers and parents and grandparents in the gymnasium-auditorium will participate. *And everyone you meet.* And for the next fifteen minutes, they do participate, and it is a sight. They forget themselves entirely.

CHAPTER 5

GTP5Core - Enriched Program – Grade Five
GG Henderson
Career Fair Pair Presentation Rubric

Names: ____________________
Career: ____________________

Presentation Criteria	4-5pts.	2-3pts.	0-1pt.
Organization Criteria • To what extent has the presentation incorporated logical sequencing to facilitate a • nd enhance audience understanding? To what extent has the presentation utilized transitional words, phrases, and techniques to ensure a smooth forward momentum? • To what extent has the presentation considered and varied explanatory and performance modes to sustain audience interest and attention?	Seamless Flawless Flowing Innovative Smooth Unified Enlightening Surprising Logical Thoughtful	Adequate	Bumpy Meandering Obvious Perplexing Transparent Haphazard Convoluted Incomprehensible Baffling Herky-jerky
Content Criteria • To what extent has the presentation included effective appeals to logos, pathos, and ethos? • To what extent has the presentation incorporated, interpreted, and explained MTCU research? • To what extent has the presentation persuaded the audience of the topic's cultural importance at present, in the next five years, and for the next generation?	Rigorous Engaging Challenging Exhaustive Illuminating Convincing Credible Insightful	Acceptable	Banal Incomplete Improbable Wrong Unsupported Fictional Illogical Specious
Visuals Criteria • To what extent has the presentation demonstrated a command of PowerPoint* template layouts, designs, and functions? • To what extent has the presentation included consistency and uniformity in heading, subheading, and text font size, colour, and design within and between slides? • To what extent has the presentation integrated photographs / illustrations to enhance visual appeal? *Prezi optional	Striking Inventive Detailed Stylish Memorable Playful Winsome Vivid Professional Colorful	Average	Insipid Flat Prosaic Commonplace Unremarkable Obfuscating Uninspired Lifeless Gaudy Typo-ridden
Performance Criteria • To what extent has the presentation demonstrated a knowledge and rehearsal of elocution, kinesics, and proxemics? • To what extent has the presentation shown cooperation, collaboration, and equity between partners? • To what extent has the presentation demonstrated adequate individual and collective preparation and rehearsal?	Smooth Inspired Creative Natural Cohesive Rehearsed Charming Animated Dramatic	Satisfactory	Awkward Self-Conscious Stiff Erratic Monotonous Ludicrous Inarticulate Uncomfortable Mannered
Comments:			/20

"Good morning esteemed Monsieur Desjardins and respected classmates."

Since they decided upon a dark foreground font on light background slides, Jennie and Darby have darkened only the bank of classroom fluorescents nearest to the projection screen at the front of the room, which ensures maximum visibility and makes sure everyone can see the *Title slide in Civic theme with a cropped aerial image photograph view of Calgary Zoo.*

"Did you know that the Calgary Zoo in Calgary, Alberta, has over 130 different species of animals and over 700 different animals?" Jennie asks.

It is a rhetorical question because rhetorical questions can be an effective way of grabbing the audience's attention and piquing curiosity with an opening. Darby clicks forward to the *Title and Content slide in Civic theme with a two-by-three-image table of six representative animals from the six animal classes.*

"Did you know that with mammals, reptiles, invertebrates, fish, birds and amphibians, the Calgary Zoo is home to six entirely different classes of animals?" Jennie asks.

This is another rhetorical question, so Darby clicks forward to the *Title and Content slide in Civic theme with vertical split-screen of West African Dwarf crocodile, North American Grizzly Bear, Komodo dragon, rhinoceros, and red panda.*

"These animals are as diverse as the West African dwarf crocodile, the North American grizzly bear, the Komodo dragon, the rhinoceros and the red panda."

Since establishing and maintaining eye contact with the audience is crucial, Darby and Jennie signed out a pair of matching Kensington Wireless Presenter remotes from the library resource centre to forward their PowerPoint presentation slides instead of relying on the tabletop computer mouse. Since also it's good to divide the speaking in pair presentations as close to an even fifty-fifty as possible and minimize distractions like having to walk back and forth to the computer on the teacher's desk, Jennie and Darby are using two different Kensington remotes and have choreographed themselves so that he will forward her slides and she will forward his. If all goes well, the arrangement will add to their Career Fair Pair Presentation on Veterinary Dentistry (NOC 3114), and they'll get full marks not only just for coordination and cooperation but also for kinesics and proxemics, which are how they use their gestures and utilize the performance space. Feed two birds with one seed; that's what Jennie said.

The plan made sense to Darby, but then back in January when they started practising their performances, it was pretty obvious to both of them that gesturing and moving around at the front of the classroom while at the same time forwarding their slides and reciting their memorized content might prove difficult. Too much coordinated synchronization can be hard to coordinate and synchronize. Jennie's solution to the problem was rhetorical questions. During particularly complicated parts of the performance, she said she would insert rhetorical questions to send Darby cues like ballet dancers and stage actors use. Thus far, during the opening audience hook and grabber part of the presentation, the plan has worked just fine.

"And do you know what these five animals all have in common?" Jennie asks.

It is a rhetorical question, so Darby clicks forward to the *Title and Content slide in Civic theme with a five-image vertical split-screen table of the five animals variously snapping, yawning, roaring, growling, and smiling.*

"Teeth," Darby answers.

This is Darby's first line, so it's a sort of joke that was Jennie's idea. She said that his earlier silence and the fact that rhetorical sentences need no answers would make his answer unexpected. Then, she explained, the shortness of his first line would seem absurdly short, and the audience would for sure laugh. Darby wasn't sure, but Jennie said he should count three beats in his head to give the audience time to laugh, which he does – one, two, three – and much to his surprise, the audience does laugh.

"The Calgary Zoo's eleven West African dwarf crocodiles each have between 74 and 80 teeth," Jennie says. "The seven North American Grizzly Bears have an average of 42 each; the three Komodo dragons each have as many as 60; the eight rhinoceros have between 28 and 30 each, and the twelve red pandas have between 46 and 54. Do you know how many teeth that is in total?"

It is a rhetorical question, so Darby clicks forward to the *Title and Content slide in Civic theme with an embedded image of a red panda scratching its brow and projecting a look of anthropomorphized bemusement.*

"Neither do we," Darby says. He counts beats again. This time, no one in the audience outright laughs as he and Jennie planned and hoped, but there are a couple of chuckles. However, everyone knows that sometimes presentation moments do not go as planned and rehearsed, so Jennie wisely suggested contingency plans. Three beats in the case of laughs and two beats in the case of chuckles and one beat in case of an awkward silence. It is better not to dwell upon setbacks, but rather instead move ahead.

Forward. *Section Header slide in Civic theme with a single image portrait of Veterinary Dentist Dr. Larissa Beaman, DVM.*

"As the chief veterinary dentist at the Calgary Zoo, Dr. Larissa Beaman, DVM is responsible for each and every one of those teeth."

Forward. *Title and Content slide in Civic with five bullets sketching biographical details of Dr. Larissa Beaman, DVM including source note footnotes from her personal Weebly website 'Genus and Species, Smile and Shine.'*

"Like many young children," Jennie says, "Dr. Larissa Beaman DVM grew up dreaming of becoming a doctor of veterinary medicine. In her hometown of Charlottetown, Prince Edward Island, Dr. Larissa Beaman DVM cared for all the cats and the dogs and the hamsters and all the adorable animals her family had as pets, but at some point in her earlier teen years, she became aware that her abilities could and should be improved by formal education."

Mr. Henderson's original assignment sheet asked that students use content that appealed to logos, pathos, and ethos, so for ethos, Jennie traces the personal biographical details and professional highlights of Dr. Larissa Beaman DVM. This portion of the presentation will last three minutes, and as they rehearsed, Darby takes a slight step back while she speaks. By stepping back, he's ensured that the audience members' attention can focus on Jennie and not on him. As Jennie explained, blocking a pair presentation doesn't have to be as complicated as planning out a whole rat king battle underneath a Christmas tree with beautiful ballerinas and a dozen *Nutcracker* extras on stage, but it is still important to emphasize the speaker and deemphasize the non-speaker through the use of movement. Once upon a time, *The Nutcracker* and desserts afterwards were annual traditions that Darby enjoyed with his mom and his dad at the Alberta Ballet in the Art Commons in Calgary, and he kind of wishes she'd used a different example to make her point, but he understands all right.

Keeping his body stock still, Darby turns to look in Jennie's general direction to feign active listening while she explains the limited job market for doctors of veterinary medicine and Dr. Larissa Beaman DVM's wise decision to specialize in veterinary dentistry in order to make herself more professionally competitive. Feigning active listening proves difficult, however, and when Darby nods slowly and sagely and furrows his brow inquisitively and appreciatively, the false gestures and expressions feel especially false. Acting is hard. It's even harder because he can't help thinking about Alexander and Them watching and judging him, which Darby knows they most certainly are.

With a quick glancing scan of the room, Darby confirms his suspicion and glances at Billy, who's not only watching and judging, but also lifting his lift-top desk. In the corner edge of his peripheral vision, Darby spots Stewart doing the same, glancing about stupidly in an attempt at furtive cunning. Alexander watches Jennie present, leaning forward with genuine interest that makes Darby feel all their presentation preparation and practice was worthwhile. As long as Alexander's happily focused on Jennie and the demands of a career in Veterinary Dentistry (NOC 3114), he can't focus unhappily on his mom's cancelation this afternoon.

When Darby's heart rate quickens and his breathing speeds up, he recognizes the feeling and identifies it as an unfortunate fight-or-flight response. His mom says the response is entirely natural and physiological, and one time when his mom said this, his dad explained that the response has evolutionary benefits to ensure the continuation of a species. His mom said that his dad wasn't helping and added that she used to get the exact same feeling in teachers' college because she had to do two different practicum teaching assignments and didn't feel at all prepared. What she suggested worked for her was to look at the back of the room far above all of the class audience members' heads and focus on a far horizon line as if it were dusk when the sky turns all slow azure and umber and yet another good day has come to a quiet close.

The strategy is worth a try, and Darby looks at the back of the classroom – back beyond Billy and Stewart riffling through their desks and back beyond Monsieur Substitute standing in judgement with Mr. Henderson's Career Fair Pair Presentation rubric in hand – and the strategy works, reducing Darby's quickened heart rate and slowing his breath.

"And from such strong beginnings," Jennie says, "Dr. Larissa Beaman, DVM worked hard to build her credentials. What are some of the most impressive achievements on her impressive curriculum vitae?"

Forward. *Title and Content slide with five bullets highlighting the educational honours and professional accomplishments of Dr. Larissa Beaman, DVM including source note footnotes from the partial profile posted on her LinkedIn account.*

Darby nods and smiles, and neither the gesture nor the expression feels false, because he has been able to stay in the moment and watch an imaginary sunset. It occurs to him how seldom he has seen the room from the front of the room, but the rarity of the perspective makes sense, of course. The rows of lift-top desks all face forward toward the white board and tensioned projection screen and teacher desk, so he most often looks forward. Sometimes he might have glanced left or right or a little bit over his shoulder when a classmate raised a hand to answer an especially difficult mixed fraction problem. Sometimes he might have turned to watch Euclid and Gauss in their cage back before Christmas break when both hamsters were still alive and well and kicked up the occasional ruckus on the exercise wheel. Maybe sometimes he might have even looked at the back wall after practice *dictée* when he passed his vocab words and phrases behind him for marking. Mostly, though, the room from the front of the room is a whole entire new room with all new and different sights to focus upon. Unfortunately, the sight Darby focuses upon most is the fish poster, which he has never liked at all.

Like the Ducks Unlimited fundraising thermometer display by the door, the very-educated-mother planet silhouettes above the whiteboard, and the Dominion of Canada timeline on the sidewall, the fish poster is yet another piece of pedagogical stimuli in Mr. Henderson's over-decorated classroom. Most days, Darby glances toward the troublesome fish poster a couple of times on his way in and out of the room, but this morning, his front-of-the-room point of view forces him to consider the image at greater length. A cartoon, the poster shows an illustration Darby has seen in a number of variations: a row of increasingly large fish arranged from left to right. On the right is smallest fish A, who is swimming along entirely contented in its workaday world and oblivious to the dangerous open jaws of fish B right behind it. With its teeth bared ferociously, fish B is approaching fast, but its predatory focus is so intense on its prey that it is oblivious to fish C right behind it – who is also fast approaching and also with teeth bared. And then there's fish D and fish E and fish F, G, H, I, J and on and on.

In Mr. Henderson's poster, the fish have trails of air bubbles running behind them diagonally to suggest motion and there's no caption or text on the poster, which probably means the message of the fish poster is meant to be self-explanatory without any necessary clarification, but to Darby's way of thinking, that's not true. The message is cryptic at best. Indeed, to Darby's way of thinking, the more he considers the illustration, the more cryptic the message grows. Something about power and the insecure nature of power? Or no matter how big someone is, there's always someone bigger? Something about how the relationship between victim and victimizer is cyclical in nature? How are any of these possible messages helpful?

"In summary," Jennie says and pauses.

Transitional words and phrases like *in summary* are useful signposts for the audience because they signal a clear shift in content material, but because he and Jennie rehearsed so much, Darby also wound up memorizing them, so he turns his head away from the fish poster and toward Jennie. She's going to say a rhetorical question soon.

"In summary," she says, "the choice to study veterinary medicine was a way for Dr. Larissa Beaman DVM to fulfil her long-held aspirations, but she was wise and practical enough to select secondary and post-secondary programs offering co-op internships so she could network within her future industry. But if you were to ask Dr. Larissa Beaman DVM her favourite part of the job?" Jennie asks. "Well, is there any better reason than beautiful and adorable animals?"

Forward. *Title and Content slide in Civic theme with embedded video upload previously recorded from the Calgary Zoo's PandaCam showing a healthy litter of six-week-old red pandas playing rough and tumble.*

As planned and rehearsed, the adorable video clip elicits laughs, chortles and chuckles, and Darby counts a four-beat pause in his head. Then – because successful presentation moments that go as planned should be enjoyed in the moment – he counts an additional two beats and exchanges eye contact with Jennie, who is grinning at him.

"Let us look at the job market for Veterinary Dentists," Darby says.

Forward. *Vertical Comparison slide in Civic theme with a two-colour bar graph and a two-colour line graph.*

"The dark green bar graph on the left shows the number of veterinary dentistry jobs that will be created in the next five years because of industry growth."

Providing key labour market information from the Ministry of Training, Colleges and Universities is its own whole subsection on Mr. Henderson's rubric, but the facts and figures are also an effective bit of contrasting and logical logos to follow up the funny pathos of roughing-and-tumbling red pandas.

"The light green bar graph in the middle shows the number of veterinary dentistry jobs that will be created because of retirement over the next five years."

Distributing eye contact with the class row by row, Darby can feel that he's maintaining audience interest, which is a heartening turn, and then when he pivots and points toward his PowerPoint to accentuate the strong likelihood of future growth and career possibility in the exciting field of Veterinary Dentistry (NOC 3114), he also notices Jennie nodding and feigning active listening in a way that doesn't seem at all feigned but actually genuine, which is even more heartening. Of all the public speaking advice his mom gave him, she said all he needed to do was fill up the whole entire room and he'd do fine, and though her tip was ambiguous and confusing as advice, Darby watches Jennie watching him, and he maybe understands his mom's words.

Then, though, with another pivot and additional scan pause, he distributes his eye contact to the far back of the room and notices movement in the small rectangular window of the classroom door. The narrow pane with its reinforced steel-wire grid darkens and seems to fill with a flourish of floral colour, which makes no sense at all until Darby sees it's actually Vice-Principal Phelps-Christianson and her stylish neckerchief scarf in the window on the other side of the door in the outside hallway. She's leaning down to peek into the classroom through the window.

Probably she has come to catch a glimpse of the presentation to see if everything is going all right, but maybe also she has come to catch a glimpse of Monsieur Substitute. Jennie has her body orientation turned to feign active listening and all the other classmate audience members are busy watching and judging, so Darby realizes two things simultaneously at once: 1) number one is that only he can see Vice-Principal Phelps-Christianson, which is good because if Alexander and Them saw her, they might snort or laugh inappropriately and 2) number two is that he has stopped talking.

"And the graph on the right-hand side?" Jennie asks.

He has stopped talking and all at once, the presentation is not going all right because he's thinking about the Volvo station wagon in the emptied-out parking lot of First Unitarian of Ottawa. Darby can't help but picture Vice-Principal Phelps-Christianson in Monsieur Substitute's lap with her face in his hair and his face buried deep into the folds of her stylish floral print scarf. Was the floral print scarf the same floral print scarf as today's? Maybe she just has a large collection of such scarves, and she mixes and matches them to go with a variety of her workday outfits. Maybe such scarves are useful as accent accessories to add variety to her workplace wardrobe, and she purchased dozens at a silk market while on vacation abroad.

"What do we think the chocolate brown bar graph on the right represents?" Jennie asks.

As with actors and extras and beautiful ballerinas fighting each other underneath a Christmas tree, it is important that everyone involved in a presentation prepares ahead and learns everyone else's part. In case someone gets sick with chicken pox and has to be kept home. Or in case someone skips a line and misses a cue. Or in case someone freezes from fight-or-flight response because he can't stop thinking of a vice-principal sitting in a substitute teacher's lap. If any of those instances happens, prepared partners and group members and actors can rush in and provide assistance.

"Maybe it represents something about the next ten years?" Jennie asks.

What the graph represents is job prospects in Veterinary Dentistry (NOC 3114) over the next ten years compared to job prospects in all of the health industries over the same period. Darby kind of understands Jennie is trying to help him with her prompts, but can't quite bring himself to say what they've prepared and practised saying.

"Do job prospects look good over the next ten years?" Jennie asks.

The question is not a rhetorical question, but in the confusion of the moment, Darby accidentally and prematurely clicks his Kensington Wireless Presenter remote.

Forward. *Title and Content Slide in Civic theme with bulleted text listing requisite and preferred education levels plus requisite and preferred licenses from provincial and federal bodies.*

"Yes," Jennie says. "So now that we know the chances of finding a job as a veterinary dentist are moderate to good, let's look at the education and certification required."

Just like she did back in the Winter Holiday Celebration Concert in the auditorium-gymnasium in front of all those people, Jennie remains in the moment and does not freeze or grow at all self-conscious, and Darby can't help but admire her ability. She pushes forward and ignores a past that cannot be changed.

"After a minimum of two years of university study in a pre-veterinary program," she says, "four years in veterinary medicine is offered by several universities in Ontario."

Darby remembers to step back and stand still, so his presence will be deemphasized and not distract the audience from Jennie. From his frozen still position, he looks off toward the far horizon at the back of the room and the fish poster, which he decides has to do with unfortunate pecking orders. Pecking orders will always be unfortunate because no matter what one's place is in a pecking order, that place always involves not only being picked on but also picking on someone else.

Everyone knows he flubbed his lines, of course, and probably everyone is staring at him even though they should be watching

Jennie. Billy and Stewart are riffling in their lift-top desks again, but Darby forces himself to stare at the setting sun horizon at the back of the room, and he wills the minutes to pass.

"In summary," Jennie says, "anyone wishing to pursue veterinary dentistry would do well to become a member of the CVMA, Canadian Veterinary Medical Association and the corresponding provincial bodies. Next, why don't we consider where the majority of veterinary dentists apply their trade?"

Forward. *Title and Content Slide in Civic theme with image of a colour-coded provincial and territorial map of Canada in three colours with a corresponding three-colour legend.*

"Each of the three colours represents the three most common specializations within veterinary dentists," Darby says. "Those working primarily with farm animals, those working primarily with zoo animals, and those working primarily with domestic pets."

As Jennie steps back to deemphasize her presence, Darby pivots toward the map, and remembers not to turn his back to the class because speakers should never unintentionally alienate or exclude an audience. He hasn't, however, got the requisite energy to gesture with enthusiasm toward the map with a flourish the way he and Jennie practised he would.

"As you can see," he says, "the specialization of veterinary dentists very much determines where they live and work."

Darby knows he's forgetting to modulate his pitch and tone, but he suspects that any attempt at enthusiasm at the moment will make his voice crack, which would be much worse than a flat monotone.

"As you might expect, those working with farm animals generally work in more rural areas and those working with domestic house pets generally work in urban and suburban areas."

From the front of the room, Darby can see everyone in the room is watching him, and so no one sees when Billy Pace removes a copy of *Oui* from his lift-top desk. The magazine comes from Darby's dad's collection of vintage pornography – the one he found back in December and the one he foolishly told Alexander and Them about back in January. The cover is bent back, the pages opened to a pictorial essay. Billy shows it to Darby for only an instant, and then he sneaks the magazine back in his desk, grinning because his mean trick has the disruptive effect that he wants it to.

"Employment at zoos is umm urban as well, but ahh the number of full time and permanent positions of this nature is small."

Darby doesn't feel up to distributing eye contact but stares straight ahead. The pictorial essay that Billy showed him was one Darby recognized: "Swing in the Mood." Like all the photograph series in his dad's collection, it had a title and even told a kind of themed story.

"Working with working animals at a farm and exotic animals in a zoo and domesticated pets in a suburb all come with different challenges."

"Swing in the Mood" tells the story of a flapper dancing all by herself in an empty dance club. The photographs show the model next to an empty stage with a half-dozen chairs and a half-dozen instruments. Although there are no musicians at all, the model dances and kicks like the music is playing in full swing, the sway of her fringed and beaded skirt revealing how little she wears underneath.

"All animals have teeth, but how much those teeth are cared for or not cared for depends a lot on where the animal lives and how that animal is used by people."

Still grinning, Billy tilts his head in Stewart Holgermonsson's direction one row over, and when Darby looks, he sees Stewart flash a folded-back magazine as well. The mean trick has been coordinated, it seems, and Stewart's picture comes from *Club* and a pictorial essay entitled "Lake Sleepaway," which tells a pornographic story with a summer camp theme. The mean trick works well because Darby's voice cracks as he asks his last rhetorical question.

"What are the challenges of each slightly different specialization?" he asks. "What are the advantages and disadvantages of each specialization?"

Forward. *Title and Content Slide in Civic theme with three column comparison layout showing bulleted lists of relative median salaries, benefits, pension, and job stability within three veterinary dentistry specializations.*

"Here are the advantages I will discuss," says Jennie.

Stepping backward, Darby looks at the floor while Jennie speaks, even though, like turning a back to the audience, looking at the floor during a presentation is a pretty fundamental error. A downward gaze at the floor not only breaks any chance of sustaining eye contact and creating a rapport of trust, doing so also can convey a lack of confidence. For some in the audience, a lack of confidence can trigger sympathy and forgiveness, but for bigger fish, a lack of confidence can also trigger antagonism, which is kind of the opposite of sympathy and forgiveness. Looking at the floor, Darby doesn't want to look at Alexander and doesn't want to see if Alexander's participating in the mean trick too.

"As you can see, relative to the average Canadian income, veterinary dentistry is a lucrative field," says Jennie.

The floor doesn't really provide an escape, so Darby brings his head up and looks again at the sunset horizon at the back of the room. In addition to the difference in perspective and angle from the front of the room, Darby also notices that there's the matter of light, which even with the fluorescents all on, mostly comes from the side windows in the classroom. Seated at his desk, Darby sees everything lit from his left and shadowed on his right, but from the front of the room, the opposite is true, and while all the faces in the audience look familiar lit from either side, the room from the front of the room does change appearances. Except for ballet dancers and stage actors and models in pictorial essays who have been genetically gifted with unusual beauty, no one's face is entirely exactly symmetrical, and the difference in light reveals changes. Looked at this way, the room is full of complete strangers whom Darby doesn't know or have any idea about.

"When it comes to job stability," Jennie says, "one has to also consider the advantages of a strong labour union."

Before turning to look at Alexander, Darby wonders which pictorial essay his former friend will be holding, and he hopes it isn't "Get off Your Throne" from *Club*. That story is a story about a naked woman reading a magazine on a fancy toilet inside the cubicle of a fancy hotel washroom, and it's a story that bothers Darby. Every time he's looked at that pictorial essay and tried to make sense of it, it's just made no sense at all.

"In summary, then," Jennie says, "those are the advantages. Potential disadvantages?"

Because the inevitable is inevitable, Darby looks to Alexander, but his former friend is not staring him down at all and his former friend does not flash "Get off Your Throne" or any pornographic magazine at all. Alexander seems only interested in watching Jennie.

Forward. *Title and Content Slide in Civic theme with triple comparison columns with bullets listing percentage of positions filled by part time contracts and percentage of positions filled by temporary contracts limited in term by negotiated and arbitrated union agreements.*

"Umm," Darby says. "The average salaries, benefits and pension numbers provided by the Ministry of Training, Colleges and

Universities are averages that look at full time permanent veterinary dentists."

Umm is a disfluency that Darby's mom says to avoid while speaking in front of an audience, and in addition, Darby realizes he has interrupted Jennie, who actually still had another couple of minutes of labour union material. Cutting off a presentation partner is not only a public speaking mistake, it's bad manners.

"Sorry," Darby says. He gestures with a nod to say that he will say no more and Jennie should finish the presentation herself and he's sorry.

"Right," she says.

Again, Jennie's ability to stay in the moment and accommodate for errors is admirable, and she steps in to recite Darby's lines.

"In summary," she says, "some disadvantages are harder to quantify than others. But who would like to go back to the Calgary Zoo?"

She clicks the Kensington Wireless Presenter remote and forwards to the thought-provoking clincher conclusion. *Title and Content slide in Civic theme with embedded video file.* The recorded clip ties to their opening attention-getter and will leave the classmate audience members with a memorable final feeling of goodwill.

"Dr. Larissa Beaman DVM was kind enough to record a short behind the scenes video of the Calgary Zoo for us," Jennie says.

On the screen, Dr. Larissa Beaman DVM waves and grins at the camera and with a sweeping hand gesture invites all of the grade five class into her lab. Stepping back, she gives a small flourish of her arm and reveals an examination table with a sedated red panda who is indeed a sleepy bear. She lifts the animal gently and brings its face closer to the camera, whisper-explaining the dangers of sweets and candies as she pulls its gums back to reveal the incisors, cuspids, and bicuspids common to most herbivores.

ON VINTAGE PORNOGRAPHY AND THE NATURE OF PICTORIAL ESSAYS

Similar to the themed stories in an elementary school language arts reader such as *New Horizons*, the plots that unfold as pictorial essays in issues of *Oui* and *Club* from 1976 to 1983 tell concise narratives that are intended to be read in a single sitting. However, while the short prose stories in *New Horizons* present conflicts as varied as Man vs. Nature, Man vs. Society, and Man vs. Himself, the plots of pictorial essays such as "Lake Sleepaway," "Sunday in the Park with Georgette," and "Out Back" are comparatively linear and straightforward. Unfolding in a series of roughly twelve to eighteen photograph panels, these scene-driven plots typically open with one or two fully dressed female protagonists who – because of an unexpected inciting incident and events arranged in a causal chain – move forward panel by panel toward an inevitable and fully undressed conclusion.

In "Out Back," for example, the opening panel of the pictorial essay presents a park ranger driving a four-wheel Honda ATV across the dusty Australian Outback. The patches on her many-pocketed vest and grizzly sunhat mark the young brunette woman as a conservation and environment officer of the Great Victoria Nature Reserve. In subsequent photographs arranged in standard grid layout as single and double-page spreads, the sweat on the ranger's brow increases incrementally, forcing her to remove her hat and unbutton the buttons of her collared shirt until she has removed the top of her khaki uniform entirely. As a responsible conservation officer, she continues to patrol on her all-terrain vehicle for the second and third photograph panel, but she must unexpectedly bring her four-wheeler to a halt by a small grove of overgrown reeds. Why? The readers of a pictorial essay cannot be told but must intuit by the visual details in the subsequent photograph: the park ranger stands bending over the ATV with the removed gas cap in hand, the material of her short shorts pulling tighter as she peers into the fuel tank. Midway through the pictorial essay, this panel thus reveals two insights simultaneously: 1) the ATV has run out of gasoline, and 2) the title "Out Back" contains an understated double entendre. In the extended denouement photographs, the ranger disrobes and wanders about the grove of reeds, skimming her hand over the long grass and smiling knowingly to herself.

While double entendres do not appear in all pictorial essays, wordplay titles often offer readers clues to not just plot but character and setting. A title such as "Ship Ahoy" readies the reader to expect a seafaring tale and provides a context to understand the nautical persona played by the dark-haired woman in uniform. Though the naval dress cannot be tied to any particular nation's military forces, readers who pay attention to the titles will immediately recognize the blue and white coveralls, neckerchief, and flap collar as a sailor's suit, even though the protagonist will shed all but the trim little white cap atop her pixie cut by the story's fourth panel. Further, titles can help establish situation and location when uniforms and costumes are not distinct enough to provide adequate scene setting. In "Straight to the Heart," for example, readers might not readily recognize the heavy grey canvas coveralls as the uniform of an EMT, but since the blonde model with a layered and feathered cut stands lit by the flashing red lights of an ambulance, her role in the plot becomes clear. A stethoscope hanging down over the crease of her cleavage and the defibrillator paddles held forth likewise complement the story's title to clarify both setting and character. In rare instances, the title of a pictorial essay must by itself suggest a good deal of exposition: in "Out for Blood," only one of the three characters begins the story clothed at all. A black-haired model wears a matching beige camisole and slip in silk, but the clothing provides no distinguishing clues that might help a reader understand her identity or her relationship to the naked twin red-headed antagonists who are seizing upon her with great enthusiasm. Readers continue unclear of context throughout the second, third, and fourth panels that follow as the naked twins grab for the wrists of the woman and lunge at her bare throat, and it is not until the fifth photograph that the import of the title becomes apparent. One of the twins bites down upon the woman's neck; a trickle of red dye runs down the front the torn camisole, and the moment comes with a satisfying ah-ha as readers retroactively understand that this particular sex story is a story of vampires and their victim.

Such gratification, however, is not guaranteed by all pictorial essays in the issues of *Oui* and *Club* from 1976 to 1983. Indeed, some provide more confusion than satisfaction. "Get off Your Throne" begins and ends with a naked woman seated reading on a toilet in a posh fancy cubicle hotel bathroom. The cryptic and suggestively scatological title will make many readers uncomfortable from the outset, but then, there is the confusion of the pictures and their unlikely visual clues: all the cubicle walls in the interior of the bathroom stall are painted a matte black, but all of the fixtures – from the toilet paper dispenser to the toilet itself – are absurdly golden. Further, unlike the styled and combed hair of most nude models in pictorial essays, the woman reading on the toilet in "Get off Your Throne" wears her hairdo uneven and short, and it appears almost as if she has chopped off her own hair. Her expression does not try to seduce or project a kind of naive agreeableness as most naked models do, and instead, her furrowed brow is scrunched together. Her grin is twisted to the side in a way that suggests the magazine she's brought with her to the bathroom bores her and annoys her both. Overall, the pictorial essay creates an unpleasant impression, and the feeling increases when readers look more closely at the final photographic panels. The disagreeable magazine that the naked woman is reading is *Oui,* and looking even closer, readers see that the issue of *Oui* she is reading on the toilet shows the same woman reading a smaller issue of *Oui* on the toilet, and then inside, an even smaller version of herself reads an even smaller version of the magazine. This unpleasant repetition of the cover continues, and "Get off Your Throne" goes on and on and in and in, which makes no sense.

CHAPTER 6

– And how fared your morning presentation, my darling?

Darby's mom wouldn't talk like that.

– How did the presentation go, darling?

That's closer, but she wouldn't say *darling.*

Waiting at the pay telephone in the Richmond East Elementary front foyer, Darby can't quite imagine what his mom will say when he calls her in the middle of the school day, but she probably won't say *darling*. In actual fact, his mother would probably say the term of endearment is an affectation that mothers and fathers and husbands and wives use in public to portray themselves in a positive light. She would definitely also add that such human flaws are understandable, and so thus forgivable. She herself sometimes addresses Darby as *love*, even though she's not British English and has never travelled to the United Kingdom. When she calls him love, the word sounds sincere, and Darby kind of likes hearing it.

– Terms of endearment are not at all important right now, love. Let's focus on the presentation. Tell me about the presentation. You're happy with how it went?

That sounds more like her, and nodding to himself and the pay telephone hand receiver, Darby feels better. The phone is ringing its second ring. After the fourth ring, it will go to his mother's voice mail, and whether or not he leaves a message, he won't get his fifty cents back from the pay telephone, which means the third ring is something of a point of no return.

– We got an A.

– Well, that sounds promising. But you don't sound happy? Do you not feel the grade was deserved? You're not happy with how the presentation went?

Holding the Career Fair Pair Presentation rubric in his hand, Darby imagines his mom's phone and its "Nice Work If You Can Get It" ringtone ringing, but he feels unsure what he will say if his mom does pick up. He can tell her about the good grade, but the good grade hardly matters even if it is recorded officially on the rubric.

But then again, Darby thinks he might be all right with using the rubric to deceive his dad since deceiving his dad means he can avoid disappointing him and the complicated and contradictory feelings associated with disappointment.

– We got an A.

– You said that already, love.

Darby nods again at the receiver. The pay telephone itself should probably have been removed from the front foyer a decade ago, and its continued presence unwisely draws attention to the age of the school and its crumbling infrastructure. The irreconcilable dilemma, though, is that the Richmond East Elementary digital device policy does not permit students to bring smart cellular telephones onto school property, but the faculty and staff also do not want students crowding the front office and bothering the front office administrators to use the school telephone each and every recess and lunch break. Thus endures the payphone.

– No, I'm not happy about how the presentation went.

– That is too bad. A shame, but I do understand. Public speaking can be demoralizing, love.

Darby's dad's opinion of terms of endearment is less forgiving than his mom's. His dad rejects terms of endearment outright because whether in public or in private, mothers and fathers and husbands and wives use such terms not only to portray themselves in a positive light, but also to deceive themselves, suppress the complexity in their relationships, and deny the complications inherent in human nature.

– Public speaking is one of the many ways we can be demoralized, I'm afraid.

Darby hangs up on the third ring because even if he leaves a neutral noncommittal message, his mother may hear something in his voice and then she'll worry. The other option is just to listen to his mom's recorded voice and hang up, but this'll make her worry as well. She'll wonder about his presentation; she'll wonder about Mr. Henderson's death, and she'll wonder about all the emergency school lockdown procedures in place to protect students from a wide range of unpredictable dangers. So listening to her voice and hanging up really isn't an option. Besides that, fifty cents is fifty cents. It's wrong to waste money.

– It's happened to you, Mom? You've been demoralized?

– Oh, yes. Everyone feels demoralized sometimes. This happens to everyone all too often.

Right now, at Woodfield Elementary, Darby's mom is either still in second period choir class providing extra help for a student who hasn't quite got the hang of reading musical notation, or she is in a lunch-hour staff assembly, committee meeting, or professional development session. Even though these kinds of meetings and sessions are voluntary and in no way required for non-unionized temporary contract faculty members, Darby's mom attends as many as possible because – as she says – she'll never not be a non-unionized temporary contract faculty member if she just spends her lunch break doing the actual work of helping students and prepping lessons and catching up on marking.

– Has demoralizing happened to you a lot?

– Oh, love. I cannot even remember how many times.

– Yeah. Sorry Mom.

– It's all right. This happens to everyone.

Because he wants to demonstrate strength and independence and self-sufficiency, Darby feels good about not talking to his mom and not leaving a message, and as it turns out, the second lunch period bell rings just as he turns away from the payphone, which means they wouldn't have had any time to talk anyway.

In between first and second lunch bell is when students gather their sac lunches from their lift-top desks or from classroom cubbyholes and make their way to the assembled tables in the gymnasium-auditorium. There is no third lunch bell, and Darby has to hurry quick. Monsieur Substitute has lunch monitor duty today, Darby notices, and the teacher stands stiff and sentry-like at the double doors' entry – so serious that he barely acknowledges Darby's quick wave greeting.

"Bonjour, Monsieur."

Oh, well. Darby finds a spot at one of the tables at the far end nearly under the away team's basketball net and backboard to settle in and unpack his Tupperware stackables one by one.

When not in use during physical education class or daily physical activity period, the basketball nets and their backboards retract back and up, so they face down toward the hardwood plank floor. This retraction is done by a clever pulley system and hand crank attached to the wall, which is no mystery at all, but just another example of how mechanical engineers enrich the lives of everyone in dozens of hidden ways each and every day. Still though, whenever Darby looks at the retracted basketball net and backboard, he thinks there is something mysterious and distinctly human in the way the contraption looks. On days when he is having a good day because a *dicteé* in morning class has gone well or he's made a classmate or his mother laugh with a silly remark, the contraption looks like it's playfully hiding its face in a giggle peekaboo game.

On days when he is having a bad day because a presentation has not gone well in morning class or because a good teacher has died, then the retracted basketball net and backboard looks like it is ashamed of about almost everything and just wants to hide away from the whole entire world.

– Maybe the distinction is the thought in your mind?

– Yeah, I guess.

– Your sad mood is making you misunderstand your world.

– Yeah, I guess. Sorry Mom.

– It's all right. It happens to everyone.

– Yeah.

– Have you thought about where you'd like to go for March Break? Perhaps we could go see *Anne of Green Gables* landmarks in Charlottetown?

Darby's mom loves to have running jokes with Darby, and lately, one of the best jokes is randomly changing topics with unlikely suggestions about March Break.

– Or we could go to Stanley Park in Vancouver and rent a bicycle built for two?

This joke is the sad-bittersweet kind of running joke because Darby's mom has already told him that they cannot afford to go anywhere during March Break, and it's even actually sadder than bittersweet because Darby knows they can't afford a trip only because his mom and dad are soon going to divorce, and divorces can be costly.

– Or we could just go to Regina, Saskatchewan and do whatever it is people do for fun in a place like Regina, Saskatchewan.

Darby thinks that what's odd about sad-bittersweet jokes is that they're still funny, and they still kind of cheer him up.

– All right.

Inside his sac lunch are Tupperware stackables containers of different sizes containing quartered celery stalks, an eighthed apple, randomly sliced red pepper, and a cheddar cheese sandwich, all of which he removes and deliberately arranges in front of himself in no particular order. Because it is wrong to waste food, he will eat each item, but if it weren't wrong, Darby would prefer to empty the celery into the organic compostables subsection of the recycling depot station by the gymnasium-auditorium door.

The problem with celery is neither taste nor texture but an unfortunate mental association: in second grade in Windermere Ridge Elementary in Calgary, Darby's class had a biology lesson in which they placed six different celery stalks in six different glasses of water with artificial food colouring. Each glass of water was dyed a different primary or secondary colour, and left to stand overnight, the stalks absorbed the colour of their surroundings. Cause and effect. The result was odd because the fibrous strings running the length of each celery stalk were a darker gradient of the colour, and although the dye was an edible food product, no one wanted to try even a bite. Since then, Darby has found celery less than appetizing.

– Carrot sticks next time? Would you prefer that?

– Yes, please. And maybe those mandarin oranges if they're in season.

– They're expensive out of season.

Pulling open the lid to his apple eighths, Darby sees the EFL immersion student from first morning nutrition break sitting three seats down and on the opposite side of the table. While it was uncomfortable and felt impolite to look at her when she sat right next to him in the library resource centre, three seats down and across the table is far enough to observe her undetected for a bit.

Like him, she's eating lunch all alone, but unlike him, she has brought something to read. Smart. It's a copy of the daily *Capital Region 24-hour Metro News Daily*, which is available free from a box at the front of the school by the public transit bus stop, which is officially off school property but no big deal. In her hand she's holding a pen pensively, and Darby watches as she reads, reads, reads – only once in a while pausing to write. She's either working on the newspaper's daily medium-to-hard Sudoku puzzle, which would be quite impressive because that medium-to-hard one is hard like cross-multiplication-pop-quiz-hard, or she is reading an article on current events, sports, or arts and entertainment and making occasional in-text and marginal notations. Darby's pretty sure his second guess is the right guess because he's seen other EFL immersion students doing the same thing other times. Reading in this way takes a lot of dedication, and in the noisy gymnasium-auditorium during lunch period, it must also take a lot of concentration, but the EFL student doesn't seem troubled at all.

Since it isn't polite to stare, Darby pretends he wasn't staring and instead scans the rest of the tables assembled in the gymnasium-auditorium. On days when they didn't go to the Good and Quick Gas and Sip, Darby sometimes sat here at the same table with Alexander and Them, and they liked to point out the utility ball straight up above in highest ceiling rafters. Wedged between the metal beams, that ball wasn't ever coming down, and it'd taken them a whole Health and Physical Education class to get it up there, they said. Alexander and Them are not anywhere in the gymnasium-auditorium today, which means they most probably sneaked off school property between first and second lunch bell, and they're on their way to behind the Good and Quick Gas and Sip. Their absence is just as well because Darby doesn't particularly feel up to seeing them and certainly does not feel up to having them see him eat all by himself.

– There's nothing wrong with eating alone, love.

– Yeah, I know.

If he hadn't tried to call his mother between the first and second lunch bells, Darby could have gone and gotten a free newspaper as well, which he kind of wishes he had done. Lunch alone on even the best of lunch hours can be a challenge.

He also didn't get the chance to tell Jennie what a good job she did on the Career Fair Pair Presentation or apologize to her for what a poor job he did. Right after first lunch bell, Vice-Principal Phelps-Christianson came to their classroom and asked Jennie if she wanted to go out to lunch at Cultured, which happens to be Jennie's favourite organic soup-salad-sandwich shop and which she most definitely did want to go to. Watching them leave the classroom as the rest of the students gathered their sac lunches from their lift-top desks, Darby worried that maybe Jennie's mom was going to take the opportunity to talk to Jennie about how often her dad went out of town for business and how sometimes people who love each other very much drift apart and grow in different directions, and maybe Jennie's mom even wanted to talk about trial separations and Monsieur Substitute, which made Darby worry more.

Now, though, Darby reconsiders because sometimes a sad mood can make him misunderstand things. Jennie and her mom might just as likely be talking about Mr. Henderson and taking comforting solace in one of the Cultured half-n-half soup-n-salad, soup-n-sandwich, or salad-n-sandwich specials. Or maybe they're just talking about how well Jennie did on the presentation. Maybe her mom was admitting how she peeked in through the window in the classroom door and she truly felt Jennie's outstanding performance surpassed even her outstanding performance at the December Holiday Concert Celebration in the gymnasium-auditorium. Darby can easily imagine they are celebrating with a Cultured add-on organic cinnamon raisin sticky bun dessert or two cookie combo.

– When did you peek in at the classroom door?

– Oh, during the portion in which you and the young Darby revealed the job market projections.

– I didn't see you.

– No, I did not in the least think that you did, so engrossed as you were. Am I wrong in thinking that the young Darby at times appeared uneasy? Did he flub a line or two?

To this, Darby imagines Jennie would just shrug. Not a gloomy, moody kind of shrug, though. More of a this-matter-is-of-little-consequence kind of shrug. Jennie isn't the kind of person who would blame another person for a shortcoming, and in actual fact, she's more the kind of person who would help someone else save their face by purposely not saying anything at all.

– And afterwards did Monsieur Substitute offer adequate and constructive feedback peppered with appropriate praise?

Vice-Principal Phelps-Christianson probably wouldn't call him Monsieur Substitute because it's a name only students use with one another. Even if she's heard students saying it, she wouldn't use it. She might call him by his first name. Pierre, Patrice, Phillipe or Pascal? But, no. Whether or not any of those names are his actual given name, a vice-principal wouldn't use it when speaking with a student even if the student is her daughter.

– And afterwards did Mr. Desjardins offer adequate and constructive feedback peppered with appropriate praise?

– Not really.

– Later in the day maybe.

– Maybe.

Would Jennie save Monsieur Substitute's face or would she show her mom the rubric? Jennie could be blunt at times and she valued good pedagogy, so she'd definitely be drawn in two opposing directions. If she's still dwelling on the pixilated discovery of Mr. Henderson in the ICU and thinking what a good teacher he was, Jennie would just let her voice trail off. Like she's reflecting about Monsieur Substitute.

There'd be a lull in conversation, and it'd be a weird moment of unspoken tension because even mentioning Monsieur Substitute to Jennie would be thin ice for Vice-Principal Phelps-Christianson. If Jennie let her voice trail off, then her mom would have to wonder if she's at all suspicious about the affair sex in the Volvo station wagon in the parking lot of First Unitarian of Ottawa. The lull in conversation would definitely lead Jennie's mom to some uncomfortable uncertainty. Just how little or how much does Jennie know about any of it? Addressing the matter head on directly would be a hazardous strategy, though, and Jennie's mom might just escape into smaller talk.

– This is a very good cinnamon raisin sticky bun.

– Yes. All of Cultured's ingredients are locally grown within a 100-kilometre radius of each franchise location.

Smiling, Jennie's mother would attempt not to think thin ice thoughts about Monsieur Substitute or about Mr. Phelps-Christianson away on business. Best not to tread too close to thoughts of her lawfully-wedded spouse and father to her only child Jennie or the potential consequences her disloyalty might well wreak. No, Vice-Principal Phelps-Christenson would halt herself on the thin ice altogether and pause, making sure her weight was evenly distributed before sliding herself back, back, back to safer shores. This is the nature of shameful secrets, Darby thinks – proximity to exposure increases both shame and potential danger

– and in this way, adulterous affair sex is not unlike pornography, smoking, and leaving school property without permission.

– A wonderful sticky bun.

– Quebec maple syrup maybe.

– *sirop d'érable.*

It's probably not a coincidence, but pornography, smoking, and leaving school property not only all qualify as secrets, but will all lead to punishments if the secrets get out. Darby feels unaccustomed to punishment because his transgressions before Ottawa never really amounted to much – forgetting to hang his wet towel in the bathroom and instead putting it in the hamper where it created mildew – and because of his parents' belief in the rehabilitative nature of discipline. According to his mom, learning from a mistake requires self-reflection and thoughtful contemplation in order to effectively lead to betterment, and so instead of taking away Darby's books or grounding him to his room, she's gotten him to write composition reflection papers, which – now that Darby thinks about them – are just like extra homework and punishments only a teacher would think of. The thing is that Darby's never minded homework all that much.

A fruit roll-up unrolled and peeled off a cellophane backing makes its own distinct sound, and hearing the pleasing sound across the table, Darby turns again toward the EFL immersion student reading and marking up her *Capital Region 24-hour Metro News Daily.* Her fruit roll-up wrapper is the yellow wrapper of a no-frills off-brand, and judging by the dark colour of the flattened fruit in her hand, Darby guesses blackberry, blueberry, or mixed berry swirl, none of which is a healthy option because they all contain processed gelatin, which comes from bones and connective fatty tissues of cattle and pigs. The unused by-products of the meat industry put to use. Darby learned this in the summer between third and fourth grade when his mom was doing a medium-to-hard crossword aloud in the kitchen and *gelatin* was one of the across answers, and even though the memory of learning trivia from his mom is a good memory, it might well have been better if he didn't learn about gelatin because fruit roll-ups now fall into the same inedible category as celery. Jell-O too.

In order to eat her fruit roll-up while still holding her pen pensively, the EFL immersion student grips the roll in one hand, bites down, and tugs, stretching the elastic fruit thin until a fragment snaps off, which kind of looks like eating taffy and mustn't be at all good for her top incisors. It isn't right to judge, though, so just in case she notices him watching, Darby pretends to stare over her shoulder and past her at the gymnasium-auditorium wall where a decorative line of handprints in repeating primary and secondary colours circles the perimeter of the whole entire gymnasium-auditorium.

The painted handprints are two years old, and they were the idea of Richmond East Elementary's administration – a school spirit and solidarity kind of thing, according to Alexander and Them – and unlike Mr. Henderson's classroom where there's too much stimulation, the handprint trim is pretty much the only decoration in the gymnasium-auditorium. According to Alexander and Them, students and teachers came class by class and added their handprints to the white cinderblock wall in a repeating pattern of red, yellow, blue, orange, purple, green, but Billy purposely wrecked the pattern by going green, blue, green. They showed Darby exactly where once, and they seemed proud of this break in the pattern – easily as proud as they were of the utility ball wedged high up overhead – but Darby didn't think the disruption was nearly as disruptive as they seemed to believe. He kept that thought to himself, though.

They would've for sure reacted negatively and maybe would have called him all sorts of swears.

– Flying Buttress.

– Chronic Angina.

– Silicone Caulking.

They're most probably calling him similar terms of disparagement right now behind the Good and Quick Gas and Sip.

– Dung Beetle.

– Two-horned cuckold.

– *Un Phoque Stupide.*

Although it may not appear cozy or welcoming, the area behind the Good and Quick Gas and Sip backs onto a steep slope and train tracks where there never seems to be any trains and is bordered by a garbage bin and an unused Goodwill donation box on its side, and so it's not only private, but also in a way comfortable. Right now, Billy and Stewart are probably sitting on milk crates and replaying how they tripped him up during the Career Fair Pair Presentation.

– Did you see the reaction shot on his face when we lifted the lift-top desks?

– Did you see his sideward glances of quiet desperation toward Jennie?

– Did you see his inability to conclude with a final thought-provoking clincher?

Stewart and Billy would keep this up a while, but Darby imagines Alexander might not pay much attention. In fact, Alexander would probably fall quiet shortly after pulling up a milk crate and drawing into his lungs the first few satisfying clouds of carcinogenic tobacco smoke. It is a dark mood Darby has witnessed more than once – Alexander turning all inward and all quiet all of a sudden – and each time, Darby has wondered at its motivation and principal cause. Nature, nurture, and a broken home probably, or maybe it just happens whenever sad and angry balance one another out.

– Why didn't you show him your magazine?

– We were all supposed to do it. Why'd you chicken?

Alexander would probably just shrug. Darby saw this mood during Christmas Break when Alexander came to his executive townhome, and the two of them were sitting in the sitting room eating butter pastries next to the gas fireplace that's never been lit. Darby's mother apologetically mentioned that the home in Calgary had been better for guests. And Darby had seen it again when school had resumed at Richmond East Elementary in January when they were eating lunch together under the away team basketball net in the gymnasium-auditorium sharing their tales of Christmas presents when Stewart and Billy insensitively observed that gifts were supposed to be noticeably larger and more numerous with kids whose parents were divorced. In both cases, as soon as the insensitive words were said, Alexander fell quiet and turned inward, which is probably what he will do if Stewart and Billy go on and on about the Career Fair Pair Presentation.

– Hey, isn't Darby's father who no longer loves his mother coming to talk about a day in the life of a mechanical engineer?

– Hey, isn't Darby's father who no longer lives with him one of the career parent guest speakers coming this afternoon?

– Hey, do you think he'll be as bad at presenting as Darby?

Although neither Billy nor Stewart is the kind to pay too, too close attention to the inner lives of others, they both have known Alexander since way back in JK, and they must have seen him turn inward plenty of times. They've probably developed their own ways and means to try and draw him out.

– Didn't Darby think he was so big when he told us about his dad's magazines?

– He sure did act the show-off, but didn't we show him?

– Sorry about your mom cancelling her presentation and stuff.

It was actually at the Good and Quick Gas and Sip that Darby first mentioned the pornography he'd found at the back of his dad's closet, and, of course, he regretted speaking of it almost right away. Darby's mom says boasting and bragging are understandable and forgivable from time to time because everyone has sudden bursts of confidence and sometimes these bursts express themselves in the form of boasts and brags, but Darby isn't so quick to forgive himself. It's probably better not to have confidence at all.

In the gymnasium-auditorium across the table and three seats down, the EFL immersion student has put down her pen and removed what at first appears to be a smart cellular telephone from her knapsack but turns out to be a handheld electronic translator. For a short, short moment, Darby momentarily imagines Monsieur or one of the other lunch-hour monitors making the same mistake and angrily crossing the gymnasium-auditorium to confiscate the device in accordance with Richmond East Elementary's digital device policy. Darby could interrupt by politely intervening to clarify the confusion and explaining away the mistake. Both the EFL student and the lunch-hour monitor would be grateful. None of what Darby imagines actually happens, though.

What does happen is that she removes a notebook with her electronic translator and writes, which pretty much conclusively proves she's reading an article in the *Capital Region 24-hour Metro News Daily*. She's collecting new vocabulary words and writing them in a notebook and categorizing them by noun or verb, adjective or adverb, and miscellaneous idiomatic terms and phrases. Darby watches long enough to confirm as she types transcribed word after word into her handheld electronic translator, and he imagines giving her a compliment.

– Your dedication and concentration are admirable.

– Thank you for saying that.

– Not at all.

Does everyone imagine playing a hero like he does? Darby feels embarrassed, but in a way, it would've been nice to intervene and help out the EFL immersion student, and really, this might be what Billy and Stewart might be trying to do with all their questions for Alexander. Although they are at root mean-spirited and destined to grow more so over time, Darby can see that their attempts to draw Alexander into conversation are kind and generous. Maybe they'd even try to use Darby's mom's strategy of changing the topic abruptly.

Maybe they'd ask Alexander to solve a three-variable quadratic equation. Or they'd ask him if he's got to World Seven, Stage Eight in *KillCraft WarMachine* and if he's yet defeated the mutant manticore-capybara boss to complete the level. Or they'd ask him if he remembers how the courtyard ducks last year laid a clutch of five eggs but only two eggs hatched and what the swell did the janitor do with the three stillborn eggs? If all these gambits fail to entice Alexander, maybe Billy and Stewart would ask him how Mr. Henderson and his asinine Nissan Leaf wound up careening off a bridge last November. Darby imagines Alexander shrugging.

Billy and Stewart would give up. They'd give up because they've tried their best and there's no point in beating dead horses. It'd be time to move on to other important matters: the newest trading cards additions to their *Broadswords of Gungnir* collections.

– I got an uncommon-to-rare yule goat with a Bronholm amulet artifact, but I still can't figure out how his enchantment works.

– Don't be such a fanny pack. Unless there's a Runic inscription on the obverse of the amulet, the enchantment's the same as a jelling stone enchantment for a yule cat. And I very much doubt an uncommon-to-rare card came with an obverse inscription.

Empty, Tupperware stackables of different sizes can be nested one inside another, and Darby enjoys packing up the ingenious food storage system at the end of every lunch period. The smallest fish cracker stackable seals airtight and fits into the carrot and celery stick stackables, two of which side by side make a square and fit into the sandwich stackables, three of which can sit one on top of another and fit inside the deep soup stackable. The containers get neatly bigger and bigger, and it's easy to imagine the size and scope of stackables increasing and increasing, soup size to cake size to chesterfield size to executive townhouse size to auditorium-gymnasium size to South Ottawa Community Centre Sportsplex size.

Feeling better, Darby notices that the EFL immersion student across from him is no longer across from him. She has gone, but her copy of the *Capital Region 24-hour Metro News Daily* remains, still opened to the same page. The newspaper should really go in the mixed paper subsection of the recycling depot station, and besides that, Darby is curious about what article she was reading and translating. With the free daily paper, the story might have been international, national, or local news, but it could also be a profile of an acting celebrity who has an upcoming movie or a human-interest story.

The article turns out to be local – a written version of the story Darby heard earlier on CBC News Radio about the family of four that burned and died in a Kanata house fire. Much of the article is underlined, and in the margins, the EFL immersion student has written lots and lots of words in characters that are either Japanese or Chinese, but might also be Korean or something. Darby doesn't know. Among the many underlined words are *accelerant*, *Remax*, *murder-suicide*, *bankruptcy*, and *synthetic oil for two-stroke snow blowers*, and there are many more. Darby's pretty sure the EFL student understood the article – as much as anyone can understand a story about a murdered family anyway.

He folds the paper lengthwise in order to insert it to the mixed paper slot in the recycling station, and as he's doing so, he again spots Monsieur Substitute. The teacher sits perched on the edge of the gymnasium-auditorium stage, a spot that's strictly off-limits to students except during scheduled performances like the December Holiday Concert Celebration, and beside him also perched on the edge of the stage sits the school nurse, who must also have been on lunch monitor duty. She's wearing a layered folk-singer skirt that sways all flowingly as she swings her legs forward and back like she's all excited to be chatting about whatever they're chatting about. Monsieur seems to like talking to her too, because he's slightly turned and leaning in her direction in a tell-tale body orientation position. That close together, they are definitely inside one another's personal space, and then Darby notices that above her white v-neck t-shirt, the school nurse wears a tied and knotted neckerchief. The print on that neckerchief is distinctly floral.

ON SCHOOLHOUSE MICE AND THE UNFORTUNATE ACCIDENT

Although generations of bucks and does once brought their litters of pinky mice offspring into the world in the darkness of the basement boiler room of Richmond East Elementary, the traps and poisons set out by school's facilities staff drove the animals upward to safer nesting grounds.

Some mice travelled to the senior art room, where the liberal and freethinking teacher-facilitator peaceably permitted mother and father mouse to curl and huddle tight together in warmth near the pottery kilns. Some mice travelled to the library and resource centre, where the carpeted floor and hallowed halls offered rows and racks of primary picture-books and junior level literacy readers for mother and father mouse to rest, generate, gestate, and regenerate unbothered in quiet cubbyholes. Mostly, though, the majority of the mother and father mice travelled to the gymnasium-auditorium, where they lived happily hidden and entirely unseen underneath the floor of the elevated stage.

Inset into the base of the stage, rolling drawers stored away an audience's worth of stacking chairs and provided nooks and crannies aplenty for new mice families to set up house and home. Onstage above, children from JK to eighth grade trod the boards repeatedly for solemn Remembrance Day observances, motivational speaker assemblies, and celebratory mathlete award ceremonies, and all the while, the shelter provided below-stage went undetected, allowing newborn mice to grow from infancy to adulthood in complete safety. Most families emerged from beneath the stage only at night and only in order to scavenge for food scraps in the many compartments of the reduce-reuse-recycle bin. With the introduction of the Ottawa-Carlton District School Board's onsite and in-school composting initiative, the most plentiful portion of the bin became the biodegradable compostables compartment – a food source as bountiful as a horn of plenty. Here, the remnants of Hostess pretzel sticks mixed with the remainders of Kraft cheese strings and Schneider snackeroni hot rods. Because young children are wont to cast off the unwanted celery, carrots, and guacamole of their lunches, the compostable compartment contained all four recommended daily food groups, and the mice did not lack or want for more. For most mice, these riches were enough. For most, the world beyond did not interest them in the least.

Two exceptions to this rule were Mother Mouse and her Souris Son, who both possessed a curiosity that extended beyond the hidden stacks of school chairs. Often, they crawled between the cracks and crevices beneath the stage so they might look out upon the greater world of the gymnasium-auditorium. With a good half-inch gap between the low-gloss varnished floor and the bottom of the stage drawers, mother and child sat in safety and watched the many and varied comings and goings of Richmond East Elementary throughout the school year. They watched as eager reader parents and children dug through disorganized cartons in the book nook section of the Annual White Elephant rummage sale. They watched as judges with clipboards walked through the Magic Magnets and Potato Clocks and Artificial Intelligence displays of the junior Science Fair. They watched as visiting constables from the Ottawa Police outreach program explained the dangerous domino cause-and-effect of truancy, marijuana cigarettes, and questionable online behaviours.

Of all the unlikely sights Mother Mouse and her Souris Son watched, though, the most enjoyable were the Health and Physical Education lessons in which classes of wide-faced kids in sweatshirts and t-shirts stood in a circle holding a multi-coloured parachute.

At least a dozen children were needed to lift the vinyl and polyester parachute, but the perimeter of the material could fit more than twice that – a class of thirty or a class of thirty-five – and everyone participated. Even the least coordinated and Phys-Ed-averse boy and girl grinned as they hoisted and pulled and lifted the round nylon sheet up up up and grinned again as it floated back down down down. The loud laughter alone kept Mother Mouse and her Souris Son watching for hours, but the activity also came with games. In Run Tag, a boy or girl ducked and sprinted across the entire diameter of the lifted parachute before it could descend down on their heads. In Shark Attack, a boy or girl hunted prey beneath the parachute's cascading cloth and grabbed at the ankles of their classmates. In Popcorn, all the boys and girls flooded the nylon surface with table tennis balls and watched as the rippling material sent the balls shooting off in unpredictable directions.

Sometimes during these games, Mother Mouse would pause and turn her head toward her Souris Son because she enjoyed watching him watch. His eyes widened and his head jumped, his whiskers twitching along in excited syncopation with the children assembled on the gymnasium-auditorium floor. Taking in her son's appreciation, she would wish and wish Father Mouse had come along. He, however, was a homebody and had stayed behind beneath the stage.

Happy to greet his family upon their return, he nodded his head and listened as Mother Mouse and Souris Son recounted their adventures from farther afield. He nudged food scraps in their direction, encouraging them to eat the lunch period leftovers that he'd collected from the front foyer refuse. Each and every day, he waited for them, and – grateful that she had married and mated so very well – Mother Mouse made sure to thank him for his waiting. In its predictability, his persistent presence felt reassuring and the reliable sight of him calmed her: the soft chestnut of his dark brown fur, the moisture of his dark brown eyes, and a whiskered twitch of his small pink nose. To Mother Mouse, his face and his chitter-squeak welcome brought certainty to the uncertain life of a small rodent. It was thus upsetting when one day she and her son returned home to find him gone.

Since sitting and stewing never did anyone anywhere any good at all, she right away suggested an excursion out of the gymnasium-auditorium to search out her spouse. A journey, a quest, an expedition. To find father, they would go beyond the boundaries of the front foyer, out beyond the school's enclosed courtyard, and down the shadowed corridors of the school hallways. They secreted themselves onto and into a rolling janitorial cart and sat for many hours waiting in hiding between paper towel stacks until an unsuspecting service maintainer Trojan-horsed them all over Richmond East Elementary. In the library and multimedia resource centre, Mother Mouse and her Souris Son peeked behind the circulation desk of the school librarian, and in the infirmary; they scurried across the examination table of the school nurse, but no matter how much they sniffed and searched, their efforts all failed, and their hopes all faded. On the brink of accepting that they might never again hear the chitter-squeak of their loved one, they and their rolling janitorial cart rolled into a grade five classroom in which a sound emanated from the front corner. It was more of a chatter-squelch than a chitter-squeak, echoing softly from across such a distance. The tiled floor played with sound in the empty classroom, and distrustful of her own senses, Mother Mouse felt uncertain, but encouraged. She and her child jumped down from the janitorial cart and took their quest in a new and unexpected direction.

Unlike the majority of rooms in the school at this hour, the grade five classroom was not unoccupied. Purple marker in hand, Gerald

Gerard Henderson sat making his way through a stack of student composition books, and he looked up just as Mother Mouse and Souris Son were scurrying quick toward the front of the room. She stopped so suddenly that her son collided into her from behind, a slapstick comedy pile-up that did nothing to diminish the fear of the moment. She felt certain the teacher was staring her down, and the unbearable eye contact reminded her just how small and vulnerable she was. How could she have forgotten that even for a moment? Her worries turned out to be unfounded, though, for the teacher smiled and spoke not to her but to the service maintainer, who was at that moment unloading a squeegee and vinegar spray bottle from his cart. The teacher made a friendly remark about all the smudges his pupils left on the windows and the service maintainer replied that he minded not at all. None of the small talk concerned Mother Mouse in the least, but she did feel grateful for the moment's distraction, and she ran closer to the mysterious chatter-squelch sound.

It came from a table in the corner near the far corner of the whiteboard, but what they found there was not Father Mouse. What they found wasn't even mouse, but hamster. Two hamsters, actually. Two classroom pets imprisoned within a cage filled with cedar chips. At that particular moment, the prisoners were burrowing and fluffing wood shavings into a makeshift furrow for an early evening nap, but when mother and son mouse drew closer, all four rodents fell silent and looked upon one another with great confusion. Their stares might well have lasted longer had the service maintainer not just then wished the departing teacher a good evening and a good weekend.

Panicked by the thought of detection, Mother Mouse and her Souris Son leapt from the cage table and dashed into a nearby knapsack backpack. Wedged inside the bag's flapped pocket sat a gradebook and a two-compartment Tupperware stackable, and with horror, mother understood these belongings belonged to the teacher himself. The padded polypropylene fabric beneath her feet moved unexpectedly and the massive gradebook by her head shifted dangerously and she understood that there was no time to flee from the knapsack backpack. Lifted up, they tumble-turned all about inside the bag's interior. The movement threw Mother Mouse off-balance, but she understood that they were in motion and the teacher had stood, the bag casually slung over his shoulder. It was a fluid motion she'd seen children perform carelessly in the gymnasium-auditorium at the end of each and every lunch period, but she'd not thought of the kerfuffle and chaos such movement created inside the bag. Shoved to the left, pushed to the right, and falling roughly down to the bag's bottom, she tried to call out to her Souris Son, and she tried not to panic while all around her, the world turned into a seismic somersault and a tectonic tumble. Then, it stopped. The commotion came to a halt, and the bag came to a rest.

Crammed between the inner edge of the zipper and the Tupperware, Mother Mouse squeezed her way through and sniffed her way to her son. She found him in a padded inner knapsack pocket, wedged in beside a highlighter and a half dozen HB pencils and he was – by some unlikely godsent grace – unharmed. The upheaval of the past few minutes hadn't allowed for coherent thought, but with her pulse now slowing, Mother Mouse felt remorse, wondering why the janitorial cart had seemed like a valid plan and a good idea. She'd not only idiotically imagined that their journey, quest, and expedition out of the gymnasium-auditorium could be an adventure, she'd thoughtlessly put her son in peril. Of course, a young boy mouse needs a father mouse, but at what cost?

The time for regret and other unproductive emotions passed quickly. An all-new threat, the soft rumble-hum of an engine sounded all around them, but Mother Mouse knew they first needed to escape the knapsack backpack. With stretchy spines and limber limbs, the mice located the zipper's end and squeezed their way through the smallest of small openings and emerged into the interior of a Nissan Leaf. Beneath their feet, the heated cushion of the passenger-side seat radiated warmth, and above them, the illuminated lights of the dashboard shone and reflected the teacher's calm expression as he eased his sensible electric car out of the faculty and staff parking lot.

The safest seat in a moving vehicle will always be the backseat, and Mother Mouse immediately sent her son from the front, thinking how she might navigate herself and her son out of this new danger. Small though she was, the element of surprise lay on her side, and she knew the teacher would not be expecting her to scurry in and up his pant leg. Five minutes into the ride, he switched on the radio, tapping along to "Someone to Watch Over Me" on the steering wheel and grinning to himself, and it was then that she attacked. She crawled up and into his sensible khaki Dockers, biting with great vengeance and furious anger as she went. The car jerked to the left and then to the right, but undeterred, Mother Mouse climbed higher and nipped at the teacher's torso as she continued up. Emerging from his collar, she clutched onto the soft cotton of his buttoned-down shirt and scramble-climbed to his shoulder. When he turned his head toward her, Mother Mouse saw the extent of Gerald Gerard Henderson's confusion, and she experienced an ambivalent ache of sympathy as she leapt for his eyes. The car jerked again, and when she looked up, what she saw was not something the small schoolhouse mouse had ever before seen – the car was rushing toward the guardrail of an elevated bridge. The rail sped closer and she braced for impact, but it did not come. The car propelled itself into air.

CHAPTER 7

On Tuesdays, Wednesdays, and Thursdays, Physical Education class follows lunch hour, but on Mondays and Fridays, it's Daily Physical Activity class. PE and DPA. Today, Monsieur Substitute has brought the grade five enriched class outdoors to play the nonsensical game of snowball soccer, a decision which only emphasizes the dramatic differences between the two exercise and fitness classes.

Darby, though, can only think of the difference between a scarf and a neckerchief. He's sitting at one end of the sideline bench, far from Billy and Stewart at the other end, and he decides that of course a woolly winter scarf is a whole entire distinct category. If, however, both a scarf and a neckerchief are the light silk or thin satin material that one might bunch or wrap or tie or knot in a stylish manner, perhaps the two are close, close synonyms? And if he and Alexander and Them could have confused a scarf and a neckerchief, could they have also confused a vice-principal and school nurse? How close up did they get to the Volvo station wagon in the parking lot of First Unitarian of Ottawa? Darby can't answer his questions with any degree of accuracy, and he kind of wishes he could talk to Alexander.

In this fantasy conversation, he and Alexander would also talk about Hannah, Mr. Henderson's death, and Alexander's mom's cancelled Career Parent Presentation. The difference between neckerchiefs and scarves would definitely come first, though.

Unfortunately, Alexander's on the field playing snowball soccer for the other snowball soccer team, so there's no chance of talking to him. Sitting at the other end of the sideline bench, Billy and Stewart might provide some insight about neckerchiefs and scarves, but they're deep, deep into a conversation about snowball soccer and there's nothing for Darby to learn there. Well, not nothing. Darby has learned that Stewart Holgermonsson's gullibility seems to increase at a rate equal to Billy Pace's inventiveness.

"Why four defense positions?" Stewart asks.

"Advance back right defense, rear back right defense, advance back left defense, rear back left defense," Billy says.

Stewart and Billy sit crouched far down at the other end of the sideline bench, but Darby has overheard just about every snowball soccer regulation that Billy has invented to string Stewart along. Overhearing what they're saying is not the same as eavesdropping because eavesdropping is rude and implies that Darby wants to listen and they don't want him to listen, and this is not the case.

"In true regulation snowball soccer, everyone has to wear snowpants," Billy says. "Or a snowsuit."

"It must be hard to move quickly."

"Goalies can wear Gortex splashpants for greater mobility."

"That makes sense," Stewart says.

That doesn't make sense, but Stewart's voice is straining to believe Billy's inventions. Darby can't see from his end of the bench, but he can imagine Stewart nodding and swaying to emphasize his understanding, which is what Stewart does whenever Billy talks. When Billy's impatience increases, Stewart's grovelling increases, and Darby has noticed this pattern many times before in class, in the schoolyard, and behind the Good and Quick Gas and Sip. Even if they're just talking about the river quests or mythical seaworms or stone amulets in those nonsense game cards they trade, Billy exaggerates or lies for no particular reason and Stewart strains to believe the exaggerations and lies. The greater the invention, the greater the gullibility. The pattern reminds Darby of the symbiotic relationships in the classroom's Biology workbook series *Science Comes Alive!*

Symbiosis: Billy = invention / Stewart = gullibility

The workbook series gives examples of different symbiotic relationships like the waterfowl that flies into the crocodile's sharp-toothed mouth to clean out the remnants of dead fish and dead turtle meat. The symbiotic aspect of the act comes in because while the waterfowl nourishes itself, the crocodile enjoys better oral hygiene and wards against tooth decay and related gum diseases. The crocodile also learns restraint, Darby supposes. Either way, *Science Comes Alive!* explained that the symbiosis between the waterfowl's food source and the crocodile's oral hygiene benefits both animals and could therefore be categorized as mutualism.

Mutualism: waterfowl = food source (+) / crocodile = oral hygiene (+).

"Goalies are the only ones who can use their hands," Billy says. "Like traditional soccer."

"Of course," Stewart says.

"But goalies most often have gloves whereas the offensive forwards and defensive backs are limited to mittens."

Since Stewart does not exactly benefit from his gullibility, the symbiotic relationship he shares with Billy does not qualify as mutualism, and so must be either commensalism or parasitism.

Commensalism: Billy = invention (+) / Stewart = gullibility (o)
Parasitism: Billy = invention (+) / Stewart = gullibility (-)

The question becomes whether Stewart's gullibility leaves him unaffected, which would be commensalism or whether it causes him harm, which would be parasitism. Darby cannot decide.

"Eight players with one goaltender and four defense," Stewart says. "So three forwards?"

"Yes, that is how subtraction works, you knob."

"Three forwards, I see," Stewart says.

"I'm glad you see," Billy says. His voice does not sound glad. It's become angry, which is often how Billy becomes with Stewart.

"Yes, I understand," Stewart repeats.

To see them from where he's sitting, Darby would have to lean all the way forward and then look down the whole length of the sideline bench. The movement would definitely call too much attention to himself and would be unwise, so instead he stares straight forward and ahead and feigns great interest in his classmates playing snowball soccer.

In the fictional playbook of snowball soccer, league rules for each team require eight players on the snow-covered field at all times, which in the grade five enriched class leaves three players on each team on the sidelines. Darby, Billy, and Stewart are sitting out together at the moment, which is unfortunate, but Jennie's playing goal, so when Monsieur Substitute blows his whistle, she'll rotate out and Billy will rotate in, which is fortunate.

So far, neither team on the field has scored a point because Monsieur's made-up DPA game of snowball soccer simply doesn't work, and it doesn't work for lots of reasons. Running in snow pants is hard. The soccer ball either skids across the snow or gets stuck in the snow. The excess of players means the forwards and the defensives run into one another. Monsieur didn't think through snowball soccer when he made it up, which to Darby's way of thinking is the main problem with Daily Physical Activity.

Separate and distinct from Physical Education, the Daily Physical Activity initiative began in an attempt to combat childhood obesity and encourage emotional and intellectual wellness through movement and play. That's how Mr. Henderson explained it back in November when Jennie asked, which mustn't have been the first time she'd asked based upon Mr. Henderson's patient-but-patient-with-an-effort answer. Unlike the objectives-and-outcome-based curricula of PE, he explained, DPA emphasized explorative movement and play – an all-fine-and-good explanation except it didn't really explain why the students passed the forty-five-minute period every Monday and Friday on such random activities. Sometimes forty-five minutes of callisthenic jumping jacks and toe touches and drop squats inside in the classroom and sometimes forty-five minutes of hopscotch and four corners and basketball outside in the schoolyard. The explanation did not explain how very arbitrary and ad hoc and spur-of-the-moment DPA felt, and it didn't explain snowball soccer.

"In Europe, is snowball soccer called snowball football?" Stewart asks.

"That's stupid," Billy says. "The sport's only in Canada."

Stewart probably wanted to make a kind of joke to diffuse potential tension, but his question has just angered Billy more, which is perhaps another aspect of their symbiotic relationship.

On the field, Monsieur blows his whistle twice in two short bursts. "Rotate," he says. "*Allons-y.*"

While he does not seem to know any actual rules about actual organized sports, Monsieur does act and sound like an actual coach sometimes. When no one rotates at a speed that satisfies him, Monsieur claps his mittened hands together in a booming way and repeats *allons-y*, which reinforces the impression that he could be an actual coach. Darby can imagine him adding a motivating catchphrase like *let's see some hustle* or *hustle up out there*, but the teacher doesn't.

Jennie rotates out and walks toward Darby but doesn't hustle. Her parka hood is pulled up snug over her head and she's cinched it tight around her annoyed face, which must've made it hard to hear Monsieur. Why she might have an annoyed face Darby can guess, and it has to do with Daily Physical Activity, which Jennie has many times said is a big personal bugbear of hers.

"Eight players on the field?" Jennie's annoyed voice matches her annoyed face as she walks toward the sideline bench.

Darby shrugs. "DPA. What are you going to do?"

"No one is ever going to score a goal," Jennie says and shakes her head.

Darby slides to the right of the bench to make room for her, and at the other end, Stewart slides even farther away. The gesture feels passive-aggressive to Darby, but passive-aggressive beats aggressive-aggressive any day, which is probably how Billy would have acted toward them if he hadn't rotated in and run off to join the scoreless snowball soccer game. Darby pats the bench beside him to make Jennie feel more welcomed.

"There haven't even been any shots on net," Jennie says. "Alexander got closest."

Even though Alexander doesn't seem to care about the game any more than most of the students, the ball arched toward the net when he kicked it. Jennie blocked the shot, glad for something to do.

"He wasn't that close," she says. "The ball came right at me."

As she slumps a bit on the bench beside him, Darby thinks to ask about Jennie's and Jennie's mom's lunchtime conversation at Cultured, but he cannot think how he might begin such a conversation. He might also ask her opinion about the differences between a scarf and a neckerchief, but such a conversation might edge too close to a conversation about adultery, so instead, he asks her about symbiotic relationships.

"In our workbook, it only talked about animals having symbiotic relationships," he says.

"Yeah, I remember," Jennie says.

"Like the oxpecker on the zebra and the goby fish in the anemone. But do you think human beings have relationships like that too?" Darby asks.

"I'd guess," Jennie says. "Like the Ducks Unlimited mallards in the courtyard help us learn about conservation, and at the same time, we're raising money for them to nest in the courtyard." She is nodding her parka-hooded head now. "So yes, I'd guess there's mutual benefit."

Mutualism: mallards = room and board (+) / student body= authentic firsthand learning (+)

Science Comes Alive! talked about only three types of symbiosis, but Darby wonders if there isn't a fourth, a category in which both halves of the relationship lose (-)(-). Yes, the teeth-cleaning waterfowl receives food, and yes, the crocodile benefits from oral hygiene, but looked at another way, the waterfowl never really learns to hunt and gather for itself, and the crocodile never learns to keep its teeth clean for itself. A lose-lose symbiosis. Such relationships do seem to exist, and that's probably why there's divorce.

"I didn't do as well on the presentation as I'd hoped," Darby says, "Sorry you had to jump in. I couldn't help as much as I wanted to, but you helped me a lot."

Commensalism: Darby = a good grade (+) / Jennie = public speaking skill (o)

From inside her parka, Jennie shrugs her shoulders, which could convey that she too feels disappointed about Darby's performance or could convey that she understands and accepts that no matter how much planning and practice goes into a pair presentation, mistakes can happen when a performance is shared between partners but thankfully, they learned one another's parts and could improvise. The fringe of her parka hides her face a bit, so it's hard to read her expression.

"I'm cold," she says.

"Did you know that your mom was going to come peek in?"

"No," Jennie says. "No, I would've told you."

The fringe on her parka still makes it hard to see her face and expression, but judging from her voice, Darby guesses it's another annoyed expression.

"She said it was just an impulse." Jennie speaks faster than she usually does. "She said she didn't plan on showing up, but I don't think her intensions matter. Because she's vice-principal, she probably doesn't need to outright ask permission to order to observe classes, but wouldn't most people ask? To be polite? Isn't that better than skulking around in the hallways and spying?"

"I don't think Monsieur would have cared," Darby says.

"No, but I don't think that matters either."

"So that's what you talked about at lunch?"

"Yes. And she said skulking was too strong a word, but she said sorry too."

"It can't be easy for your mom to say sorry," Darby says.

"You're right about that."

Darby grins at Jennie because her annoyed tone has faded, but also because he's relieved. It seems that the conversation at Cultured did not touch upon Monsieur Substitute and trial separations or Mr. Henderson and funeral services. Darby thinks it'd be all right to ask about the half-n-half soup-salad-sandwich specials, but then she turns to him.

"Mr. Henderson only assigned us as partners because no one else would work with me," she says. "Did you know that?"

From inside her parka hood, she makes eye contact with Darby, and she's probably waiting for him to talk because she wants him to agree with her. She wants him to admit this truth, but Darby won't.

"I think he assigned us together because I was new," Darby says, "and I had no one to work with. Arriving late in the semester was a hassle for me, but it must have caused organization troubles for Mr. Henderson as well."

"Maybe," she says, "but maybe both reasons too." Jennie is not modulating her pitch or tone, and her voice is flat.

"And I was lucky to be partnered with you," Darby says in a rush. "We got a good grade because you said we should reach out to Dr. Larissa Beaman, DVM for strong logos and ethos content. And because you knew about organizing PowerPoint slides with bullets using parallel sentence structures. And because we practised each other's parts in case of mistakes and you knew my part well and were able to step in when I had a fight-or-flight response. You got us a good grade."

Stewart leans forward from the other side of the bench to stare, and Darby realizes he has raised his voice a bit too much and probably sounds desperate to convince Jennie, but he doesn't care.

"I was lucky to have you as a partner," Darby says again.

"Yes," she says at last, "but you didn't want to have me as a partner."

"Umm."

Darby's disfluency trips him up. He can see that Jennie does not feel good about herself and a sin of omission won't work to make her feel better about herself. What is needed in this situation is a benevolent lie, but Darby can't think of one quickly enough.

"Umm."

"It's all right," Jennie says.

On the field, Monsieur Substitute blows his whistle twice. "*Allons-y*. Let us have hustle," he says, and he blows his whistle a third time. "Rotate."

When Darby doesn't move, Jennie points out that it's his turn to rotate in.

"It's your turn," she says.

When he still doesn't stand, Stewart stares and shakes his head.

That's what she and her mom talked about at Cultured at lunch, Darby realizes. They talked about how no one wanted to work with her on the Career Fair Pair Presentation.

"Go," Jennie says.

"You are such a dumbwad." Stewart says.

Darby at last stands and jogs onto the field, but his snowpants and snowboots make jogging hard so he's just sort of trotting. Most of the snow is tramped down and a bit slippery too, and Darby takes his spot at the left forward position. Billy has rotated to the centre forward, and Monsieur's there holding the soccer ball waiting to restart the game.

"*Commencez*," he says.

The ball hits the snow with a slap, and as soon as it does, Billy charges toward it. He kicks hard, and the ball smacks into the other team's centre forward, who steps backward startled. As Billy charges toward the ball, more and more players from both teams step back. No one wants to risk a kick in the shins, and so everyone pretty much lets Billy push his way forward to the goal. He seems to have learned that softer, short kicks with little running bursts works better in the snow, but Darby only half-watches as the action moves away from him.

He's dwelling on his failure with Jennie – his inability to lie to her well and make her feel better about the presentation. Letting her down by freezing in fight-or-flight felt disappointing, but freezing with a disfluency instead of benevolent lying felt discouraging, and because bad thoughts most often lead to worse thoughts, Darby remembers something else from back in early January.

To fill class time after Mr. Henderson's unfortunate accident, Monsieur was bringing the students to the library resource centre for presentation research and preparation every second period. At the multimedia centre, Jennie would talk and talk about Veterinary Dentistry, unable to contain her enthusiasm or control the volume of her voice. She made a display of her excitement, which made Darby uncomfortable, but he knew to keep his reaction to himself and not injure her feelings. Sometimes, over a lunch hour behind the Good and Quick Gas and Sip, when Billy or Stewart teased him and ridiculed his presentation partner, Darby would admit to his embarrassment, but for the most part, he said not much and endured their remarks with an all-in-good-fun grin.

One day, Billy or Stewart wondered aloud what ridiculous clothing she might wear to discuss Veterinary Dentistry, and Darby only shrugged. Maybe it'd be that super-styling blue jean coverall-skirt combo she wore at the December Holiday Concert Celebration. Or maybe she'd find a pantsuit somewhere. Alexander had fallen quiet, Darby noticed. Maybe no one would even notice her clothes, Billy said, because everyone'd be too busy staring at that shrimp-scampi-looking hearing aid stuck on her ear. The remark was the kind of ugly thought all people have once in a while but know better not to say aloud. Darby noticed Alexander looking at him, and it was like they both knew they should interrupt Billy and stop him. They didn't.

Standing on the snowball soccer field, Darby thinks about how unkind his silence was, and he wonders if Jennie hasn't somehow sensed his secret unkindness. A flush of shame warms his whole face.

Parasitism: Darby = a good grade (+) / Jennie = self-image (-)

According to Darby's mom, it's best for people to forgive themselves for their mistakes. According to his dad, people are crummy.

"Show hustle, Darby," Monsieur yells.

The teacher claps his mittened hands together in a booming way again, and Darby notices that most of the students on both teams have collected down at the other team's net. No one is playing their assigned positions, but since DPA is more about movement and play than proper sports and regulations, Darby doesn't suppose it matters. More students are running for the ball, and more students are paying attention, and it seems as if Billy's enthusiasm has caught on.

Jogging toward the goal, Darby watches Alexander from the other team as he tries and fails to pass the ball. It thuds against a patch of trampled snow and the player's legs scramble on a slippery spot. Most of the students chuckle good-naturedly in unspoken agreement that snowball soccer is mostly ludicrous, but everyone may as well enjoy themselves.

"Stop it," Billy says. "Stop laughing." He speaks in a bark that brings all the chuckles to a halt. Players from both teams turn to look at Billy, but he keeps his head down, avoiding eye contact and charging forward. He's either unaware of his inappropriately aggressive-aggressive behaviour, or he has worked himself into such a temper tantrum fury that he does not care. Darby cannot tell which, but he watches as Billy kicks his boot against the ball harder and harder to little effect.

"Stop laughing," Billy says again.

Wedged into an uneven patch of snow, the soccer ball turn-spins as Billy kicks, but it doesn't move forward or back or left or right, and its immovability frustrates Billy more. As he kicks harder at the hard-packed patch of snow, he grunts out in anger and sends the players nearest him a step or two back.

"Dumb mother, dumb mother, dumb mother."

Strictly speaking *dumb mother* is not an actual profanity, but it is close enough to directly evoke the actual profanity, and the students look away embarrassed and alarmed and grinning. Everyone's waiting for Monsieur to blow his whistle or intervene somehow, Darby figures, and no one wants to watch another kid getting in trouble.

"Dumb motherfuck."

When Monsieur still does not blow his whistle or intervene in any way, Darby wonders how long Billy's outburst is going to last. A teacher can't pretend not to notice such obviously and openly inappropriate language. A teacher can't allow such behaviour to continue certainly. Monsieur pretty much has to intervene, doesn't he?

"Motherfucker."

Monsieur doesn't intervene, though. Alexander does. He steps close and puts a hand on Billy's arm.

"Take it easy," Alexander says.

Darby has seen Alexander calm Billy down a couple of times before, but this time it doesn't work. Instead, Billy flings his arm back to throw Alexander off him.

"Don't," Billy says.

The reaction saddens Darby as much as it surprises him. Whenever he's witnessed Alexander calm Billy in the past, Billy has always let himself be calmed. Darby wonders what has changed and what the tension is all about, but then realizes that the tension must be about him. Billy's still angry that Alexander didn't participate in the mean trick during the Veterinary Dentistry presentation, and that's why he's reacted as he has. That's why he's staring down Alexander as if double dog daring him to say more. Alexander doesn't say any more, though, and instead just walks away.

Only now does Monsieur Substitute choose to intervene, blowing his whistle twice as he trots over to the clusters of students.

"*Ca suffit, ca suffit,*" he says and toots one more time.

Though it isn't time to rotate and it isn't his turn to rotate out, Alexander walks off to the other team's sideline bench, and there's something in his slumped shoulders that Darby recognizes. This is how he looked when he saw Darby with Hannah at the Southgate Bayview Mews Mall gazebo.

"*C'est bien,*" Monsieur Substitute says and claps his hands. "*Continuez.*"

ON THE STAGES OF FALLING FOR A FRIEND'S OLDER SISTER

Because of hormones and sentimentality and proximity, an eleven-year-old boy might develop romantic feelings toward his friend's eighteen-year-old sister in any number of ways. Indeed, when a boy in the prologue to his pubescence catches sight of a young woman in the afterword of her adolescence, such feelings emerge easily after a certain number of afterschool and weekend encounters, but in actual fact, the evolution of the boy's ardour follows a series of three distinct and identifiable stages.

a. Stage One

The initial and spontaneous infatuation of the first stage might flare up on an evening, a month before Career Day, that a boy and his friend journey together to the friend's apartment in order to review the conversion of mixed fractions to improper fractions for an upcoming algebra unit test. For the boy, his friend's apartment has grown into something of a safe refuge – a cramped low-rise retreat that provides escape from the inescapable anxiety that follows him from room to room at his own broken townhouse home. There, the boy's mother worries after him at every step, but such hovering concern does not pervade his friend's low-rise apartment. While the term *latchkey kid* and the parenting style it implies have fallen decades out of favour by the time of these get-togethers, the term fits well enough for the friend and the life he leads in the low-rise apartment. Essentially unsupervised, the latchkey friend's days might be both isolating and unhealthy, but the situation also allows for great freedom. Unlimited electronic games, inappropriate cable television dramas, and even the occasional out-in-the-open cigarette on the fourth-floor balcony. For the boy, such greener grasses make the low-rise apartment an idyllic setting where his heart will open to new possibilities.

On the evening of the boy's first infatuation, he and his latchkey friend enter the apartment in a rush, unslinging their knapsacks, kicking free their snow boots, and tumbling forward to laugh together about the ridiculous cold of the cold school bus. Here, all-of-a-sudden-and-out-of-the-blue, the friend senses something amiss or hears something in the air, and happy grinning, he holds up his finger. In the silence, he calls out.

"Hey sis, you here?"

From behind the closed bathroom door the older sister's voice comes. She's soaking in the tub, she says. Her shift at the mall pet store was cut short, she says. She picked up microwavable pizza bites on her way home, she says.

Sweet, says the latchkey friend, for pizza bites make good study food, and from his knapsack, he removes *Unknown Quantitative Qualities*, an interlibrary loan that explains the *xyz* of algebra better than any textbook ever found in any fifth-grade classroom. The friend turns toward the hall to his bedroom and says they can work in there, but the boy's attention remains unfocused, for he is imagining a young woman soaking luxuriously in a bathtub.

Hills and valleys of foaming bubble-bath surround her, and she's reclined, her head resting on a washcloth at the head of the tub and her feet propped up on the faucet. Although loving the animals at Chez Animaux comes easy to her, the boy imagines that no retail job is an easy job. Maybe the assistant manager has a strict policy against sitting behind the cash, so the sister soaks in the water in order to unwind. Weary and tired and naked. The warm water would relax more with some sort of bubbled scent, he imagines, and through his mind's nose, the boy breathes in traces of vanilla, a BodyShop scent available in lotion and bath beads and bath salts and bath bombs.

After a half hour, the boy smiles. With his friend's help, he has come to understand the essence of common denominators, and his friend smiles too, jumping right into how to flip fractions for algebraic division. They stop studying, though, when they both hear singing. Drifting in from down the hallway, out through the closed bathroom door, the older sister's voice sings the mournful chorus of "Miss Otis Regrets" absentmindedly and up and down. The friend explains that his sister does this sometimes. She sometimes gets to reading in the bathtub and she sometimes forgets herself.

The new information spikes the boy's imagination more, for not only is the older sister a reader – and everyone loves a reader – but also the song she sings is Cole Porter. The boy recognizes it from a compilation CD he and his mother listen to in the mornings, and he imagines the older sister with her heels propped up on the faucet, the toes of her bare feet swaying to the tune. Probably the water around her has grown cold by now, and probably she has to stretch with her toes to turn the faucet and add hot water to warm the tub. The imagined scene makes the boy's face flush. At eleven years old and still unbalanced by his parents' trial separation, he has grown susceptible to such eruptions of exaggerated emotion. At home in the townhouse, such sentiments must be stifled lest he worsen the situation, but here in this low-rise apartment, he can let his imagination run to wherever it may go. He enjoys imagining his friend's older sister; he feels fondly about the bathroom scene he has set her in, and it lingers in his mind hours afterward. After he has readied himself for many math problems, after he has finished off many a pizza bite, and after his mother has come to bring him home.

Without at all realizing what has occurred, the boy completes the first stage of his first love without yet meeting or speaking to or setting eyes upon the object of his affection.

b. Stage Two

Following the first stage by a matter of days, the second stage of romantic development advances from the abstraction of the young boy's idealized imagination toward a more concrete specificity. He meets the older sister in person, and through the encounter, her singing voice and her vanilla aroma take on a more individualized physical form. The setting for this meeting will not be the apartment refuge, but the nearby Southgate Bayview Mews Mall.

On the Saturday in question, the boy and his friend begin their get-together with four hours of *KillCraft-WarMachine*, completing the entirety of the game's primary narrative and wandering the unchartered territory of a bonus level. They have thus far discovered nothing but ruins, and so they decide that they might do some wandering beyond the apartment, striking outdoors to travel and discover what they may. Well, not outdoors, but across the road to the Southgate Bayview Mews Mall. After all, late December in Ottawa can be cold, and neither the boy nor his friend is the type to traipse heartily up and down tobogganing hills even if such fanciful fun were readily available nearby. No, the boy and his friend would much rather be browsing through Plot's End, the used bookstore housed between the Dollarpalooza and an emptied-out retail space that was once either a Hallmark Cards or a Carleton Cards but is now out of business.

In between the narrow aisles and shelves of moldy second-hand books, the boy and his friend pick up and put down leveled readers and middle-school chapterbooks, discovering they shared some favourites in common. While these young-reader titles might have embarrassed them a short while ago, the boy and his friend openly mock themselves, growing closer with each unlikely book they compare. The adventure about the introvert campers who subvert the counsellors of a rival camp who are plotting to cheat at the inter-lake water Olympics? The dramedy about the snarky dyslexic boy who uncovers his school administration has been fudging the standardized testing results to embezzle funds from the school board? The science fiction about the musical theatre clique at the Andromeda Arts Academy who learn a valuable lesson about cross-species empathy? They grin at the absurdity of middle-grade storylines, and they nod at titles and cover illustrations in the way other boys might intone *got-it-got-it-need-it* through a collection of trading cards, and though such incidental connections might represent little, the accumulated coincidences bring both joy.

Then the boy comes across *Animal Farm*. Miscategorized amongst the middle-grade books, the edition differs from the two decades-old editions the boy grew up with in his childhood home. One copy was his mom's and one was his dad's, and each parent brought a copy to their marriage, but they decided to keep both, doubling up in the basement bookshelves in Calgary. A family favourite, the book was read, reread, and chatted about, but the boy does not at first recognize the edition in his hands at Plot's End. The cover of this edition shows a tranquil landscape in oil paint with an aged barn at sunset and a field of calm wheat blowing in the background breeze. In the foreground, eating together from a shared trough at the barn's open gate, the farmyard cast of horse and sheep and pig stand in shadow, but the peaceful scene isn't one the boy connects with the story in his memory. This cover design lies, but he holds it up to show his friend anyway.

He knows the book, but hasn't read it, the friend says. His sister's got a copy, he says. It's a novel pretty much everyone has to read in secondary school, he says, but his sister read it on her own when she was in middle school. Like Cole Porter, the book is an insignificant and unsubstantial bit of happenstance. The boy, however, feels the coincidence as a connection, and so when the friend suggests they swing by and visit her in the Southgate Bayview Mews Mall's Chez Animaux, the boy says, yeah, that sounds good. He's always liked pet stores. Who doesn't like a pet store?

As the friend and the boy approach, the older sister brightens, her face lit and genuinely gladdened by their unplanned appearance during her shift. She is beautiful, the boy notices, her dark hair cropped short with a dyed blue streak. The angry jewelry she wears in her brow and lip and nostril seem to want to hide her good-natured grin, but none of it does. The boy also notices her open affection with her brother – a squeezing sideways hug and a haphazard peck on the side of the head – and the boy wonders at such feeling, glad to learn that his friend receives such sibling warmth.

Business at Chez Animaux has been slow all afternoon, it turns out, and the assistant manager has granted himself an extended lunch break in the food court. Would the boy like a tour of the pet store? He nods and all three journey together through the glass aquaria containing tropical fish, the noisy cages containing birds of a feather, and the tubular bubble mazes containing small rodents. At the back wall of the store, the six windowed homes of puppies and kittens offer endearing sights: litters of toddler animals piled on top of one another in a lazy sibling slumber and litters of toddler animals frantically tumbling all over one another in a right-good rumpus. In the window enclosure closest to him, the boy sees a calico kitten pawing on the inside of the glass, mewing and trying to break through the fourth wall, which prompts the sister to check her watch and announce that it's quite close to feeding time. Would they like to come into the back and help out?

Behind the scenes, the appealing windows of puppies and kittens becomes a narrow corridor storeroom with inventory shelves against one wall. Pulling open a cabinet door on the opposite wall, the sister reveals the animals. With filled water dishes and measured scoops of kibble, the boy gets to reach and stretch into the puppy and kitty enclosures. As he bends forward, he can see outward through the windows that face into the store, looking upon the world from these small creatures' points of view. Neat. The gratitude he feels toward the older sister is great, and thus his affection for her passes through to the third stage.

c. Stage Three

The third stage involves marijuana. On a Saturday afternoon after a movie matinee, the boy and the friend return to the apartment to find the sister once again home early from Chez Animaux. Reading on the chesterfield, she's still dressed in her work uniform – a black half apron worn over a green golf shirt with the store's animal paw insignia. Her schedule was five hours, but the assistant manager sent her home after three because the store was slow.

A cost-saving measure the guy is trying out, she says. He wants to run a smoother staff with greater efficiency, she says. The guy has been reading some self-betterment small enterprise and medium business management book, she says. Her voice reaches for playful mockery, but the boy hears disappointment there too, and his mind transforms the store supervisor into his very own personal arch nemesis. Crap assistant manager.

The book open on the older sister's lap does not sound like a book one should read when one feels down. *Hospice and Palliative Care for Companion Animals.* It's a school text she's reviewing for a unit quiz. The boy and the friend nod, but say nothing. They planned on taking over the chesterfield for a couple of hours of television, but they can't very well say this if she's being all responsible and mature and studying. In silent agreement, the friend and the boy turn toward the hall, but the sister shows them a zip-lock baggie containing two hand-rolled cigarettes. The top edge of the baggie is yellow on one side and blue on the other, and when ziplocked together, the top of the baggie appears green to ensure an airtight seal of freshness, and the boy recognizes it as the clever brand his mom sometimes buys even though Tupperware is better for the environment. Such are his thoughts when the older sister asks them if they want to smoke, and he agrees without truly deciding to do so.

The three of them pass the first cigarette around in a counter-clockwise direction, and even though the boy feels sure he feels nothing out of the ordinary and even though the drug does not seem to have affected him, the group activity and the cooperation of the hand-to-hand motion gladden him. After kindergarten and the age of five, no one makes a big deal about sharing, but there is something reassuringly generous and proper about carefully taking the cigarette from the left, inhaling, and then conscientiously handing it off to the right. When the cigarette burns short and is difficult to pass counter-clockwise from hand to hand, the older sister removes from her pocket a pair of decorative hinged tweezers, and she clips in the remaining end of the cigarette. The top of the tweezers attaches to a brown beaded leatherette string with frayed ends, and the boy wonders where one might purchase such a specialized device.

Before lighting the second cigarette, the friend suggests they forage for food, and from the cupboards and fridge crisper, they collect green peppers, red peppers, a can of marinara, and two types of pasta. Penne or fusilli? They settle on fusilli and repeat the word repeatedly, stretching out the *sssilly* and laughing together, and the boy wonders if maybe he does feel something and maybe the drug has affected him. With the pasta on boil, they sit again in a circle to share the second cigarette, and the boy and the friend launch into a shared story. It's an anecdote about a classmate who doesn't know how to swear but constantly wants to swear and comes out with unlikely improvisations. *Dipwad. Assmother. Christ of Jesus.* Smoking and snickering together, the three create further unlikely curses – *son of a bastard, in loco parentis, paterfamilias* – until the second cigarette is down to a short end and the sister's clip is once again needed.

From the hallway, a loud repeated beep whines, cutting off the laughter and stopping the giggles and locking boy, friend, and older sister in a confused eye contact. *Whaaaaa?* their faces all ask.

A fire alarm, the boy says. Something's burning, the older sister says. In the kitchen, the friend says. The friend at last stands, running off and running back to report that the penne is burnt to ruin and beyond repair. The boy is pretty sure his friend means fusilli because they all three agreed upon fusilli, but he keeps the thought to himself. Correcting other people needlessly can be rude, and he is a guest in their home after all. The sister shrugs and tells the boy that the fire alarm has a hair trigger. Goes off every time anyone wants darkly toasted toast. The friend flees to wave a dishtowel at the ceiling alarm, and sure enough, the beeping whine stops a moment later. The older sister shrugs again and passes the last of the cigarette to the boy, who inhales only to find the ember has burned out.

Alone with the sister on the chesterfield, he realizes he is alone with the sister on the chesterfield, and together they pass through silence – so much that the boy wonders at the friend's absence.

Maybe he's gone to bed to lie down and rest a bit? The sister shrugs beside him, dismissing the question, and she says she's hungry. In the kitchen, they decide on the red and green peppers for snacking, even though slicing them might not be a good idea because they'll have to use sharp knives and neither one of them is in any condition to telephone 911 if the blade slips and nips off the end of an index finger or – goodness forbid – hits a vein and does even more serious damage. Next thing the boy knows, they're back on the chesterfield snacking on their red and green pepper slices, and that's when he notices that time isn't working in its usual chronological way. He also notices that the chesterfield cushions sag in the middle, so the sister and he are not only sitting together but are also huddled together, her side slightly pressing into his side, and the feeling is a fantasy.

She reaches for the coffee table, and he thinks she's reaching for *Hospice and Palliative Care for Companion Animals*, but she retrieves a comic book instead. Reclined on the chesterfield, she holds open the comic book in invitation. *Mutant Mutation Generation.* It's an innocent invitation to read together, which strikes him as a generous gesture for which he is greatly grateful, so he too reclines. Side by side, they turn the pages and scan the illustrated panels as the story comes together bit by bit.

Reading together, the boy slides deep into his third stage of infatuation, and his crush is complete and total and entire by the time they reach the end of the story. The final denouement panel shows the mutant demonoid tween protagonist tucked in and sleeping safely in her bed after her adventures are done, and with this final scene finished, the older sister closes the comic and turns to the cover. It's a natural progression that the boy has enacted numberless times but never before considered. Once a story is done, the next logical step is turning to the cover for moment of quiet reflection.

In this case, the illustration on the cover of *Mutant Mutation Generation* shows the main character in her bedroom, sitting criss-cross on top of her bed reading a comic book. The bedspread beneath her shows a repeating bunny-doggie-kitty pattern, and the posters of fictional movies and imaginary bands cover the bedroom walls behind her. The setting is idyllic, the boy thinks, but then he notices the comic book cover inside the comic book cover, which shows the same demonoid tween protagonist reading the same comic in the same room with the same patterned bedspread and postered walls. And on the cover of that smaller cover is another smaller cover, again a smaller version with another smaller version inside. The repetition goes on and on and in and in, which makes no sense.

A panic quickens in the boy's blood, and he can feel his body tighten. The picture makes no sense no matter how much he tries to make sense of it. Sitting as close as she is with her side pressed into his, the older sister notices his panic. It's the cover, he says and points. Oh yeah, picture in a picture. *Droste* effect, she says. Lots of comic books use it, she says. Her calmness calms him, and she tells him there's even a French art term for the effect. *Mise en abime.* She touches his forearm, and he feels better. Everything is funnier in French, he thinks, and he falls for her more.

CHAPTER 8

1. On Workplace Relationships. Would you rather have a job where you work by yourself or on a team? Discuss in a 250-word paragraph with specific examples.
2. On Workplace Environments. Would you rather have a job where you work indoors or outdoors? Discuss in a 250-word paragraph with specific examples.
3. On Workplace Customs. Would you rather have a job where you work more with your hands or with your mind? Discuss in a 250-word paragraph with specific examples.
4. On What You Wish. Write a 250-word paragraph on a topic of your choice.

Monsieur Substitute must have written out the choice of topics for Afternoon Reflection and Composition at some point over lunch because they're waiting on the whiteboard for the students to get right down to work after DPA. Just like Mr. Henderson used to do, Monsieur Substitute offers a choice of four topics every day, which makes Darby think that maybe Mr. Henderson has written down a whole long list of topics somewhere in a lesson planner and Monsieur is just copying them out, but that's all right.

The fourth topic choice always offers the students their own choice, so it really shouldn't be fourth. The correct ordinal number should be the infiniteth choice, except when Darby thinks of it that way, the word sounds deliberately immature like preschool talk. Better to think of it as the nth choice. Before today, Darby has never once chosen the nth choice because Afternoon Reflection and Composition period is only a half-period lasting thirty minutes, which is tight for 250 words, and selecting one option from a finite list of three will always be more time efficient than selecting one option from an infinite list of n.

Today, however, Darby decides upon the fourth choice because he wants to write to Alexander. A composition and an apology – feed two birds with one seed. Maybe in choosing the topic, he will even be able to make his former friend back into a friend, which is maybe not a selfless motive in keeping with the spirit of apologizing, but maybe that's all right.

Darby can draft the apology in his pastel green Daily Afternoon Composition cahier and then recopy it in loose-leaf pages to pass to Alexander before afternoon nutrition break. That's the plan, and since thirty minutes for such a plan is not a lot, he knows he has to focus right away, but still, he's distracted by the French language map of Canada on the cover of his *cahier d'exercises.*

According to his mom, each and every parent in Ottawa wants their child to be beautifully bilingual, and parents in Ottawa sign up for the early entry French immersion program classes with good intentions. After the first few primary grades, however, enrollment inevitably dwindles down, which must leave the school board with leftover surplus *cahiers.* What Darby figures is that the school board created Daily Afternoon Composition period as a way of working through the notebook surplus, and while he believes the reuse-recycle practice makes good economical and environmental sense, the belief won't get his composition written, so he forces it from his mind.

> *I am sorry I developed feelings for your sister without your permission first. You were nice to try and cheer up Billy during snow soccer. Even if it didn't work. Sorry your mom can't come do her presentation on the importance of social services. It would have been good. Thank you for not doing the mean trick with Billy and Stewart this morning. Do you think maybe the scarf*

woman with Monsieur in the parking lot of the church might not have been the vice-principal but a different woman like the school nurse? Sorry about your sister again too.

According to Darby's mom, the ability to apologize is a gift, and gifts must be given with honesty and sincerity. It does no one any good to apologize without self-awareness and careful consideration. According to his dad, apologizing too much makes every apology more-or-less meaningless. According to his mom, this is why his dad has such trouble apologizing and perhaps such a quality isn't ideal. Darby rereads the start of his note and decides to start again.

The map of Canada on his *cahier d'exercices* workbook is actually a *carte du Canada*, and at some point, when he first arrived in Ottawa, Darby doodled two roadside billboards on the cover. The first one says *you are here* in a comic-strip-font with an arrow pointing to Ottawa and the second exact same sign with *you were here* points to Calgary. Both doodles were in ink pen and couldn't be erased when he later wanted to erase them. Now, when he sees them, Darby understands how foolish and immature the drawings are. He wasn't just feeling sad; he was kind of indulging in feeling sad. He was feeling sorry for himself; that's what Darby's dad would tell him. His mom would tell him it was all right to feel sad, and it was normal to let his mind wander.

I don't really know why I talked to Hannah too much but it has something to do with the nose-piercing and her lip-piercing, which both are ~~lovely fetching~~ nice and which I can't seem to stop thinking about after I see her. And that was why I decided to go to her work and talk to her without your knowing. Then she was happy to talk to me too and that has never happened before so that's why I kept going back to meet her in secret. So I am sorry.

An effective apology requires not only honesty, but also empathy, and so Darby decides he can't very well tell Alexander that a big part of the reason he met with Hannah was probably puberty. Honesty of that nature would be counterproductive to the apology.

The silhouette *carte du Canada* doesn't really show a map of the country, Darby notices. What it shows is thirteen separate silhouette maps of the provinces and territories all neatly organized up against one another. On the cover of his pastel green *cahier,* the pastel green borderlines between the provinces and territories are not lines at all, but his brain forming the separate shapes and empty spaces into Canada. It's the trick of negative space. Now that he's seen the picture this way, though, seeing it as anything but a map of Canada is hard. His brain will not be untricked.

Ahead of him to the right, Jennie writes in a pastel blue *cahier,* and farther to the right, Alexander writes in a pastel purple *cahier.* Jennie writes her composition the way she always seems to – one smooth uninterrupted cursive stream of 250 words. Alexander writing, though, looks more like Darby imagines he himself looks – all starts and stops and starts, scrawling out a sentence, stopping to stare at nothing in particular, and then reluctantly starting again as if the nothing-in-particular that he was staring at gave him a sort-of and close-enough answer. The problem, as Darby sees it, is that whereas Alexander eventually gets himself moving again, Darby's own stops stretch out for longer than his starts. According to his mom and his dad, the challenge is focus.

Someone in the quiet classroom opens and closes their lift-top desk, which makes a soft creak opening and an even softer bump closing that nonetheless draws attention. From the front of the room, Monsieur Substitute glances up and glances down in partial concern. He sits perched on the edge of the teacher desk in a way that Mr. Henderson did when he held forth his opinion on matters of current events. With a red pen pinched in his hand, his hand pressed into his chin, and his eyebrows crunched,

Monsieur Substitute appears greatly focused and concentrated on the work at hand. The work at hand, though, is actually only the daily advanced-to-expert word search he didn't finish during this morning's Silent Reading Period. The Dell puzzle booklet is the bus station and airport magazine shop sort, and today's word search must be particularly troublesome because the red pen in Monsieur's hand hasn't moved from his chin in at least a few minutes.

While plenty of students in the enriched class enjoy a crossword and sudoku during their downtime between periods, no one would ever dare to bring a word search book onto Richmond East Elementary school property, and it'd be pretty easy to make fun of Monsieur Substitute for his low-to-moderate ambitions, which at the Good and Quick Gas and Sip, Alexander and Them actually do. *Quelle surprise and zut alors, the words, they run backwards and they run diagonal!* Sitting on the overturned milk crates, they rubbed their chins and shook their heads in fun.

> *What tricky terminology do you think is making Monsieur Substitute wrinkle his brow? Sorry your feelings got hurt about your sister. Do you think the word search has a particular theme or subject? Like geographical words or terms of parliamentary government?* Thème *or* sujet?

Making fun of Monsieur and his word searches might distract and thereby downplay the difficulty in giving and accepting an apology, but the strategy feels unkind and culturally insensitive. In the end, this version of the note might solve one short-term trouble, but it might also cause more long-term guilt.

Jennie's own opinion of the word searches isn't at all critical, and she has pointed out that to a francophone, the advanced-to-expert word searches probably contain uncommon to rare vocabulary, so even though a word search cannot challenge in the way a cryptic crossword might, it is educational. Monsieur Substitute has to hold a translated word in his mind while hunting it out on the word search letter grid, and in this way, he reinforces the uncommon words he knows but does not often use, and he can build his bilingual vocabulary by collecting rare words. Explained this way, the word searches seem kind of almost admirable.

Darby looks over at Jennie and sees she's still working away on her composition with her pen moving steadily across the page. Alexander's still stopping and starting. Though the two approaches look outwardly different, Darby recognizes a similarity there because they've both told him they choose the nth choice each and every day. The similarity must say something about Jennie and Alexander, Darby decides, and then he remembers another similarity.

The indigo table. Before he got to Richmond East Elementary and became the twenty-second student in the gifted and talented class at the end of October, Mr. Henderson had arranged the twenty-one students in the class into seven groups of three. Though the groups of three weren't really tables and were really just clusters of three desks pushed closer together, the teacher called them tables and named each one after a colour in the Roy G. Biv colour spectrum. Red, orange, yellow, green, blue, indigo, and violet. Jennie and Alexander both sat together at the indigo table with Sarah Underhill.

Seating Jennie and Alexander together makes sense because Mr. Henderson would certainly be the kind of teacher to assign seating strategically. He would separate students whose symbiotic parasitism brought out the worst in one another, breaking up Alexander from Billy and Stewart, and he would unite students whose symbiotic mutualism brought out the best in one another, placing together Jennie and Alexander. Her enviable focus and serious studiousness would shame Alexander into doing better. His agreeability and patience would tolerate the extremes of Jennie's stubborn tendencies.

Imagining them together at the indigo table is easy. If Alexander was slacking and loafing and not taking a Language Arts reading comprehension group exercise seriously, Jennie would have thrust a Collins classroom dictionary into his hands and insisted that he look up the definitions of new keyword vocabulary words. If Jennie got herself worked up and added unnecessary steps to a cross-multiplication calculation, Alexander would have watched silently and suggested shortcuts with tact and respect so as not to upset her. Darby imagined them illustrating and labeling a cross-section diagram of the respiratory system together, each of them grinning and co-sympathizing at their shared lack of artistic flair and ability. Together through all of September and well into October, their personalities would have complemented and supplemented one another just as Mr. Henderson had hoped.

But then Darby came in the last week of October, and with twenty-two students, seven tables of three no longer worked. The classroom desks were rearranged into rows, and Alexander wouldn't have gone out of his way to spend time with Jennie. It was much easier to fall back in with Billy Pace and Stewart Holgermonsson. Then Mr. Henderson had his unfortunate accident, and Monsieur Substitute came, and Monsieur doesn't at all care about using students' complementary personalities and academic aptitudes to form productive paired partners and small work groups. Make your own groups if you want to – that's what he always says.

Sorry about your sister. I was a jerk. Do you want to stay inside and sit with me and Jennie during afternoon nutrition snack break today?

Darby folds the loose-leaf note lengthwise and widthwise three times, and with the message safely folded inside, he writes

Alexander's name on both sides of the outside. As with cellular smart phones and swear words, Monsieur Substitute tends to look the other way at notes passed in class – not worth the trouble to stop them – but today he's still absorbed by the advanced-to-expert word search. The teacher doesn't notice, so he doesn't have to pretend not to notice as Darby pokes Kamil Gendry in the desk to his right. Darby watches as Kamil pokes Sarah Underhill and passes the note along. In this way, the note travels hand to hand baton style two rows to the right and three desks down.

It's a risk, he knows. If Alexander gets the note of apology and recognizes the handwriting, he might just rip it end-to-end into two without bothering even to unfold it. If Alexander reads the note of apology and identifies Darby's regret and invitation as a transparent ploy at self-protection, he might be all the more incensed. If Alexander accepts the invitation and joins him and Jennie for afternoon nutrition break, he might talk about going off school property or smoking or pornography or marijuana or Hannah or any number of secrets Darby would rather Jennie didn't know about. Several possible outcomes are unhappy outcomes.

"*Ça suffit,*" Monsieur Substitute says. "Please close your *cahier d'exercices maintenant.*"

For the first time this school year, Darby has not completed his afternoon composition. He knows for sure that the four drafts of inadequate apologies he has completed in no way satisfy the requirements of Mr. Henderson's assignment. He also knows that it almost for sure doesn't matter.

After the unfortunate accident back in November, Mr. Henderson's purple pen comments in the notebooks disappeared. No more marginal appreciative exclamations or attentive questions. Monsieur distributed and collected the class's *cahiers d'exercises* daily, but he was not staying late or taking them home to read through the compositions. Fair enough. Darby's dad would say if the Ottawa District Carleton School Board chooses not to pay short-term contract teachers a sufficient living wage and chooses not to grant dental and medical benefits, then it can hardly expect too, too much evaluation and assessment outside of in-class time. Darby's mom would agree, but she would say it's a shame too, which is what Darby kind of thinks.

As November became December and the likelihood of Mr. Henderson's return grew less likely, students in the enriched class caught on about the compositions. Some like Billy stopped going through the motions and writing anything at all, and others like Stewart pretended to write but didn't care what they wrote. Darby could see their point because really why bother? Like Jennie, though, he kept writing his daily compositions, but unlike her, he did increasingly wonder why. Maybe because school had always conditioned him this way, or maybe because he didn't know what else to do, or maybe because he was scared what might happen if he didn't do what he thought was expected of him.

"*Cahiers* to the front of the row, please," Monsieur says.

Darby closes his notebook to pass it forward and watches Alexander do the same. With second nutrition break coming, everyone is lifting their lift-top desks, putting away pens into pencil boxes, and pulling out snacks, and in the commotion, Darby loses sight of Alexander. He wrenches his neck to see better, but then the first afternoon bell rings and people start standing, so it's no use at all. His own snack for the afternoon is grapes and a nut-free s'mores granola bar in a twin snap Tupperware stackable. Darby's mom says healthy and unhealthy treats should always be paired, and Darby lifts open his lift-top desk to get them both. In the opening, he somehow misses Alexander crossing the room toward him.

"Yeah," Alexander says.

"Yeah?" Darby asks.

"Yeah. All right." Alexander says.

His voice sounds low, the same as it did on the snowball soccer field, and Darby right away thinks about explaining how he saw Monsieur and the school nurse sitting close to one another inside one another's personal space on the gymnasium-auditorium stage. That'd cheer Alexander up at least for a bit anyway. Before Darby gets to say anything about anything, though, he notices Billy looking at them across the classroom and making an *ah-what-the-hell* look of pissed-off perplexity, and then, Jennie is right there standing beside Alexander looking at Darby with a *well-this-warrants-explanation* look of incredulous confusion.

"Alexander's going to sit with us for snack break?" Darby says.

"If that is all right?" Alexander says.

"Alexander is going to sit with us for break." Jennie nods in agreement, but with a slow skepticism. "That's all right, I guess."

Over Alexander's shoulder, Darby sees Billy and Stewart snatching their coats and boots to stomp outside, which Darby figures is fortunate because otherwise they'd be glaring and glowering threats throughout the whole entire second nutrition break. In all, about half the class goes outside and half stays inside, so the room isn't so super quiet that Darby and Jennie and Alexander have to whisper-speak in hushed tones of discretion, but also they don't have to project loudly or lean in close to hear one another.

"I don't think a mandarin orange needs to be in a container," Jennie says. She points at her snack, which sits inside a snap-top stay-fresh container. "I mean, the whole point of a snack orange is that it comes with its own skin wrapper."

"Bananas are like that too," Darby says. "Avocados as well, but avocados would be an odd school snack."

Darby realizes that Alexander hasn't unpacked a snack and sees that Jennie has noticed too at almost the same time. Offering to share would be the obvious move, Darby thinks, but then sometimes even small acts of generosity can be taken the wrong way.

"I had a Twix this morning," Alexander explains with a shrug. "But I ate the whole thing. Guess I should have eaten just half. I mean, there's two pieces in a Twix. It's right there in the name, so yeah." His voice trails off.

Darby breaks his s'mores granola bar in half and points toward his grapes, and thankfully, no one treats the sharing like a big deal.

"You know what's dumb?" Darby asks. Neither Jennie nor Alexander asks what because the question is a rhetorical question, and they wait for Darby to continue instead. "The school garbage-free lunch policy. We're supposed to bring everything in reusable containers to reduce waste, but really it doesn't work that way because whenever I have a granola bar, I wind up just unwrapping the granola bar at home and then putting it in a Tupperware container. I still have to throw out the wrapper into the garbage."

"And then you have to wash the Tupperware," Alexander says.

"Which just wastes water." Jennie says.

"That's exactly what I mean, yes," Darby says. "Thank you."

They snack in quiet for a moment, which makes Darby worry, but he reminds himself that the three of them sitting together is an entirely new social dynamic and so some conversational lulls are to be expected.

"You guys did good on your presentation this morning," Alexander says.

Jennie and Darby both say thank you, but Darby is pretty sure Jennie's gratitude sounds more genuine because she sounds almost embarrassed.

"Jennie did much better than me," Darby says, and it doesn't even bother him to say it.

Alexander shrugs in a *c'est-la-vie-que-sera-sera* sort of way, but then adds that they must have spent a lot of time preparing together. "And you embedded the video right into the PowerPoint slides," he adds. "I always mess up when I embed .mov files."

"Thank you," Jennie says again.

"No big *rien*," Alexander says.

Darby thinks maybe he might show Alexander the wholly inadequate rubric that Monsieur gave Jennie and him, and they could all share a laugh about how little work the teacher does. *An A with no feedback, quelle surprise* – but then, Jennie probably wouldn't approve of having a laugh at Monsieur's expense, and she is probably right, so Darby keeps the unkind thought to himself.

"Yeah," Darby says instead. "Thank you."

"I think Mr. Henderson would've really liked all the work you did."

The mention of Mr. Henderson runs the risk of souring the conversation, and Darby worries that the whole afternoon nutrition break might turn south, but it doesn't.

"He did like hard work," Jennie says and nods. "He liked it because he always worked too hard himself."

"Oh yeah," Alexander says, and he nods along with Jennie. "Guy went way overboard."

Darby's mom says that agreeing and mirroring a conversational partner can be a way to facilitate social interactions, and he wonders if this is what Alexander is doing with Jennie.

"I agree too," Darby says with a nod.

"In September when school started, we spent like a whole morning playing parachute games in the gym."

Jennie grins and nods at Alexander's memory as if it's a fond one. "His icebreaker activity," she says. "Most teachers just do two-truths-and-a-lie or a scavenger hunt worksheet, but Mr. Henderson had us play parachute games. They're meant for younger kids, but still fun."

"Remember how Billy got all carried away and competitive?" Alexander asks, and the question makes Jennie chuckle.

Darby feels uncomfortable, but he's not sure why. Probably because thinking about Billy Pace reminds him of the guy's ah-what-the-hell look of pissed-off perplexity, but probably also because missing out on Jennie's and Alexander's good parachute memories makes him feel jealous. Darby's mom and dad both say jealousy is an unproductive and illogical emotion but entirely human and therefore forgivable.

"Yeah," Alexander says. "Mr. Henderson understood what makes a good icebreaker."

Jennie chews on a wedge segment of mandarin orange, and Alexander lets his words hang in the air, but both of them are probably thinking too much about Mr. Henderson, so Darby strategically decides to ask about their Afternoon Reflection and Composition topics.

"Did you both write on the fourth choice?" he adds.

"I always choose four," she says.

"Yeah?" Alexander asks. "Me too. I always choose the fourth option."

It turns out that while both of them wrote about what they wished, they also both sort of stayed on the topics of careers, which makes sense to Darby, and he thinks would have pleased Mr. Henderson since personal reflection about career paths was probably one of the curriculum outcomes he had in mind when he planned Career Day in the first place.

"I was thinking about this picture book that my sister and I used to have," Alexander says. "*Maybe You Should Fly a Jet! Maybe You*

Should Be a Vet! It was like a rhyming list of jobs and the message was that you had to pick one. Anyway, I was thinking about the strangeness of the book's title, and then I realized that Hannah is in school to become a vet."

Darby focuses on a grape, peeling its skin with his fingernail a bit so he doesn't have to make eye contact while Alexander talks about Hannah.

"Do you think her choice is connected?" Jennie asks.

"Probably not. The book was kind of obnoxious, and she used to make fun of it while she read it to me. Once in a while in between listing jobs, the narrator repeated 'you have to pick one job' and 'you can't just be nothing' and Hannah would do an extra serious-pushy voice. I would laugh whenever she did it. Which is probably why she kept doing it."

His voice turns low, and Darby thinks maybe Alexander is thinking about him, so maybe he should apologize again because maybe an apology aloud counts more than one in a note. Darby can't tell.

"What I liked most about the book didn't have anything to do with the story really. It was just that feeling of being little and sitting beside her and listening to her read to me, you know?"

Apologizing about Hannah aloud in front of Jennie could cause confusion and could lead to all sorts of unwanted questions and an uncomfortable conversation that Darby would rather not have, but he decides the risk is worth it.

"Sorry about Hannah," he says.

"No big *rien*." Alexander nods and looks toward Jennie. "Anyway, that was my Afternoon Reflection and Composition. What was yours?" he asks, which effectively and fortuitously deflects the chance of confusing questions and unwanted conversation.

"I wrote about my dad's job at the Ministry of Agriculture. When I was little, he was a senior analyst, and I wasn't sure what he did, but then he was promoted to managing consultant. I still don't really know what he does. Something about livestock information and statistical studies."

Now it's Alexander's turn to pay close attention to his grape because although Darby feels almost entirely certain that Jennie's dad is not a cuckold and there is thus no need to feel nervous as she talks about his job at the Ministry of Agriculture, Alexander doesn't know this at all.

"His newer job means more travel and time away from home, but he didn't know that when he accepted the promotion, or he wouldn't have taken it. I think he should just go back to his old job, but my mom said it doesn't work like that. Going backwards isn't possible. Which made me think about Zoology because that was what he studied in school. He couldn't find a job in it, so that's why he started at the Ministry of Agriculture in the first place even though he didn't want to. So now, if he wanted to get what he wanted, he'd have to go backwards even farther."

"Zoology?" Alexander asks. "Is that why you chose Veterinary Dentistry for your presentation?"

Jennie nods.

"I didn't know that," Darby says. Knowing wouldn't have changed or affected his performance in the Career Fair Pair Presentation, but Darby still feels foolish that he didn't know.

"I thought you did." Jennie's eyes look up as if that's where her memory is. "I thought I told you that."

Darby realizes that he might now have to admit that he didn't write anything for Afternoon Reflection and Composition, and he can't remember why he brought up the topic in the first place, but nobody mentions it, which feels like getting an out-of-nowhere reprieve.

"Sorry your mom had to cancel today," Jennie says. She gestures toward the white board.

- Financial Advisor and Asset Manager Terence Gendry
- Dental Hygienist Cintia Holgermonsson
- Mechanical Engineer Harold Tamm

Alexander's mom's crossed-out name has been erased altogether, but he shrugs and says it's no big *rien*. Whether or not this show of calm acceptance is sincere, Darby can't be sure, but he envies it because just then he remembers his dad is coming in a few minutes, which pretty much does away with his reprieve.

ON SETTING AND THE SOUTHGATE BAYVIEW MEWS MALL

Of the many settings where human industry and social endeavours can unfold, few are as maligned as the suburbs – those peripheral stepchild communities that surround the more glamourous city centres. Standard attitudes toward the suburban compromise of neither-here-nor-there and neither urban-nor-rural tend to be sneering uncomplicated clichés that disparage the conventionality and conformity of architecture and ideology. Such easy insults only intensify if the city in question is itself of modest ambitions – a suburban setting on the outskirts of a medium-sized city like Calgary or Ottawa is doubly maligned – and additionally, within such an unimportant location, the easy insults intensify further if the specific setting-within-the-setting is a suburban mall. The least important locale within the lesser important location within the less important setting. A place of no consequence at all.

And yet, even an eleven-year-old boy knows that there is very little logic behind such logic. Even an eleven-year-old boy senses that if examined closely, such hierarchies of setting do not hold up to reason. Commonplace and widespread assumptions might reach far and wide, but common sense insists that settings should not exist in a hierarchy any more than human beings should. No matter the setting, hearts and minds open equally everywhere. Affection and love and insight can bloom at the mall as well as it can anywhere else. An illuminated store directory, a Wild Beanz coffee kiosk, a food court gazebo. Anywhere can become a locus of humanity's best qualities.

a. At the Illuminated Store Directory

Standing inside the corridors of the downtrodden Southgate Bayview Mews Mall, an eleven-year-old boy gazes up at the store listings and runs his finger down the Leisure and Entertainment subsection to find the pet store Chez Animaux. He has lied to his mother and said he was taking the OC Transpo from Richmond East Elementary to his friend's home, but he has lied also to his friend. It was a week before Career Day. The bus line he truly took has brought him here to the unprosperous mall and its illuminated directory. Masking tape covers the names of two shops in the Leisure and Entertainment subsection, though they remain legible when the boy leans closer. Hobby Farm and Colour Me Crafty. Only two businesses have survived: Plot's End, a used book and second-hand magazine shop, and Chez Animaux, the pet shop where the object of the boy's affection works. In the illuminated map above, the boy searches for the pet shop and notices that one of the sign's interior bulbs has burnt out. A blur of shadow covers the entire anchor store at the mall's northernmost reach. The sight of such failed economy should be discouraging, but affection endures, and the boy finds his way.

He finds his way to an indoor park bench situated across from Chez Animaux, where he can watch the storefront unseen. From this angle, he sees little of the store's interior – a free-standing cubbyhole shelf of dog treats, a fiberglass Humane Society donation sculpture in the form of a St. Bernard, and a sliver of the front cash counter cluttered with impulse-buy cat toy displays. A ceiling-high glass box takes up most of the pet shop's storefront, an animal enclosure that curves outward into the mall corridors so passersby might be tempted by newly arrived puppies and kittens. The glass box sits vacant at the moment, and as the boy looks into its emptiness, a shadow of a doubt darkens his thoughts, and he questions the wisdom of his quest.

He planned to wait at the entryway to the pet shop, where his friend's older sister might just happen to pass by and where the boy might just by happenstance look up as she passed, and through such a manufactured chance encounter, they would thus spend fifteen minutes together. She might say *what a surprise* and explain that she was just off on her break. He might say *what a funny coincidence* and suggest that they share an Orange Julius. Or perhaps a Booster Juice if she prefers? She might never look beyond the façade of his charade, and at some point, he will present the gift he bears within his school knapsack backpack. A round jar of BodyShop body butter in French Vanilla ice cream scent. In the boy's dreamy fantasy mind, this first encounter might be the first encounter of a long series within the idyll of the Southgate Bayview Mews Mall, and he might present her with any number of thoughtful and meaningful presents. A waterproof bookmark for long bathtub reads. A novelty Zippo lighter with the *Mutant Mutation Generation* team logo embossed on its shiny steel sides. A heart-shaped nose stud in silver.

But the boy understands that his plan breaks down with the body butter, for the gift of the lovely scent ruins the pretense of an accidental meeting. The doubt that clouds his heart like a burnt-out bulb forces him to accept the unlikelihood of his quest and the plot holes in his plan. He doesn't even know when her break is, and his mom will be picking him up at the entry to his friend's apartment in just over an hour. How could he have thought his heartfelt expression of affection would bring love? She is eighteen, and he is but eleven.

Thus distracted, the boy fails to notice the hidden door inside the glass storefront display opening and shutting; he fails to notice an employee step into the empty enclosure with a bucket and cleaning sponge, and he fails to notice that that employee is her. The young woman he has travelled so far to see. When finally he does notice, he feels his chest cavity constrict and he feels unsure what to do with himself. Sitting straight across from the glass front, he'll certainly be noticed if he stays on the park bench, and yet fleeing at that exact moment might also draw her attention too. From inside the glass enclosure, she would certainly see his mad and awkward scramble of flight from the park bench.

With no obvious action to take, inertia wins out and the boy sits in stasis while the young woman washes the floor and the interior walls of the display. She does not seem to spot him but goes about her soap and water work in her green golf shirt and black half-apron, the uniform of all Chez Animaux employees. Not even when she exits the glass box and re-enters with a spray bottle and rag and cleans the inside of the glass, erasing the paw prints and slobber smudges left by the previous tenants. She's preparing and disinfecting the storefront box for the newborn new arrivals, the boy thinks, and he is right. When all is spic and span, she removes an orange grease pencil from her half-apron and writes on the inside of the glass. Working slowly in large stylized all-caps, she shadows each letter as she goes, adding a three-dimensional effect to her font. All the letters come out alike in size and design, the consistency impressive. *LABRAD*. Midway through the word, the boy realizes that she writes each letter so slowly and so carefully not only because she cares about her work, but also because she is writing backwards. From within the glass enclosure, she writes her painstaking letters to catch the eyes of passersby in the outside corridors of the plaza. She writes backwards. *LABRADOODLES*.

Stepping back, she admires her work. A well-earned moment in the boy's opinion, and then he watches more as she sets her face in a twist of concentration and returns to work, carefully crafting an *H* with the same steady hand. *HIDA. HIDAR.* The boy feels sure he could watch her work for hours, but he checks his watch to see how much time he has left. *HIDARBY. HI DARBY.* Hey, the boy knows that name. It's his name. Just as the thought enters his mind, the young woman steps back and grins, making eye contact. He holds her eye contact, and unsure of what else he might do, the boy waves an embarrassed hello. She probably saw him before he saw her, but the surprise of it was that she doesn't seem surprised. She doesn't seem to mind.

After a moment's pause, she removes a napkin to erase away the greeting, replacing it with *THREE FEMALE, TWO MALE, SPAYED AND NEUTERED*, and right there in the Southgate Bayview Mew Mall, the boy's affection blossoms into love.

b. By the Wild Beanz Coffee Kiosk

When the boy once again journeys by OC Transpo to the Southgate Bayview Mews Mall, he isn't thinking about the meeting as a second date, but neither has he entirely dismissed the fiction. While they did not actually talk on the evening of the first-non-date first date, she did encourage him with his name writ large across the storefront glass. Thus, even though he knows that no singer-songwriter has ever strummed and sung of the romance between an eleven-year-old and an eighteen-year-old, his French Vanilla gift remains secreted in his backpack knapsack, and two days later, he returns with his offering.

Moving through the corridors of the shopping plaza once again, the boy reconsiders his position on the indoor park bench. Sitting in wait and watching in indecision has never helped anyone, he decides, and he strides purposefully past the mall's central fountain, a broken water feature that has not featured water in years. At the threshold of Chez Animaux, he slows only to gaze sideward at the curly golden labradoodle pups rolling and grappling and knocking over their water dish. Inside the store, the object of the boy's affection kneels beside a wall of aquaria with a mesh net in hand, scooping out unfortunate floaters from the tank of small feeder goldfish, but upon the boy's entry, she turns her head to him right away. They grin at one another, but before the longed-for reunion can occur, a voice from behind the front cash counter intercedes.

"Good afternoon, and *bienvenue* to Chez Animaux."

The assistant store manager. He wears Chez Animaux's standard uniform half-apron, but his dark grey golf shirt signals his authority to all. It is the fellow who keeps cutting the young woman's shifts short in order to save on labour costs. The villain. The boy's nemesis. Pinned to his chest he wears a badge declaring *ask me a question*, but the boy cannot think of one and glances away toward a spinning rack of paperback pet-care manuals. *Your New Corgi. Healing Heartworms. Reptiles!* The boy imagines himself in the market for a reptile, and as he imagines becoming such a person, questions do occur to him.

"Can you tell me the similarities and differences between skinks and newts and anoles and bearded dragons? What are the advantages and disadvantages of each, and which would you recommend for a first-time reptile owner?"

The assistant manager smiles his retail smile and suggests they take a look at the store's lizard selection. With an impatient flutter of his hand, he beckons over the young woman, telling her to cover the front cash counter, and as she passes by the boy, she lets her arm brush against his. A secret signal of closeness and conspiracy. She voices her play-along opinion and says she generally recommends newts for novices.

Cramped in beside the assistant manager in the reptile aisle, the boy feigns attention while the assistant manager points out each species inside their glass tanks. A good half of the lizard inhabitants hide away, decorative driftwood protecting them from prying eyes, but the assistant manager maintains his sunny salesmanship. The fellow reads from the information stickered to the side of each tank, and the boy realizes that his nemesis knows little of skinks, anoles, newts, and bearded dragons. Encouraged, the boy blurts that he's leaning toward a skink. Maybe a fire skink or a garden skink. On the fence, he says. Also, if he were to purchase a male and female breeding pair, how long could he expect before they reproduced? Further, if the pair successfully bred, how long would the gestation period last; approximately how many newborn skinks could he expect in a first litter, and how much time would pass before a second litter?

The flustered assistant manager reaches for the rack of spinning manuals and retrieves *Skinks Are My Favourite People*, reading aloud that the male and female garden skink have different colours on their stomach. Flipping to the glossary, he files his finger down the page, says he's sure that there'll be breeding tips somewhere, but then he pauses in apology. The print is too small, and his reading glasses are in the back office. His voice trails off, but the boy remains sunny and decides not to let the matter go.

"That'd be great. Thanks. I'll wait."

Once alone, the boy and the young woman let themselves laugh. He chuckles and shrugs his shoulder. She chortles and shakes her head. Her break will be in a few minutes, she says, if he's got some free time, and – easy as that – their second not-really-a-date date is all set. Downstairs in the rotunda near the escalators at the Wild Beanz coffee kiosk? She adds that skinks are actually pretty high maintenance pets. A hamster is much more doable.

Tucked away from the higher traffic areas of the mostly empty mall, the four tables surrounding the Wild Beanz coffee kiosk are reserved for paying customers only and provide a sense of privacy for the whole entire fifteen-minute break. There, the boy does not have to feel self-conscious as he presents the circular jar of French Vanilla body butter, which she accepts happily and without an explanation. Perhaps this is because of her age, the boy thinks. Perhaps after adolescence, people learn not to expect and require an understanding of the world around them. If true, that would be wonderful.

Twisting the jar open, she scoops out a dollop of body butter and rubs it into her bare elbows. One of the driest and most sensitive skin bits on the body, she explains, and she gestures for the boy to roll up his sleeves. Wide-eyed, the boy tries to slow his runaway heart as she rubs the scented skin care lotion on his elbows. Then, she pushes her spiced chai tea toward him and tells him to take a sip. It's herbal and doesn't need milk, she explains, and when he tastes it, it doesn't taste bitter or strong like the orange pekoe Red Rose that the boy's mom drinks. It tastes sweet.

When their all-too-fast fifteen minutes together comes to a close, they stand together at the top of the escalator, and as if off-handedly, she says he should come by again next week. It takes him a moment to realize the remark is an invitation, and his first thought is to ask for an explanation, but he stops himself and only nods in assent. Sounds good, he says.

c. Inside the Food Court Gazebo

On the mezzanine food court at the Southgate Bayview Mews Mall, clusters of patio tables encircle a grandly elaborate gazebo at the centre of the dining area. Once upon a former time in the mall's more salad days, the gazebo housed public fundraising events for the Salvation Army, Goodwill, and St Vincent de Paul, but in recent years, all that has sat inside is a single café table. Since dining or dawdling in such an elevated and singular location leaves mall shoppers exposed to all passersby, the table most often sits unused.

However, on the Tuesday that the boy carries a plastic tray of coffee, milk, and muffin and the young woman stands by his side, the gazebo seems the only option. While the dining area does not appear busy – only two mothers with three strollers sit talking tiredly and two teens with three skateboards sit talking tiredly – the wrappers and remains of meals litter the vacant tables. Whoever clears and cleans and wipes the food court after the afterschool rush has not yet arrived, so the young woman points to the gazebo and the table for two inside.

The boy pauses. By nature and nurture, he prefers not to take centre stage of anyone's attention, but beyond such personal predilections, the gazebo presents a risk. In a city around one million people, anyone might at any time bump into anyone else. Unexpected and accidental encounters happen all the time. She does not notice his worried mind, though, and already before he might even articulate his fears, she is moving towards the inevitable setting of their non-date third date. It seems that she does not suffer from the same self-consciousness as he, and walking beside her into the shaded light of the gazebo's interior, he realizes he has learned a useful lesson about the young woman. Not five minutes into their meeting, he has learned of her admirable and enviable confidence.

Soon after this first lesson, they sit and sip their beverages, and he learns yet another lesson. She holds strong opinions. Because her mind remains on Chez Animaux and work, the strong opinions she currently unpacks for the boy are on the crossbreeding of dogs like labradoodles. Mixed breeds have been around as long as dogs have been around, she explains, and she can sort of understand varieties that serve a specific utility. A collie and sheepdog bred for practical work purposes, for example. Too often, though, the creation and continuation of crossbreeds have little to do with utility and practical needs, and more to do with ridiculous and shallow wants. If two breeds produce offspring naturally, that's one thing, but when people engineer crossbreeds for their own whims, isn't that another thing? Pet owners want poodles because the puppies are fluffy and curly haired and hypoallergenic. Pet owners want Labrador retrievers because they're hearty and active and up for a good long jog or a tussle on the floor. So a crossbreed is tailor-made to suit aesthetics and one's active lifestyle? Such motives come from an entirely selfish place, certainly.

Throughout her monologue, the boy nods in agreement, for as far as he can tell, he does agree. As with her confidence, he finds her strong opinions both admirable and enviable, but while listening and peppering his nods with *yeah*, *yes*, and *that's true*, he also waits for an opening. He waits for a pause during which he might present her with a gift. Though the bookmark, zippo lighter, or heart stud would have moved her, what waits hidden in his knapsack backpack is music.

Once, while the boy and his friend played video games, she was soaking in the tub and singing "Miss Otis Regrets" and he heard her voice drift out sweetly through the bathroom door. He knew the song, for the song played often in his family home, and way back before his parents' trial separation, his dad had once gifted his mom with a homemade compilation of Cole Porter cover songs. With some digging, the boy found the CD still sitting in an unpacked box of music abandoned in the storage space in the walkout basement of the executive townhome. His father's tightly slanting handwriting listed the illegally-recorded-and-reproduced song list on the front on the jewel case, and sure enough, track seven said "Miss Otis Regrets / Just One of Those Things." The boy feels certain the gift will go over as well as the French Vanilla body butter, and he need only wait for an opening in the conversation.

Before such an opening can come, though, the young woman presents him with a gift of his own. From her shoulder bag, she retrieves a book entitled *#SkinkLove* and grins. Chez Animaux just sold its one remaining copy of *Skinks Are My Favourite People*, which might be the more popular manual, but she's heard good things about *#SkinkLove* too. In case he ever does decide upon a home collection of reptiles. She grins mischievously and counts off the many crucial lessons contained within the book. Setting up a happy home and habitat. Settling on proper plants and foliage for reptile décor. Selecting suitable crickets and mealworms for feed. The text contains helpful chapters for responsible skink enthusiasts of every level.

The playfulness of her voice makes it clear that she enjoys his company, and realizing this, the boy learns a third lesson about the young woman. While she certainly understands that skink ownership will never be part of his future, she delights in giving into and playing along with the fantasy – just as he has delighted in thinking about their first, second, and third non-dates as dates. Part of him knows he's only playing at pretend, but he enjoys doing so.

She grins at the Cole Porter CD when he passes it to her, and she reads the track list aloud. The small ring she wears in her right nostril is different from the one she wore on their last non-date date, he notices. The metal of this one is smooth and engraved with some sort of curling and overlapping pattern that encircles the loop. She catches him staring, but doesn't seem to mind and unclips the loop. It was a flea market find, she explains, from a craft show in Gatineau. Two years earlier? Three maybe. She also bought a small gemstone stud from the same stall. Not a real gemstone, but a dark purple colour she liked nonetheless.

The enthusiasm in her voice continues, and the boy understands that she's glad to talk and have someone listen to her talk. To encourage her and to hear her voice more, he asks about eyebrow rings, and she says she's bought most of hers from an online site recommended by a classmate, but her very favourite pair were from a harbour front market in Halifax. She got her first tattoo on that same trip, and since then she's gotten more. A ring of ivy around one ankle, a napping Hobbes tiger on her right calf.

Reaching across the gazebo table, she pats the boy's forearm enthusiastically and asks him if he likes breakfast cereal. The non sequitur puts him off balance, but only for a moment. Sure, he likes breakfast cereal. All sorts of flavours really, but Toasted Bran Nut Clusters especially. Although marketed as an adult cereal, the clusters contain a honey taste that comes out in the milk. She grins and nods as he explains, but she also stretches down the collar of her Chez Animaux golf shirt, revealing the base of her neck and bare collarbone. The unexpectedly and utterly unannounced appearance of skin stifles the boy's speech, putting a stop to his explanation about the varied buoyancies of cereal clusters, crispies, and flakes. He doesn't at first quite understand what he is looking at, but then he does. A full colour tattoo of Toucan Sam. The spokesbird for Fruit Loops smiles happily, his oversized beak angled downward toward the young woman's small shoulder. *Just follow my nose, it always knows.* A thin cord of satiny cloth runs over her shoulder too, and seeing his confusion, she tells him the shoulder string connects to a camisole.

"A camisole," he repeats, as if understanding.

He nods, but turns away so as not to stare too, too much. In turning, he sees someone he knows. It's the boy's only real friend.

The young woman's little brother. He holds a plastic tray, and he stands unmoving. Without his mother and his sister home for dinner, he probably walked here for a slice of cheese pizza. Staring across the food court, his head tilts to one side as he looks into the gazebo, but he still hasn't moved. He's unnaturally still like someone just tagged him out in freeze tag, his crinkled forehead trying hard to comprehend what he sees. He wants to understand what he sees. His friend and his big sister. What he sees doesn't make any sense, and his shoulders slump in sadness.

CHAPTER 9

Halfway into afternoon nutrition break, Monsieur Substitute asks the students who've stayed inside to help him rearrange the lift-top desks into a semi-circle arch.

"So the parents can stand in the centre of a U-shape," he says and gestures with his hand in a semi-circle arch motion.

The Career Parent Presentation parents will sit on the stacking chairs while they wait to present, Monsieur says, but everyone is already dragging and scraping the desks against the tile, which makes a hubbub and a racket, so practically no one really hears. Darby makes sure his lift-top desk sits beside Jennie's on her right side near her good ear, so they can chat. He kind of hopes Alexander will drag his desk over to their side of the U and Jennie probably hopes this too, but asking feels like it'd be too much of a big deal goodwill gesture, so Alexander just stays on the other side. Billy's and Stewart's desks sit on that side as well, which Darby realizes might feel uncomfortable because the position means they'll be looking right directly across at him while the parents present on their chosen professional fields. An unhappy happenstance.

With the classroom all rearranged, Darby settles back into his desk, and only then does he notice that his dad has come in at some point during the hubbub and racket. Standing at the white board right underneath the Dominion of Canada timeline banner, Darby's dad is talking with Monsieur and Stewart's mom, the Dental Hygienist, and the sight causes an upswell of worry and panic. What are the chances they're all talking about Darby's performance on the Veterinary Dentistry presentation and his dad feels disappointed in him? But then, his dad turns toward Darby and raises a hand, waving a subtle hello of greeting.

"Your knee is bobbing up and down," Jennie says.

"It sometimes does that," Darby says.

"It was good to invite Alexander for snack break."

"Yes."

Darby wonders when he might get a chance to talk to Alexander about the school nurse and her printed neckerchief and realizes it won't be for a while. Probably not until Monday after weekend visitation.

"I imagine he'd always sit with us," Jennie says, "if we ask."

She smiles like this idea has just occurred to her and is not of any great consequence to her either way, but Darby just nods.

"Do you realize that Monsieur has made a thrust stage performance space?" she says.

"The desks?"

"Yes. I imagine it was inadvertent," Jennie says.

Darby nods to agree that the desk arrangement was most probably not on purpose, but he can see that the empty negative space around the rearrangement of lift-top desks does resemble a thrust stage performance space. Across from them, he sees Alexander has removed his *New Horizons* reader from his lift-top desk, and he's flicking through the pages.

"Did you see your father brought a prop?" Jennie asks. "A prop in a box."

She points to Darby's dad sitting at the front of the class. He and Stewart's mom continue their chatting, and on his lap sits a square Fed-Ex box with the flaps closed in an overlapping pattern. When no tape is available, the overlapping flap pattern can be an effective way to close a box. Darby's dad showed him how to do it when they moved from Calgary to Ottawa.

"Props can enhance a presentation," Jennie says, "as long as they're used right."

It's another piece of public speaking advice from Darby's mom – a truism that he and Jennie have already agreed is true. When used purposefully and with practice, a handheld visual aide can enrich an audience's understanding of presented material, but a prop used to create nothing more than busy stage business will detract from the overall material.

"Yes, a prop must be integrated into the content of a presentation," she says.

Beside his father in front of the white board, Stewart's mom Cintia Holgermonsson has her own box in her lap – not a reused door-to-door courier service box, but a reused running sneaker shoebox with an energizing Nike swooping checkmark on the side and a separate shoebox lid, so the overlapping flap close technique isn't necessary. Inside, she too probably has a prop, Darby would guess.

"If the empty negative space is a thrust stage performance space," Jennie says, "then the whiteboard would be the proscenium arch area."

"What do you suppose the props in the boxes are?"

Jennie shrugs her shoulders and tilts her head to the side in a playful gesture to ask *I don't know, what do youuu think?*

"Probably related to their careers?"

"Well, yeah. That goes without saying," she says.

"Well, maybe my dad has a prop to explain the distinction between cantilever and suspension and arch bridges because no one but mechanical engineers really knows the difference."

Darby means to make a joke, but as soon as he says it, he realizes his guess might be close.

"And Stewart's mother?" Jennie asks with a tilt and a shrug. "What prop would a dental hygienist bring?"

Sitting beside his father, Mrs. Holgermonsson isn't just smiling politely at Darby's dad. She's chuckling at whatever they're chit-chatting about.

"I don't know," Darby says.

Between his mom and dad, his dad has always been the less friendly-and-outgoing-with-strangers parent, so it's odd to see him entertaining Mrs. Holgermonsson. Before November, Darby was used to his mom doing all the talking for them both, but lately, his dad seems to be making more of an effort. He forces himself into conversations with grocery store clerks and servers and museum ushers, and even though the result often feels awkward and the conversations don't go anywhere, Darby wonders if maybe all that time alone in his low-rise apartment complex has not somehow changed his dad's personality.

"Some sort of dental hygienist prop?" Darby says. "I don't know."

"I know you don't know," Jennie says. "That's why you're guessing."

Mrs. Holgermonsson has come to Career Day uniformed in her dental hygienist clothing, which is a matching set of aquamarine scrub tops and bottoms. At the dentistry office that Darby went to for the first ten years of his life in Calgary and at the dentistry office that he has visited only once so far here in Ottawa, all of the dental hygienists and the dentists have dressed similarly during all of his check-ups, cleanings, and fluoride treatments. Such consistency leads Darby to conclude that all dental professionals everywhere wear similar dress, which seems to him oddly formal.

"Maybe a paper face mask?" he says. "People in my dentist office all wear those paper hospital masks."

In the two times he has visited hospitals in his life – once when his dad had a benign cyst removed from his shoulder and once when his dad's dad's health was inevitably declining in old age – all of the doctors, nurses and related medical staff wore less formal scrubs. Darby remembers tops and bottoms with all sorts of small dot patterns, large polka dot patterns, and multicoloured sailboat patterns, which kind of made their scrubs look more like pajamas than uniforms.

"Surgical masks?"

"Yes, those," Darby says. "Though I don't know why dentistry people wear surgery masks."

"It's bad breath," Jennie says. "Dentists and dental hygienists wear masks to protect from bad breath."

"Oh."

"All right," Jennie says, "if her prop is a surgical mask, why would she put one of those in a box? She could just fold it up in her purse."

Darby nods. "Maybe she's brought a paper mask for everyone in the class then? Maybe she's going to explain the spread of good and bad bacteria within the mouth?"

"Then at a crucial point," Jennie says, "when she takes a dramatic pause, she brings out the masks?"

Jennie sweeps her hands in a magician's *ta-da* sweep to illustrate her point. In Darby's experience, Jennie does not often let herself be silly, but when she does, it's worth seeing.

"No. First, she does a scan pause," Darby says. "Makes fleeting-but-meaningful eye contact with each and every one in the class while asking a rhetorical question about the problem and spread of good and bad bacteria in the oral cavity." Darby pauses to count three beats. "And then, she opens the box to reveal surgical masks. She doesn't say anything at all, though. It's just all visual representation. Problem and solution. Cause and effect. *Et violà. Bob est votre oncle.*"

Jennie grins and nods. "Yes, our imagined Mrs. Holgermonsson has exceedingly good presentation skills. She deserves a rubric with a *très, très bien.*"

The mention of the rubric makes Darby grin, and he realizes he doesn't feel as bad about the presentation as he might. Making good fun of bad news might be all right, he decides.

"*Très, très bien*," he says with a nod. "*Avec deux* exclamation marks.

"Free samples make a presentation memorable. And you know what else?" she asks with a grin. "Your knee has stopped bobbing."

Darby realizes that he has not been worrying, which means Jennie has successfully distracted him, and for her effort, he feels grateful. When he thinks to express his gratitude, though, he stops himself because doing so would acknowledge her effort and detract from it.

Also, Billy and Stewart just then re-enter the classroom, so Darby's newly-won calm has lost a bit of its shine. He imagines Billy and Stewart glaring at him as they cross to their seats, but actually, it's only Billy. Stewart has spotted his mom and she's spotted him, and the two of them exchange a subtle wave much the way Darby and his dad did.

"You are wrong about the surgical masks, though," Jennie says.

"Pardon?"

"Mrs. Holgermonsson hasn't brought masks."

"No?"

As he watches Billy slip into his lift-top desk close to Alexander, Darby doesn't feel like guessing, but he does anyway.

"Maybe toothbrushes for everyone? With the name, address, and telephone number of her dental office stamped into the handle?"

"No. Inside the box is a set of oversized prop teeth with an oversized prop toothbrush." Jennie mimes holding a regular-sized toothbrush to her regular-sized teeth. "Mrs. Holgermonsson's going to use them to demonstrate how to brush properly."

Billy glares at Alexander, who's still immersed in *New Horizons* and doesn't seem to notice.

"So you've seen the giant teeth demonstration before?" Darby asks.

"Yeah. She came to our class last year. And before that in grade three, two, and one. Pretty much every year."

"And you made me guess all those wrong guesses? Cheater."

"You weren't wrong about the free samples, though. Last year, at the end, she gave everyone a fun-sized pack of dental picks."

Across from them on the other side of the thrust stage performance space, Billy Pace has lifted his lift-top desk and is mucking about inside, which probably doesn't mean anything good. Stewart sits watching his mom at the front of the room by the white board, so at least whatever meaner-than-mean trick Billy has in mind, Stewart probably won't be part of it. If it has to do with Darby's dad's pornography again, though, that'd be way worse than him finding out the truth about the Veterinary Dentistry presentation.

"Your knee's bobbing again," Jennie says.

Darby looks over to Alexander. His focus on *New Horizons* makes him look disconnected from just about everything, which could either mean that he is absorbed and has escaped deep into one of the anthology's collected fictions or that he is deliberately staring at the pages in an evasive stratagem because he doesn't want to deal with Billy. Both maybe.

"I like dental picks," Darby says.

"The waxed kind. Fresh mint flavour."

"Even better."

"That fellow there knows samples," Jennie says. She points to Kamil Gendry's financial advisor and asset manager dad, who just then crosses to the white board to shake hands.

"Mrs. Holgermonsson, this is Mr. Gendry," Monsieur Substitute says. "Mr. Tamm, Mr. Gendry."

"Yes, thank you, Mr. Desjardin," Kamil's dad nods.

Darby glances over at Kamil, who has also noticed his dad's entrance and looks ready to exchange a subtle wave of greeting, but he doesn't get the chance because his dad right away falls into handshaking with the other adults.

Like Stewart's mom, the financial advisor and asset manager wears a uniform of sorts, but his consists of navy-blue slacks, a beige button-up, and a cream coffee sports blazer, so his clothing doesn't stand out and stick out in the classroom setting as much as hers. With two parents wearing uniforms and his father not, Darby recognizes that his dad didn't get at all dressed up, but maybe he should have. His red plaid shirt and plain jeans aren't at all appropriate and do not at all identify him as a mechanical engineer like a uniform should.

"Good to meet you. Nice to meet you, yes."

With handshakes done, Kamil's father distributes business cards to each and everyone, and he still hasn't exchanged a wave with Kamil, who seems to still be waiting for one, which makes Darby feel bad for him.

"Last year," Jennie says, "he brought not only pens with his business contact information, but also promotional stress balls. Samples can be props."

Darby sees his dad pulling a face at the business card in his hand, which makes sense because his dad doesn't believe in networking. Well, maybe he believes in it; he just doesn't approve of it because he says networking requires an unacceptable level of insincerity. Looking at the other adults, Darby understands that his dad's reaction is the one that's out of place. His dad is the one who has trouble playing his role.

"A pleasure to see you again, Mrs. Holgermonsson," Kamil's dad says. "A pleasure to meet you, Mr. Tamm."

Although Darby has heard others address his father as Mr. Tamm before and he knows the title is natural, the sound of the name continues to make him uncomfortable, and sitting in the classroom with Jennie, he thinks he knows why, and it's because of roles. Like props and uniforms, Mr. Tamm is something of a put-on role, but it is not a role that Darby's dad acts for Darby. For Darby, his dad plays only the role of dad.

While the different and distinct roles are all well and good when acted out separately, coming to the classroom for the visiting career parent presentations means both roles must be acted out all at once simultaneously, and it's the all-at-onceness and simultaneity that probably make his dad seem uncomfortable. The trouble comes from identity management because both roles together reveal the falseness of each role separately.

"The pens and the stress balls were red and white," Jennie says. "Parliament Insurance and Investments."

Darby's about to ask what sample props she thinks Kamil's dad will distribute this year, but the room grows quiet.

"*Votre attention, s'il vous plaît,*" Monsieur says to the class. "Good afternoon."

Glancing over across the U-shape, Darby sees Alexander reluctantly putting away the *New Horizons* in slow motion, reading while he lifts the lid of his lift-top desk. It's a problem Darby recognizes because lots of times he's been immersed and didn't want to stop reading but had to, and it's like having one's attention divided between the story inside the book and the outside actual world.

"*C'est bien,*" Monsieur Substitute says. "We will begin. Each of the parents has only fifteen minutes, and we must make sure they each get their time. So we will begin."

With his book put away, Alexander leans forward to rest his chin on his arms on the desktop.

"We all need to pay our close attention today." Monsieur's voice contains a stern command, which is an unpleasant tone, but not his normal unpleasant tone, which is annoyed but not all that interested. The teacher probably wants to impress the visiting parents, and probably that's why he re-arranged the classroom desks as well – because he needs to play the role of responsible teacher and needs to impress the visiting parents. Plenty of times, Darby's mother has said that the relationship between a teacher and the parents of the pupils in a teacher's class can be strained and awkward, and it's because of lots of different reasons having to do with suppressed power struggles.

"Our first speaker this afternoon will be Terence Gendry."

Monsieur Substitute unfolds a piece of paper and reads from it, which is a public speaking crutch and a misstep because it's better to use cue cards with bullet point reminders of the material. Or it's even better yet to memorize the material like Jennie did for the Veterinary Dentistry presentation.

"Mr. Gendry has worked as a financial advisor and asset manager for Parliament Insurance and Investments for fifteen years," Monsieur says, "which is longer than everyone in the class has been alive."

This morning on the way to get water, Jennie said that Monsieur might now want to be the fulltime and permanent grade five enriched class teacher, which Darby realizes might also be a reason the substitute wants to impress. Benefits and a pension and unionized job security. Mr. Henderson has died in his sleep without waking, and Monsieur might well try to benefit from the misfortune. If that's the case, though, he should do better than using a public speaking crutch like reading from notes.

"Mr. Gendry is here to tell us about what education you need to work in finance, what his job is like on a day-to-day basis, and why it is important to handle your money wisely."

Though his refolding of the paper looks as clumsy as his unfolding did, Monsieur handles the hand-off well, and Kamil's dad stands up just as the teacher recedes back to the teacher desk. With his hand on the front of his sports blazer, Kamil's dad unbuttons it as he walks to the centre of the thrust stage performance space – a gesture executed so smoothly that Darby suspects it must be something he does often.

"I know all of you have heard your parents discussing their RRSPs and RESPs every year around tax time in April," Mr. Gendry says. "And I know many of your parents have spoken with you about the importance of putting aside a certain percentage of your weekly allowance, birthday money, and holiday cash gifts from extended family for long-term investment?"

As far as Darby can remember, his dad has never spoken to him about the importance of any of that. At the whiteboard proscenium arch, his dad is still glaring at the business card in his hand, and Darby doubts his dad will ever discuss long-term investments with him.

"However, even knowledgeable investors need assistance from a professional from time to time." Mr. Gendry stops for a dramatic pause, and the effect is effective enough to draw back Darby's attention for a moment. "And this is when a financial advisor's expertise can be helpful and why asset management is an essential life skill."

Although Darby doesn't think asset management will be a career he will ever grow interested in, he does try to listen. He does try to pay attention, and he does try to understand the advantages and disadvantages of Guaranteed Investment Certificates and Extended

Trade Funds. He fails, though. He fails and his thoughts drift a bit, but he figures that's all right.

In Calgary, Darby accompanied his parents to the bank two separate times, and they all sat in one of the back hall offices with a financial investment advisor. Both times, his mom and dad seemed to have trouble paying attention. The first time was when his father's father died with money left behind, and the second time was when they sold their Calgary house for below market value because they were moving to Ottawa in great haste, so neither time was a pleasure. Afterwards, though, his mom and dad teased each another about their lack of interest, and they seemed happy that their failing was a shared failing.

Perhaps an immunity to financial advice runs in his family, Darby thinks, and perhaps it's only natural he loses track of the presentation, his wandering mind meandering around the faces in the room and over to the side windows. Through the window and across the schoolyard, someone sits crouched reading on the steps of the farthest portable where he and Jennie started their day, and Darby sees it's the EFL student from lunch and the library. Her teacher probably ends the day with free reading time, and with less than an hour to go until final bell, the EFL student has found herself a quiet spot away from everyone else. Despite the cold, she's retreated from her class, and whatever book she's reading, she isn't stopping to take notes or write marginal translations. She's reading for pleasure most likely, and Darby wonders what the book is, but his speculation is cut short.

His classmates are clapping for Kamil's dad, who has wrapped up his presentation after only some six or seven minutes, well under the allotted fifteen minutes. He responds to the applause with smiling nods and moves around the inside of the u-shape with pens for everyone in the class. His presentation has definitely come to a close, and in the mutters of *here you go* and *thank you, Mr Gendry* and *here's a pen for you*, Jennie leans in close to Darby.

"Networking," Jennie says. "Networking is an essential life skill."

When Darby and Jennie receive their pens, they turn out to be red and white with PI & I insignias, but they also turn out to be double-sided writing utensils – a blue ballpoint on one end and an orange highlighter on the other. Impressed, Darby clicks his pen two, three times before deciding he will pass it along to his mother. Teachers always need more markers and pens, and he can give it to his mom on Sunday after weekend visitation when both of them usually need cheering up. Even if the promotional pen turns out to be the cheapie kind that dry out too quickly or writes all splotchy, the gesture will please her.

Sometimes Darby wonders what his mom does when he's not there on weekends and how she spends her hours away from him, but anytime he wonders this, he feels bad for not wondering the same about his dad. His dad lives almost all the time by himself alone in the low-rise apartment, so Darby's decided it's probably best to put such speculation from his mind altogether.

Back in his seat by the proscenium arch whiteboard, Kamil's dad thanks the class one more time and Monsieur Substitute steps forward. Yet another smooth hand-off. Stewart's mom opens her less-than-mysterious mystery shoebox, and as predicted, she removes an oversized set of teeth and an oversized toothbrush. Beside Darby, Jennie probably wears an *I-sure-called-it* grin, and he glances her way to nod, granting her the compliment due to her.

"Yes, thank you very much indeed," she whisper-speaks.

On the other side of the U-shape, Stewart watches his mother, sitting up and straightening his posture in a way that makes Darby like him a little bit more.

"Brush your teeth, every day, brush your teeth, twice a day," Monsieur Substitute reads. He sing-speaks as he reads from his notes, so his wooden voice sounds even more wooden. Such failed attempts at levity can only make everyone uncomfortable, and in a moment of second-hand embarrassment, Darby looks down at his desktop.

"Cintia Holgermonsson," Monsieur continues, "is here today to talk to us about the career of a dental hygienist."

Probably the teacher had more to say, but since his joke failed, he just wants to get off stage as quickly as possible. As he steps aside, Stewart's mom pats his shoulder and thanks him very much for the introduction, which seems like a kind gesture meant to make him feel better. It's easy to see the resemblance with her son because she's kind of squat, and unfortunately, her aquamarine hospital scrub pajamas only accentuate her squatness. Darby worries that between her enthusiastic expression and her unfortunate stature, someone will for sure make a cruel remark to hurt her. Billy Pace most probably. Any remark will injure Stewart as well as his mom, and while Stewart's not exactly a good guy and he just hours earlier pulled the mean trick, Darby hopes Billy will stay quiet.

"Three volunteers," she says with three fingers in the air. "I need three volunteers to show me how they brush their teeth. Everyone has their own way, and I want to see your own personal technique."

Her voice sounds more confident and steady than Darby would have guessed, and when Stewart's hand shoots up, she makes a pretty good joke.

"I've seen you brush your teeth many times, Stewart."

She gets a genuine laugh from the class, and since it's the kind of laugh that isn't laughing at anyone and everyone gets to be in on, the moment makes for an effective opening grabber introduction in Darby's opinion. Impressive.

With the ice broken around the classroom, several hands go up to volunteer, and Stewart's mom the dental hygienist points smiling to Jennie and Sarah.

"You. And you. And?"

Waiting a beat, she points to a pleasingly embarrassed Monsieur Substitute, and he becomes the last volunteer. With the giant teeth and toothbrush, the three volunteers one by one demonstrate their techniques. Jennie circles counter-clockwise top, bottom, left, right, inside, which Stewart's mom calls *very thorough,* and Sarah brushes in a series of upward and downward flicks top, bottom, left, right, inside, and out, which Stewart's mom calls *efficient.* With the prop toothbrush in one hand and the prop teeth in the other, Monsieur Substitute looks silly in the way that Stewart's mom probably wants him to look silly, and he freezes and stammers an apology.

"I use a battery power brush," he says. "So I am afraid that I do not know what my personal technique might be." With his voice trailing off and away, Monsieur looks to Stewart's mom. For her help? Her approval? Darby isn't sure, but Monsieur doesn't seem to be sure either, and Stewart's mom uses the opportunity for yet another laugh. She raises her eyebrows at him and pauses the smallest of pauses.

"Well, those electric toothbrushes can be a godsend" she says, "And in fact, they are not entirely different from some of the tools we use in the dental clinic for polishing and buffing teeth."

Without really missing a moment, Stewart's mom has transitioned into an explanation of some of her favourite parts of her daily routine at the dental clinic, taking the giant tooth model and giant brush from Monsieur's hands and signaling all three volunteers to return to their seats. Subtle and smooth. From there, she asks individual students what they like and don't like about visiting the dentist, which leads to even more audience interaction.

She fills up the whole entire room, Darby realizes. This is what his mom meant.

At the end, when everyone claps for her and she mime-curtseys with her non-existent skirt, Darby glances to Stewart to confirm that he looks pleased and proud, which he does. Darby's dad claps right along with everyone, grinning in a way Darby has seen before. His dad tends to be happy when others are happy, and all twenty-two students in the classroom seem to be happy, but there is something else on his dad's face too, and it's worry. Though unexpected, the emotion makes sense because he'll probably not present as well as Stewart's mom, and he's up next. Kamil's dad sits next to his dad, and unlike everyone else in the room, Kamil's dad is not clapping in appreciation for the presentation. He's checking his smart cellular telephone, which is impolite and actually not allowed in the classroom.

Before retaking her seat at the proscenium arch white board, Stewart's mom says she has small samples for everyone, and they turn out to be travel toothbrushes with 10 ml travel tubes of toothpaste and very clever engineering. The bristle end of the brush folds downs and into the handle of the brush like a saw blade in a Switzerland Army knife, and the tube of toothpaste slides into a secret cylinder space at the end like a toothpick in a Switzerland Army knife. Darby imagines slipping it into a carry-on suitcase on rolling wheels and walking through an airport to fly off to a work conference in another city. Or maybe he zips it into a backpack side pocket as part of his carry-on luggage because his mom surprise announces that they're going to fly back to Calgary to see his old friends over March Break vacation next month. Neither of these daydreams are all too likely or probable, Darby knows, but he also knows that's what daydreams are for in the first place.

As with the PI & I pens, all the students murmur their *thanks* and *that's swell* and *even better than last year's minty dental picks*, and they put away their free sample gifts in their lift-top desks. Putting his away, Darby notices that the name and address and contact information stamped into the side of the handle of the brush says *Dr. David Holgermonsson, DDS*, which most probably means that Stewart's father is the dentist in the same clinic where Stewart's mom is the dental hygienist, which is a connection that he knew before but forgot he knew. Darby wonders why Stewart's dad didn't come for Career Day and how weird it must feel for his mom to work for his dad, but according to Darby's mom, other people's lives contain mysteries and multitudes, and he's pretty sure she's right.

"Thank you very much, Madame Holgermonsson." Monsieur Substitute holds his own travel toothbrush and gives it a shake in appreciation that does seem genuine. "Our next presenter is Mr. Tamm, who works as a mechanical engineer. He has been working in the field for fifteen years, and up until last fall, he worked for a variety of oil and gas companies in Alberta. He and Darby moved here because he started working with Iogen Engineering here in Ottawa."

As Darby thought would happen, his dad's opening grabber introduction is neither as effortlessly smooth nor as immediately compelling as Stewart's mom's. Really, he has no introductory opener at all. Instead, he starts with a pause – not a scan pause to command attention and start well, but an awkward pause followed up by a look down at his shoes. Standing in the middle of the thrust stage performance space, he seems to just then consider how he might begin. He begins with a question.

"Can anyone give me some examples of mechanical engineering that are in the classroom?"

The awkward pause that follows may not be as long as his dad's first awkward pause, but it certainly feels longer. Darby knows that sons are supposed to sometimes be embarrassed by their dads and sons are supposed to sometimes be proud of their dads, but he's pretty sure sons aren't supposed to feel sorry for their dads.

"Um," his dad says, "objects designed by mechanical engineers use force combined with internal components?" The improvised question triggering no response, he adds that internal components might be levers or gears or springs.

"The stapler has a spring in it," Alexander says.

He hasn't put his hand up before saying this, but no one seems to mind.

"Yes, a stapler is a good example," Darby's dad says. "The arm of the stapler is a lever and inside the arm of the stapler is an internal mechanism that contains a spring." Darby thinks his dad should probably make eye contact with Alexander or say thank you and express some sort of grateful acknowledgement, but he doesn't. Instead, he looks at the ceiling as if the blueprint patent instructions for a stapler are written up there among the fluorescent lights.

"When we push down on a stapler," he says, "the force of our push activates the force of the internal spring to release a staple, and then the force of our push propels the staple through the paper."

Beside Darby, Jennie raises her hand, and at first, his dad doesn't seem to know how to react, but then he nods at her.

"The clock," Jennie says.

"Yes, clockworks are complicated and involve dozens and dozens of gears and springs. The forces used in a clock vary. There's wind-up and pendulum clocks, of course. If the clock is battery powered or electrical or solar, the mechanical engineering of the clock will be combined with electrical engineering."

As more hands go up, Darby's dad explains the gears of the turning handles and the hinges that move the side windows open and shut, the complexity of the coiled projector screen that ascends and descends unpredictably, and the spigot end of the inverted water bottle from which the classroom hamster drinks. No one seems to notice that his dad lacks presentation skills and has trouble with eye contact, and though he didn't plan on engaging with the students, their examples and his explanations look nearly indistinguishable from interaction. When the examples slow down, Darby's dad looks to the door of the classroom.

"Your classroom doesn't have a wall-mounted pencil sharpener," he says, "but when I was in grade school and in secondary school, our classrooms all had these wall-mounted pencil sharpeners. With a small kind of hand crank on the right side and a hole on the left where you stuck in your pencil tip to sharpen it. As you turned the crank, the pencil got nicely super sharp and the wood and lead pencil shavings dropped into a kind of outer cover doubled as a kind of cupped receptacle. I remember sharpening my pencils more than I probably had to because the sensation of turning the crank and the decreasing resistance of the friction of the pencil wood felt so very pleasurable. And then once in third or fourth grade, I saw my teacher emptying the machine. I guess I hadn't considered how it was emptied, but the cup part just turned and popped off and you just shook out all the pencil shavings. Taking the cup off revealed the inner mechanisms as well, and inside were two gears with these licorice-like textures twisting around them, so when you cranked the handle part, the gears moved in circles but also in two opposing directions and the whole effect was kind of hypnotic. I don't know what I'd imagined was inside the pencil sharpener, but it wasn't that. Later when I learned how it worked, I figured out that what I was thinking were licorice gears are actually called helical gears, but then I figured out that they weren't helical gears at all but cylindrical blades with helical patterns. But inside, between the blade parts and the crank parts, there were actual regular round spur gears hidden away."

Glancing around the room, Darby sees that the students are paying attention, and his dad has again stumbled into engagement.

"What is in the Fed Ex box?" Alexander asks, which makes Darby feel grateful.

Since his dad left the box in his chair by the white board proscenium arch, he has to turn his back to the audience to retrieve it, and then he ignores the audience while unflapping the overlapping flaps of the Fed-Ex box. He gets away with both these gaffes, though, by talking the whole time.

"A lock. I forgot. I made a lock to show you a simple example of mechanical engineering. All classroom doors have locks, but I imagine they are all key locks, which contain a different kind of internal mechanism. The kind I made to show you is a three-stage tumbler. It's the kind for school lockers."

With the flaps up, Darby's dad lifts out a construction made mostly of basic red and blue and white Lego bricks, but with a few modern Technic pieces mixed in as well – ridged black rods and grey gears.

"Those are the spur gears I was talking about." He points to the centre, unaware that the students can't see from where they're sitting. His obliviousness has an advantage, though. All the students lean forward, and Darby realizes that his dad in his own way fills up the whole entire room.

"The main component parts are the three flat circular disc shapes in red. They attach to the crank on the outside." He points as he explains the reverse order of the three discs and their connection to the three digits of a combination padlock, highlighting where the open slots in each disc are and how they line up with each subsequent turn. "That's why you have to turn clockwise, then counter-clockwise, and then clockwise when you open a combination lock. Each disc has a catch that turns the next disc. Once all the slots are lined up, you slide out this bolt piece, aaaaannnd open the lock."

For a moment, Darby thinks he understands. He thinks he understands, and he can see how the component parts of the mechanism relate to one another and activate or do not activate when turned clockwise or counter-clockwise until the negative space slots are organized in a line. Then, though, just as he believes he has a hold of the thing in his mind, understanding slips away, and he cannot see at all. He doesn't get it. That's all right, though.

"I get it," Alexander says.

Everyone is giving his dad nearly all of their attention. Well, not everyone. Kamil's dad is writing something on his phone, but it probably has to do with an asset management, so Darby doesn't blame him.

"Neat," Sarah says. "I can see it too."

As a few more classmates chime in to confirm their understanding, Darby knows he doesn't understand and probably won't or can't, but the thought does not trouble him because he pictures his dad working on the lock. Lego works well for symmetrical heights, widths, and depths, and it simplifies angles, but getting all the working parts of the lock to work could not have been easy. His dad would have had to make three or four or more attempts before getting the model the way he wanted it. The component parts of the lock are colour coordinated to make the explanation easier, which means his dad must have thought of and planned for the model ahead of time. Maybe he made several versions of the construction until he settled on this one for the Career Parent Presentation.

In his mind, Darby can see his dad coming home from his new work at Iogen to his one-bedroom apartment in the low-rise apartment complex. Since he's new at the company, his dad doesn't know any of his co-workers too well yet, and no one has yet invited him out for an after-work beer or coffee and bar finger food snacks. Maybe Darby's dad hasn't talked to too many people all day, and at night alone, he sits in the quiet and dark apartment kitchen with Lego bricks spread out around him on the table. Some of the bricks come from Darby's collection, but his dad would have had to buy a few specialized pieces for the tumbler lock model. Probably he constructed the model on weekends when Darby wasn't there. He would have hidden the project away when Darby came over for visitation weekends, so it'd be a surprise for the presentation. His dad, Darby realizes, doesn't want to disappoint him.

"So this is one example." Darby's dad pauses, uncertain. "One example of mechanical engineering and how it appears everywhere every day around us."

He hasn't thought of a clincher closing final thought conclusion. "Which is why mechanical engineering is important."

He's petering out and his voice is trailing off, and Darby thinks his dad should just stop talking because that'd be better all around. "Important to me anyway. Why I chose it."

Everyone understands this is the end, and so everyone claps. It doesn't much matter how effective the closing-clincher-final-thought conclusion is, Darby sees. People will clap regardless and Darby claps too, which makes his dad grin, which is good. Since the mechanical engineering presentation not only finishes off the Career Parent Presentations and Career Day, but also signals the end of the school day and the end of the school week, it makes sense when Darby feels the energy in the room wane and fade.

"I'm afraid I don't have anything to give the class." Darby's dad shrugs. "I didn't think to bring any kind of sample to give you."

"I did."

The voice comes from the hallway, and standing in the doorway, Hannah holds a shopping bag and a box in either hand. As everyone turns to look at her, she lifts the box slightly, showing the Chez Animaux paw logo on its side. No one seems to know how to react to her unplanned appearance, and the room turns quieter. Looking to Alexander, Darby sees he didn't expect Hannah either.

"I brought something from my work," she says.

She hasn't entered the room, and she just stands in the doorway in her winter coat and boots as if waiting for permission to enter. Although Alexander probably didn't expect his sister to appear at the end of Career Day, he's grinning and Darby sees him give Hannah a small nod, which feels very much like the wave Darby's dad gave him. She nods back at Alexander and holds up the Chez Animaux box and shopping bag.

"It's for the whole class," she says.

On the side of the box, circular breathing holes surround the store logo, which means the box is a critter box. All the students stare at it, which Darby figures is a natural response. All-of-a-sudden-and-out-of-the-blue, the energy in the room is no longer waning and fading and everyone seems to be waiting for her to say more. Well, not everyone, because Kamil's dad keeps typing and reading on his smart cellular telephone. But almost everyone seems to be waiting for her to say more.

"Since our mother can't come," she says, "I thought I'd come and present instead."

Heads turn again, this time looking toward Monsieur Substitute and looking for approval. Can someone who is not a parent present a visiting Career Parent Presentation? As an expert and authority on nothing at all, he probably does not know, but he seems to understand all the expectant faces in the room expect an answer, and at last, he welcomes her inside.

"*Bienvenue.*"

With the flaps of his Fed Ex box refolded in an overlapping pattern, Darby's dad smiles to himself and to Hannah, conceding the thrust stage performance space as he retreats to the background of the whiteboard chairs.

"I'm Alexander's sister," she says and shrugs as she enters the room. "I don't really have a career as such, but I do work at Chez Animaux, and I do study veterinary care." Her voice trails away. "So, I can tell you about that."

As she removes her coat and hat, all eyes follow the critter box, wondering what might be hidden away inside behind its cardboard walls. Everyone follows it down to the tile floor and then up and through the room as Hannah walks to the centre of the thrust stage performance space. She notices everyone staring and grins.

"Um, you seem curious?" she asks

If an appropriate and well-integrated prop can grab the audience's attention, then a mysterious prop unexpectedly introduced will really pique interest. Darby wonders if she planned this opening, but he doesn't think so.

"Can I set it here?" she asks, gesturing to the lift-top desk just directly in front of her, which just happens to be Sarah Underhill's desk. Like the lucky someone chosen by a celebrity magician to assist in a particularly engaging illusion, Sarah nods repeatedly.

"I started working at Chez Animaux in grade eleven right after I turned sixteen," Hannah says, "because I needed pocket money and I needed to save money for university, but also because I'd already decided I wanted to study animal care in school. And so when I think about it now, cause and effect kind of blur. Did I grow more interested in the job because of my future goals or did my future goals increase my interest in my job?" She shrugs but it is a confident shrug. "I don't know, but then, you know, I don't need to know."

Hannah wears the thin silver loop in her eyebrow but not the thick silver bolt in her cheek, and her hair has changed since Darby last saw her a few weeks ago in the Southgate Bayview Mews Mall. The ends have grown out a bit and curl inward near her neck in a kind of bob with a wide purple-blue streak running down the left.

"I've been working at Chez Animaux for two years now, and I'm now in my second semester of veterinary science, and you know, I don't have much time to think about cause and effect or anything like that. I mean I'm usually too busy, but once in a while, if the store is slow and all the cleaning and stocking and feeding are done and I'm studying introductory domestic animal anatomy, well then – sometimes all the memorization makes my mind wander, and I do wonder about how the job I have now relates to the job I want to have in the future. And I've decided that working in the pet store will make me a better veterinarian in the long run."

She speaks a bit too quickly for a presentation, but it's hard to tell if the speed is part of public speaking nervousness or just her normal extra enthusiasm. Darby decides both probably, and either way, she's won over the class.

"What's weird, though, is that I think the reason why Chez Animaux will make me a better veterinarian is both positive and negative. Washing and feeding small rodents will make me more comfortable with small rodents later, and having to learn and explain the subtle differences between newts, skinks, and salamanders to customers will later make me more comfortable with clients who have newts, skinks, and salamander pets. Cats shouldn't drink milk; dogs shouldn't eat chocolate, and rabbits need never touch avocados. I've picked up lots of positives that will make me a better veterinarian, but I have also picked up lots of negatives that will make me a better veterinarian as well. Like the way you can learn from a bad teacher and a good teacher, if that makes sense? Anyway, the store sells poodle breeds with clipped tails, which people don't seem to know is a bad idea. The store makes referrals to clinics that declaw cats, which people don't seem to know is a bad idea. The store stocks an aquarium of feeder fish for piranha owners and cages of feeder mice for large reptile owners, which, you know, I'm pretty sure is, you know, problematic?"

Her tone of voice has turned serious – probably because she's suppressing anger – but the modulation works well for public speaking.

"Nevertheless and nonetheless," she says. "I can see everyone is looking at what I brought?" Hannah places her hand on the top of the critter box. A few students laugh uncomfortably and confirm her suspicions.

"Well, then, I won't wait."

Like the overlapping flaps of a used box, the closure at the top of the Chez Animaux critter box is clever. A four-sided pyramid, the top uses two longer flaps that come together along the length of the box and two shorter flaps along the width. The two longer flaps have handles in the middle and grooves at the end, and the shorter flaps have slots. Closed altogether, the slots fit into the grooves and the handles are strong enough to carry a kitten or small breed puppy like a terrier or rodent like a hamster.

"Here we are," Hannah says, and scoops out a hamster with golden brown fur. "The specific breed is Syrian hamster. Long hair

Syrian. Because of the colour and the fuzzy hair, it's most often called a teddy bear hamster."

Cradled in her palms, the animal sniffs its pink nose about and darts its dark eyes about, stepping forward to the edge of Hannah's hands. At the point of drop-off, it stops and turns its snout down, curling itself into itself.

"Alexander told me your class used to have two hamsters called Euclid and Gauss but your Euclid died over Christmas time, so I thought I'd bring the class a replacement. Maybe a Pascal or a Fibonacci?"

As they did with the model of the Lego tumbler lock, everyone leans in to get closer to the teddy bear hamster. Darby glances at the faces of his classmates and sees that they're chuckling and smiling and grinning – a reasonable enough response to the sight of a small and vulnerable animal of unquestionable charm, but the sight also speaks well of human nature, he thinks.

"Unless anyone has a different idea for a name?" Hannah says.

"Aesop," Alexander says. "I always thought Aesop would be a good name for a pet."

Hannah looks at her brother and nods. "Nice," she says.

"Aesop here is a female. From a litter that's maybe three and a half or four months old. A human year is approximately twenty-five hamster years, so about eight or nine now. Not that much younger than all of you, actually. She'll get to be 6-7 inches when full-grown, but she's still just a puppy now."

Darby looks to the proscenium whiteboard and see Kamil's dad raises his eyebrows with a smirk. Stewart's mom lets out an audible *well, oh my goodness* as she chuckles. Darby's dad nods slightly as he smiles. After these happy initial reactions, all three parents look to their children to take in their reactions, as if their responses feel incomplete until they include their children's response. Kamil's dad looks over at Kamil and snaps a picture with his phone. Stewart's mom looks and Stewart and gives a cheery thumbs-up. Darby's own dad looks at him with a furrowed-brow expression that Darby can't quite decipher. Wistfulness?

"Young hamsters are puppies; adult males are bucks, and adult females are does, which, you know, is odd. I've no idea why or how they got these names. I also don't know much about their anatomy either. We did basic dog and cat anatomy in first semester, but we don't study rodents until third year."

"Do you know why they eat their own crap?" Billy Pace asks.

Hannah has not yet invited questions from the audience and her presentation may not even include a Q and A session at all, so the question feels a bit abrupt. Additionally, in Darby's opinion, even though *crap* isn't officially a swear word, he senses the word is close enough to a swear word that it colours the abruptness of the question with a touch of aggression. His sense of this is confirmed when all the faces of all the students and visitors in the classroom shift in unison from the adorable teddy bear hamster toward Billy Pace, who sits slouched behind his lift-top desk.

"What?" he asks, flipping his hands up as if he did not just say *crap*.

Since Monsieur says nothing and everyone is waiting for him to say something, the quiet discomfort in the room stretches out a few moments longer until Hannah answers.

"Because of the desert," she says. "Hamsters were originally desert animals, and like a lot of desert animals, hamsters will sometimes eat their own droppings to conserve water."

Responses to this answer range from groans to murmurs of *ewww* and *cools*, and Stewart's mom repeats *well, oh my goodness*, but order has been restored in the classroom and Hannah has successfully smoothed over Billy's attempt at disruption.

"Why don't we introduce Aesop to Gauss?" Hannah says. "Hamsters are social by nature, so they should be fine in the same cage."

Turning and moving to the front of the room, Hannah once again holds the attention of the entire class, which probably explains why almost no one sees Billy Pace's expression. His jaw tightens, and his eyes widen, and Darby suspects the look is a look of fury – fury because Alexander has been growing apart from him and Stewart over the past while, fury because Alexander didn't participate in the mean trick this morning, and fury because Alexander chose to stay inside with Darby and Jennie for second nutrition break. All of these reasons might explain why he decides upon that moment to play the meaner-than-mean trick, but perhaps the main reason is Darby's laugh.

Darby doesn't mean to laugh because Billy Pace's anger has isolated him in the class, and laughing is unkind. Darby doesn't mean to laugh at Billy Pace because a more appropriate response would be sympathy, but there's just something comic in Billy's tightened jaw and widened eyes and fury, and so Darby laughs.

Cause and effect, Billy removes a full-page spread from one of Darby's dad's vintage pornography magazines. As he did earlier in the day during Darby's and Jennie's Veterinary Dentistry presentation, he holds the magazine down low between his body and the desktop of his lift-top desk because he wants only Darby to see it. By threatening to expose but not quite, Billy wants the meaner-than-mean trick to strike fear and inspire terror, and, of course, Billy knows that Darby's dad sits no more than twenty feet away at the proscenium arch whiteboard. Billy knows how to best exploit his ability to shame Darby.

Glancing up and scanning the class, Darby sees that everyone else has turned toward the corner of the room where Monsieur

Substitute lifts the pet cage to help Hannah. The teacher grunts an exaggerated *urmph* as he lifts the hamsters' home to make a joke. Hannah and Aesop have spread goodwill throughout the classroom, and it is to the teacher's advantage, Darby thinks. Whether or not Monsieur feels himself responsible for Euclid's death over the holiday break in December, he's probably aware that the students blame him, and a new pet will mean his past transgression will be forgiven and forgotten. The *urmph* joke works and a few students giggle.

Darby looks back at Billy, who still holds the pornography picture out. Though Darby's heart rate races, no one else yet sees what he sees, and this is at least a relief.

"Hamsters rarely react negatively to a new companion, but they might stick to opposite ends of the cage for a while," Hannah says. "It can take them time to warm to one another. Two or three days usually."

Though the magazine is bent back at its spine and the cover invisible, Darby identifies the publication as *Oui* and can see that the photograph features both a woman and a man. Of the vintage pornographic magazines that Darby borrowed from his father's collection at the back of the bedroom closet in the low-rise apartment, very few contained pictorial essays of couples. Well, not really couples. The focus of the photos was always the woman, and the man always played an extra nonessential role in the narratives, positioned on the outskirts of the composition and either clothed or shown only from the back with buttocks bare.

"Oh, Gauss and Aesop seem to be getting along just fine. They've cuddled together good and tight under the exercise wheel."

Sunday in the Park with Georgette. That's the title of the pictorial essay. It tells a story that Darby returned to a few times before foolishly lending the magazines to his friends. In the opening photographs, red-haired Georgette in the brightest of yellow sundresses wanders through a park playground, gliding down the corkscrew slide and mounting the jungle gym climber. The disrobing begins in the second or third photograph when she walks to the swing set, but it is not until a couple of pictures later that the male voyeur in shorts and a t-shirt appears. He hides crouched in the shrubbery at the edges of the playground where Georgette can't see him spying. As the story progresses and Georgette further explores her outdoor adventures, pumping her legs on the swings and leaning way, way back to kick higher and higher in the air, her smile widens and intensifies. She throws her head back in happy laughter and in the amusement of a light heart. Though the voyeur watches her naked throughout, the hidden man's expression remains fixed and serious, his intense gaze staring but communicating no emotion that Darby could see. In the penultimate page of the story, the red-haired Georgette has tired herself out from exertion, and she sits unmoving on the swing with her back hunched forward so her bare tummy creases and her bare legs dangle bored in front of her. This is the photo Billy Pace holds up to threaten and torment Darby in the classroom. Then, Billy turns the page.

"Syrian hamsters can survive for long stretches with little water, but you should change water in the bottle from time to make sure it doesn't stagnate."

The next page that Billy turns to is the final photograph of *Sunday in the Park with Georgette*, another full-page photo. Naked red-haired Georgette and the voyeur make eye contact for the first time. The look on her face shows surprise and the look on his face is guilt, and the story ends abruptly, not really revealing if her surprise will turn to anger or fear or further light-hearted amusement. It's kind of a fight-or-flight moment in the pictorial essay, and when Darby looked at it in the past, he thought that moment could go either way.

What he notices now is that Billy Pace has stuck something to the pages of the photo. They're label stickers – the kind used for file folders and icebreaker getting-to-know-everyone's-name labels – and Billy has stuck them to the magazine photo. The stickers will definitely wreck and tear the pages, but Darby supposes he doesn't need to worry about that now. On the labels, Billy has written words.

"It's all right to leave a large bowl of feed pellets with a weeks' worth of food," Hannah says, "they won't eat it all at once like a dog. But it's better to feed small portions twice a day."

On the label sticker next to the voyeur, Billy Pace has written *The Frenchman*, and on the label sticker next to Georgette, he has written *Your mom*, and when Darby reads them, he realizes that Billy Pace hasn't been threatening and tormenting just only him, but also Jennie.

"In the long run, a small portion of feed pellets twice a day is better for their metabolism and health."

Darby glances back at Jennie and sees that she sees. Whether or not she understands Billy Pace's label sticker is unclear. Whether or not she looks at the label stickers and the soft-focus pornography and tries to make sense of them is uncertain. Whether or not she reads the names and thinks about the many business trips that her father takes out west while her mother remains at home in Ottawa all alone and lonely is unknowable.

Darby wants to tell her not to draw any conclusions that might be wrong-headed and hasty. A scarf and a neckerchief are not the same; her mom has not made her dad a cuckold, and there's been a misunderstanding. Darby wants to explain, but he doesn't. Instead, he jumps from his lift-top desk and pushes his way through the U-shaped audience of classmates toward Billy.

"Darby, did you want to hold the hamster?" Hannah asks.

Hannah has turned toward Darby in confusion, but he passes through the thrust stage performance space without looking toward her. He reaches out toward Billy Pace's face and grabs, pulls, punches hair and eyes, hardly noticing all the other faces turned toward him. Probably Stewart looks confused and scared, and probably Alexander looks confused and sad, but Darby's confused mind doesn't think clearly. To the extent that he's thinking at all, he hopes to clutch onto Billy Pace's head and bring it down sharply against the top of the lift-top desk. The thing with anger and physical violence, though, is that they aren't nearly as easy as they look. Instead of slamming Billy's forehead down with great force and furious anger, Darby clutches hold of a few strands of hair and hooks his pinky finger inside the guy's ear, which is kind of gross. Billy pulls back, and the look on his face is confused but also amused disbelief – a mixed emotion that Darby does not have time to consider. After his initial attack fails, he punches.

"Darby, what?" asks Hannah.

"Darby, don't," says Jennie.

"Darby, stop," says Darby's dad.

"*Merde*," says Monsieur Substitute.

Because Darby punches with little punching experience and no particular plan, he swings in Billy's general direction but he does not connect the first, second, or third time. The fourth time, though, he does connect. He hits Billy in the neck, and the hit lands well enough to erase Billy's confused and amused expression.

"What's wrong with you, you freak?" says Billy Pace.

"Don't," says Jennie.

"Stop," says Darby's dad.

"*Ca suffit*," says Monsieur Substitute.

Darby understands that the new expression on Billy's face should probably frighten him, as it is clear that Billy wishes to do him harm as soon as possible, but Darby remains distracted by his own anger. In releasing his anger, he has realized just how often he has not released it, which his mother says can be detrimental and lead to psychological and physiological harm. Darby has often seen his dad express his anger at city motorists who drive in a careless, selfish, and /or aggressive manner and thereby demonstrate the poorest of all human characteristics. For some reason, though, Darby has always felt the need to deny anger entirely, which is odd and he wonders where such a need came from.

"Motherfucking asswipe dickwad," Darby says – or something to that effect. He might also be yelling some of Stewart Holgermonsson's nonsensical swears. Asswad, or douche wipe, or eldest son of a bitch. Whatever he says, he says it while he continues his punching and escalating his attack. At some point, he climbs up onto the desktop of Billy's lift-top desk and grabs him by the head and shoulders, which turns out to be an unwise strategy because the maneuver unbalances Billy, desk, and Darby. They fall and topple together, hitting the tile floor as one.

"Ugh," Billy Pace says.

"Holy moly," Stewart says.

Jennie says nothing at all.

At some point, Billy drops the copy of *Oui* he has been using to threaten and torment Darby, the magazine forgotten and face down on the floor with only the back-cover advertisement for mentholated cigarettes showing. During the tumble of Billy, desk, and Darby, however, seven to eight copies of *Oui* and *Club* spill out and slide onto the tile. While only Darby and his former friends recognize these as the vintage pornography magazines that Darby stole from the back of the closet in his dad's low-rise apartment, Darby's dad may well put two and two together when he spots the titles all asunder. The other students and adults may not put two and two together, but still – they most likely suspect something is amiss. In the normal course of events, the enriched grade five class does not include sex and violence.

"It's all right," Alexander says. "It's all right."

Although he's lost in the moment and although his friend speaks softly, Darby hears him and feels Alexander's hand on his shoulder.

"It's all right," Alexander says again.

Because Alexander has spoken with concern, Darby slows down. He begins to realize what he has done, and he begins to regret what he has done, but in slowing down, he's also left himself exposed to Billy's first counterattack – a backhand slap that turns out to be much more precise than any of his own attempts at violence. Also as it turns out – receiving hits and smacks and punches is as unpleasant as giving them. *Ow.* The sharp pain feels like a bit of a revelation.

During the brief moment of revelation and sharp pain that will most likely bruise and leave a purple swelling, Monsieur Substitute intervenes. He grabs Darby by the arms, pinning them at his sides, and while the teacher probably intends only to restrain him and deescalate the situation and he has the best of good and pure intentions, the grip allows Billy to slap Darby a second time. This slap connects with Darby's ear, which stings as much as the cheek and also leaves an unpleasant ring in his head.

"Ow," he says.

The second hit brings Darby's dad from his seat at the white board proscenium arch, and he moves on Monsieur Substitute, grabbing for one of the hands grabbing Darby. He's trying to protect Darby – an act of protectiveness that probably shouldn't please and amaze Darby as much as it does because such protection is a basic and fundamental function of parenthood – and although Darby hasn't got a clear angle on his dad's face, he imagines a jaw tightened and teeth gritted in fierce determination. According to Darby's dad, there is never a good reason to strike or put unwanted hands upon another human being, so this bit of impulsive protectiveness is a kind of a violation of his own personal and reasoned code of ethics, and the moment brings up a swell of emotion in an already-emotionally-heightened moment.

Unfortunately, Darby's dad's grip on Monsieur causes Monsieur to tighten his grip on Darby.

"Ow," he says again.

"What are you doing?" Monsieur Substitute yells at Darby's dad.

"What are you doing?" Darby's dad yells at Monsieur Substitute.

The room fills with a good deal of yelling, but Billy hasn't slapped Darby a third time, for which he feels fortunate. When Darby turns to see why, he sees Stewart and Alexander restraining Billy, and again, the sight touches him and makes him feel protected. With Monsieur pulling one arm and his dad pulling the other, however, Darby also feels a sharp ache in between his shoulders. The room fills will more and more yelling, but Darby realizes none of it is his yelling, and his fury fades.

ON *LE PARC SAFARI* AND THE UNFORTUNATE ACCIDENT

In Hemmingford, Quebec, a quick fifteen-minute drive south down from Montreal, at *Le Parc Safari*, one of the province's preeminent tourist attractions and a fun-for-the-whole-family entertainment centre offering a drive-through jungle environment, children's zoo, midway, and water park from Victoria Day to Labour Day, a summer student by the name of Alexandra-Madalene Laroche-LaPierre was working away in the humid stink of the last days of August in *La Ferme des Cinq Continents* and was in the midst of attempting to feed two species in one trip – at once bearing a whole entire bucket of nutritional grain pellets for the llamas, alpacas, and Anatolian black goats and a whole entire jug of vitamin-C-and-sedative-enriched hydration solution for the fallow, roe, and spotted deer in the walk-through petting zoo enclosure, even though properly speaking, each separate task should have been performed separately and should have been overseen by an experienced senior staff member by the name of Ted, the zoological technician who had been assigned to designate roles and responsibilities to temporary staff members and to supervise their activities and who, for reasons unbeknownst to Alexandra-Madalene, had not turned up for his eight-to-four shift that especially humid August morning – when she noticed that she had failed to secure the single hook latch that firmly shut the gate to the large and small rodents enclosure in *La Maison Sud-Americaine*, a serious, costly mistake that would not cost summer student Alexandra-Madalene her position at the park because she could hardly be blamed for poor judgement when left abandoned, under stress, and responsible for the most helpless of all of God's small creatures, but would rightly cost zoological technician Ted his position when it was later discovered that he, the holder of a Master's degree in Animal Biology and a one-time potential candidate for the lucrative and prestigious position of Veterinary Dentist (NOC 3114) at the world-renowned Calgary Zoo in Calgary, Alberta, had missed work simply because he had decided he'd had enough of the indignity and shame and self-loathing of perpetual underemployment, and on the particular morning in question, he'd said aloud *no more world* and would remain nestled in the false comfort of his sofa bed until he bloody well felt like getting up and the rest of all and sundry would just have to deal, and a serious costly mistake that inadvertently offered the twin gifts of freedom and self-determination to a nutria, a Brazilian opossum, two chinchilla rats, and a family of three capybaras, and though the opossum – for personal reasons that would remain private all its own – remained nestled in the false comfort of its hay and wood-chip home sweet home, the more brazen rodents seized the day, hoping to leave behind *La Cage des Grands et Petits Rongeurs*, *La Maison Sud-Americaine*, and all that bad feeling for adventures farther afield and fled until the amber alert rang out throughout the drive-through jungle environment, the children's zoo, the midway, and the water park to alert all-and-sundry *Le Parc Safari* employees – from the highest of the high Executive Liaison of Tourism in the front office to the lowest of the low *Wild Beanz* Barista in the zoo food court – to stop what they were doing and join in the search amongst the wild reeds of the duck pond, where the nutria was later found making a nuisance of itself, around the outside barriers of the common chinchilla hutch, where the chinchilla rats were later found standing amazed and reunited with their far-flung cousins, and along the banks of the winding lazy river, where the family of three capybaras were not later found because they had escaped *La Ferme des Cinq Continents*, *Le Parc Safari*, and all that rot.

As the humid warm of summery summer gave way to the chilly cold of autumnal autumn, when *Le Parc Safari* shuttered its front gates for yet another successful tourist season and the last of the maintenance and grounds crew finished final clean-up and passed along the front gate keys to the off season gate-keepers and security staff, after two weeks of hiding in the woods and shrubbery adjacent to the fun-for-the-whole-family entertainment centre's picnic grounds where they had been surviving on a diet of grasses, common elderberries, red-berried elderberries, and a shrub of St. Johnwort since the day of their great escape from *La Maison Sud-Americaine,* the mother, father, and son capybaras found themselves apprehensively adrift on an incredible journey and instinctively adrift in a southerly direction toward the nearest source of freshwater, Lake Champlain, whose shores bordered the northern states of New York and Vermont and provided potable drinking water and whose lush wetlands provided edible and fibrous flora for so many peaceful-and-easy salad days that mother and father rodent both came to believe that fleeing *La Cage des Grands et Petits Rongeurs* had been the right and correct choice and that they had stumbled upon a newer and better, safer and sounder setting in which to raise their young offspring rodent, lulling them into a false sense of security and leaving them vulnerable to the ill fate and reversal of fortune that came in the form of a timber rattlesnake bite, upon whose tail father capybara accidentally tramped roughly with his hoof and whose venomous bite released a toxin that led to father capybara's fainting, infection, and death within one single September week, and thus left alone to their own devices, the over-sized mother and son rodent headed aimlessly north, once again disregarding international land agreements and once again evading both Canadian and American agencies of border patrol, and while they came to and crossed numerous streams and rivers of freshwater, the experience with the Yankee timber rattlesnake that had made the South American mammals a widow and an orphan had also made them leery and cautious, reluctant to settle in any one place lest their family suffer more, and thus, they rambled and waltzed matilda onward and directionless, their days spent foraging for the scant natural food supply of shrub, grass, bush, and weed offered up by the Precambrian shield terrain and the unnatural food supply of Wendy's and Harvey's and Timmies thrown from car windows along the 417 highway, oftentimes following the sun and winding west, but other times intent only on evading the populated pockets of populations scattered between the bright lights and big cities of Ottawa, Ontario and Montreal, Quebec – where the capybaras were more than once on the troubled minds of Alexandra-Madalene Laroche-LaPierre, who still blamed herself for the unfortunate escape in August and whose guilt and anguish led her to change her area of study at McGill repeatedly and erratically from Animal Biology to Chamber Music to Choral Music to Musical Education to Mechanical Engineering, and of Ted, who relocated from his basement apartment outside of Hemmingford, Quebec to a ground-floor unit in a low-rise apartment complex whose location allowed for daily walks to the Westmount Library and surrounding park where he could sit and read outside and where he thought of Veterinary Dentistry (NOC 3114) and of the dual losses of potential and dignity only when the occasional squirrel paused to rest and share his park bench – until one November evening when mother and son capybara might well have found themselves wandering and foraging inside the outer limits of the nation's capital where acres of dense forest were unexpectedly broken by rural roads, crossings, and concessions, and they perhaps came upon a bridge over troubled waters that they could only but cross, not at all expecting to see a careless, selfish, and aggressive Gerald Gerard Henderson driving a Nissan Leaf toward them at a speed that sent mother and son, car and driver over the side and to their shared fates.

CHAPTER 10

With his furious anger diffused down to reflective regret, Darby looks around and sees his classmates scattered around the room. Some have remained by the hamster cage, and some have moved back to the thrust stage performance space, which no longer much resembles a thrust stage because too many of the lift-top desks have been bumped and moved and now face different directions. Billy's desk still sits sideways, the lift-top lid open like a forgotten cabinet in a kitchenette, which Darby's mom always worries about because bumping your head into the corner of a cabinet door can be painful.

Although Darby feels he should apologize and he opens his mouth to mutter an apology, nothing seems to come out. The absence of sound alarms him, but he realizes also that no one would have heard him even if he'd talked anyway because too, too many people in the room are already talking and talking too loudly. All around the hamster cage and all around in the now disorganized scramble of desks, the students all seem to be either accusing and blaming him or Billy, a disorganized debate in which no one at all follows the proper parliamentary debate format points of information or points of order. Everyone just argues.

"Are you all right?"

Though the voice isn't all that louder than the other voices, Darby sees his dad is the one asking the question. Darby also sees that his dad no longer grips his arm in an uncomfortable squeeze, either. His hand sits on Darby's shoulder, which is a gesture of concern that matches the concern on his dad's face. Now that Darby thinks about it, neither of his arms feels squeezed, and Monsieur seems to have let go, too. When this happened, Darby is unsure.

Both the teacher and his dad were grabbing so tight that there's a shadow trace of the pain on both his arms.

"Are you all right?" his dad says louder.

"Yes, I'm all right," Darby says, and again, no words come out. He nods his head, though, so his dad seems to get the gist of the message. Darby wants to thank his dad as well, but all he manages is a nod.

"We should all calm down now," his dad says in an even-more loud voice. He talks to the whole room, and though he does sound authoritative, ten-and-eleven-year-olds sometimes choose not to listen even when they hear.

"Yes, *ça suffit*," Monsieur says. "Calm."

The teacher has no more effect than Darby's dad. Glancing over at Hannah, Darby sees she's trying too, mouthing *take it easy* to those closest to her, but only when Cintia Holgermonsson speaks does the room grow quieter.

"No," she says. "No more. Enough. No more."

Stewart's mom still holds her giant prop toothbrush, and she shakes it as she speaks – a sight that catches the students' attention and cuts off most argument.

"Stop. No more. No."

A couple of kids still mutter and argue on, so Stewart's mom points at them with the giant toothbrush, waggling it aggressively.

"Enough. We sit down now. Now we sit down."

Obedient and embarrassed, most everyone sits at the wrong desk, and a couple of Darby's classmates take the Career Parent presenters' seats at the front of the class by the whiteboard, which makes the moment kind of like musical chairs. Monsieur and Darby's dad are left with no choice but to squeeze into the too small lift-top desks, their knees sticking out to the side.

"Billy Pace," Stewart's mom says. "Lift up your desk right now and put those magazines away."

Darby realizes that Stewart's mom must have years of experience dealing with Billy. Maybe she's been patiently holding her tongue ever since Billy and Stewart were four or five years old since they became friends sometime in JK, and they've probably had dozens and dozens of playdates and get-togethers. Stewart's mom maybe had to scold Billy on dozens and dozens of playdates at her own house, and she knows the exact pitch and tone of sternness that he'll obey.

"Lift up your desk, Billy."

The giant toothbrush she wields should somewhat undermine the threat in her voice, but Billy only shrugs defiantly and does what he's told. With everyone under control, the dental hygienist relaxes her shoulders and lets herself sit as well, but she doesn't seem to know what to do next.

Glancing at Alexander, Darby sees his friend exchanging smirks with Hannah, whose eyes widen in mock terror. The brother and sister both seem to know how inappropriate and what a bad idea laughing would be at this exact moment in this particular circumstance, which probably makes it harder not to laugh, and not for the first time, Darby wishes he had a sibling too.

"We should call the front office," Jennie says. Her words come across as peevish because she's annoyed that no one else knows the proper next thing to do and next obvious step in their present situation. Darby decides she's right to be annoyed because there are plenty of adults in the room. Adults should know what they are doing.

"*Oui*," Monsieur says. He swings his legs out to stand from the cramped lift-top desk but pauses with a glance at Cintia Holgermonsson. Mounted on the wall by the front whiteboard, the PA intercom callbox is located all the way on the other side of the room. Does he require Stewart's mom's permission to stand and cross the room? The question feels illogical, but the teacher seems to be waiting for an answer.

"Go," Cintia says, which makes both Alexander and Hannah tighten their mouths and stifle grins. They wisely refuse to make eye contact with each other, but when Alexander turns and looks toward Darby, his throat makes a croak. Darby whisper-speaks a *thank you*, and he can hear his voice.

"Hello," Monsieur says into the small box. "I am calling from room 107."

Like speakerphone Bluetooth telephone calls in the car, PA intercom conversations feel too much like eavesdropping to Darby, and he looks to the tile floor in order to give Monsieur and the front office reception some privacy. The gesture does nothing and has no meaning, Darby knows, and yet it feels more polite than watching the teacher bent forward over the callbox.

"We need assistance, I believe."

His formal tone strikes Darby as odd, and sure enough, when he looks at Hannah and Alexander, both stare at the floor, almost but not quite holding in their smiles.

"Does the situation require lockdown or safe-school procedures?"

"No, no," Monsieur says. "No. No alarm procedures. But perhaps could I speak with Madame Phelps-Christianson?"

The receptionist on the other end of the PA says he will fetch the vice-principal, and then, the vice-principal says she will be in the classroom in a minute, and throughout both uncomfortable exchanges, Darby feels himself returning to normal.

"I need to leave?" Kamil's dad says. He speaks to the room at large but remains seated. Uncertain whom to address, he turns to Monsieur standing at the callbox. "An appointment," he explains, gesturing with his smart cellular telephone as if to explain and apologize.

"I think maybe we should wait for a moment?" Monsieur says but he sounds unsure.

"We will wait," Stewart's mom says. She has put down her giant prop toothbrush, but the authority in her voice remains convincing.

The wait does not last long because Vice-Principal Phelps-Christianson appears in the doorway only moments later, speaking calm and slow with a reliable authority figure's smile. While she isn't pleased, the smile says that neither is she in anyway at all angry. Today's disturbance will be nothing more than an additional task to accomplish. This little upset need not be overly upsetting, and her smile will guide them all through it as efficiently and professionally as possible.

Darby thinks she must take her job very seriously to be so calm, which makes him realize how off base he and Alexander and Them were about the church parking lot at lunch hour. How could they have misunderstood so much?

"Hello everyone," she says, "I am told there's been a bit of trouble?"

"Yes, bonjour," Monsieur says, "We have had a bit of trouble, I am afraid."

"All right." Her voice sounds neither stern nor threatening, and yet Monsieur seems threatened nonetheless. The exchange, Darby realizes, is the first time he has seen the teacher and the vice--principal interact, and he again understands how little he previously understood.

"I really need to leave?" Kamil's dad asks. "I've got a work appointment."

"Yes, Mr. Gendry. One moment, please," she says. "Mr. Desjardins, will you join me in the hallway a moment, please?"

It is unlikely that the vice-principal knows all the family names of all the parents in the school. More likely, she either knows the family names of all the parents who are visiting for Career Day, or she knows all the family names of all the parents in her daughter's class. Either way, her ease with names impresses Darby, and he watches the vice-principal through the small rectangular window in the classroom door.

The first end-of-day bell rings, and since today's Friday, the first end-of-day bell also means the weekend. On most Fridays, the bell means hurry to finish the tasks at hand and hastily pack up whichever texts and notebooks need to go home for homework, and sometimes the anxious students head to the door to line up so they can be closest to the exit when the second bell rings. No one gets up from their desks today, though, and just in case the message isn't clear, Mrs. Holgermonsson emphasizes the point.

"We will wait," she says.

When Vice-Principal Phelps-Christianson opens the door, her calm smile has not changed, and in an unchanged voice, she tells the students they should get themselves ready for the end of the day.

"We don't want any of the bussers missing their ride home," she adds in a playful voice. "I do need Alexander Andrews, Billy Pace, and Darby Tamm to stay behind, though. And Mr. Tamm? Would you mind joining Mr. Desjardins and me in the hall a moment? Mr. Gendry, I apologize for delaying you."

Though she's not outright pointing at people and ordering them what to do, the effect is the same, which again makes Darby think the vice-principal does her job well.

"Mrs. Holgermonsson, would you mind staying for a moment longer while we chat in the hallway?"

Understanding the request as a great responsibility, Stewart's mom nods once, which is when the vice-principal notices Hannah for the first time. As she is neither parent nor student, Hannah gives the vice-principal pause.

"I'm sorry," the vice-principal asks, "you are?"

"Alexander's sister?" Hannah says. "I work at a pet store?" She points to the Chez Animaux shopping bag as if to explain.

"You came for Career Day?" Vice-Principal Phelps-Christianson asks. "Good." The vice-principal pauses again, taking a moment to decide whether to invite Hannah into the hallway or keep her in the classroom.

"I can stay here." Hannah decides for herself. "I'll wait with Alexander."

"Yes, good." With a place for everyone and everyone in their place, the vice-principal turns again to Darby's dad. "Mr. Tamm?"

Darby's dad tells him he'll be right back, and though Darby feels pretty sure his full voice has returned, he only nods. With the classroom door closed, the adults leave to talk in the hallway, and for a moment, Darby worries that Monsieur might tell his dad about the morning presentation – about how Darby froze and how Jennie had to step in and save the day from wreck and ruin. The moment and the thought disappear, though, and once again, Darby can hardly believe how little his former self understood about anything at all. He was foolish to worry about his dad's disappointment. Out in the hallway, they definitely aren't talking about Veterinary Dentistry, and Darby can only imagine what they are talking about.

MONSIEUR SUBSTITUTE:

Like an animal, the boy was flying over the desks and attacking his classmate with great ferocity. Never before I have seen such a behaviour.

VICE-PRINCIPAL PHELPS-CHRISTIANSON:

Has your son acted out physically in the past, Mr. Tamm?

FATHER:

No, but something has clearly upset him.

VICE-PRINCIPAL PHELPS-CHRISTIANSON:

I would have to agree with that assessment, yes.

MONSIEUR SUBSTITUTE:

A tiger or some sort of cat from a jungle. The boy pounced up on top of the desk, and he flew. He flew at the other boy. Out of control but also determined.

FATHER:

Yeah, all right. I get it. I was there.

MONSIEUR SUBSTITUTE:

Like the mongoose. The boy is an unruly little animal. A mongoose with fierce strikes.

FATHER:

Yeah, I saw what happened. Thank you.

MONSIEUR SUBSTITUTE:

It was unexpected. Like his fangs were bared out.

VICE-PRINCIPAL PHELPS-CHRISTIANSON:

Yes, Mr. Desjardins. Thank you.

MONSIEUR SUBSTITUTE:

De rien.

VICE-PRINCIPAL PHELPS-CHRISTIANSON:

How has Darby been dealing with stress at home, Mr. Tamm? It cannot have been easy for him to come to a new school last semester?

FATHER:

No.

VICE-PRINCIPAL PHELPS-CHRISTIANSON:

And forgive my intrusiveness, but I understand you and Ms. Tamm no longer live together?

FATHER:

No.

VICE-PRINCIPAL PHELPS-CHRISTIANSON:

Well, I'm sorry for your troubles. I am afraid we'll need to sit down with your wife and Billy Pace's parents as well. I will telephone them to meet us in the office, and I'm sure together we can all find a fair resolution for everyone involved.

MONSIEUR SUBSTITUTE:

The explicit magazines as well. Do not forget we must get to the bottom of the obscenity magazines. We must uncover from where the little beast got such filth.

FATHER:

Yes.

When the second end-of-day bell rings, Darby watches Monsieur reopen the classroom door and come in by himself, bidding *adieu* and *à lundi* to the line of students filing out of the room. In no time at all, the bustle and noise of the grade five classroom has transformed into an emptied-out awkwardness. The handful of remaining students and adults don't seem to know whether or not they should speak.

Hannah reaches into the pet cage, letting her hand rest there until both hamsters waddle over. She makes a clicking sound with the side of her mouth, grinning as they sniff her open palm curiously. Though he wishes he hadn't made such a mess of his friendship with Alexander, Darby feels glad he's gotten to know Hannah, and he's still watching her when his dad and the vice-principal re-enter.

"Thank you for your help, Mrs. Holgermonsson," the vice-principal says. "And thank you for coming to Career Day today as well."

Turning his head, Darby sees his dad has noticed him watching Hannah. His dad smiles as if he understands something, but Darby has no idea what that might be.

"Billy Pace," the vice-principal says, "I'm going to ask you to sit with the school nurse while we wait for your mother and father."

Billy slumps down in his desk but nods, looking up only when Stewart and his mom leave. The vice-principal's other directions are for Darby and Alexander, who are to wait in the outer office anteroom together.

"Jennie can sit there with you two if she likes, and Mr. Tamm will wait with me."

The vice-principal turns to the hamster cage and pauses as if just then reminded of Hannah's presence. As neither adult parent nor child student, she again causes a moment of uncertainty for the vice-principal, but again Hannah decides for herself.

"I'll go with Alexander and Darby," Hannah says. "If that's all right."

"Yes, certainly." Vice-Principal Phelps-Christianson nods, seeming relieved not to have to make another decision. "Thank you. From what I understand, Alexander wasn't involved in today's disturbance, but it may help if he could wait."

With Billy off safely secured in the nurse's room, everyone else walks together to the front office where the vice-principal gestures to a set of chairs and asks the children to wait in the anteroom. Well, the children and Hannah. With four anteroom chairs and four of them, the seating works out well, but Darby also sees that no matter who sits where, he'll have to sit across from someone, and he'll have to make eye contact, which he isn't sure he's up to just yet. In the end, he and Jennie sit side by side, and across from him, Hannah and Alexander are avoiding Darby's eyes. Probably they're doing it on purpose, for which Darby is grateful.

"We'll be no more than a few minutes," Vice-Principal Phelps-Christianson says as she slips into the inner office and closes the door behind her. Neither Monsieur nor Darby's dad says anything at all, but Darby again feels his dad touch his shoulder.

Once alone without the adults, no one says anything, which is something else to feel grateful about. At some point during the trip from the classroom to the front office, the furious anger that slowed into reflective regret has changed yet again and become a brand-new discomfort, and Darby recognizes this new discomfort as embarrassment. He cannot recall how many ineffectual punches he tried to throw or how long he was trying to throw them, but he kind of sort of remembers the side of his hand catching Billy's ear. Similarly, the specific profanities he yelled out are blurry, but he kind of sort of remembers using the phrase *asswad*. He definitely remembers Billy calling him a freak.

According to Darby's mom, it's best not to worry about other people's opinions too, too much, and according to Darby's dad, there's much more to worry about than what other people think, and Darby can see the validity in both points of view, but if Jennie, Hannah, and Alexander right now think he's a freak too, Darby feels pretty sure he will actually tear up and embarrass himself even more.

A muffled voice comes from behind the inner office door – either his dad or Monsieur, Darby would guess – and another muffled voice responds. The words are too indistinct to be understood, but none of the voices is raised or angry either, which Darby takes to be a good sign.

"That's your mom?" Hannah asks Jennie, interrupting the quiet in the anteroom. "The vice-principal is your mom?"

"Yes," Jennie says.

"Good mom." Hannah says and pauses as if she's considering her own assessment and then firmly agrees with herself. "Good mom."

Looking up, Darby sees Jennie grin. "Yes, thank you," Jennie says. "I think so too." She's pleased by the kind words, of course, but she's also glad to be talking to Hannah, too. Jennie's voice contains a nervousness Darby hasn't heard before, and he realizes why – on top of being eighteen and way on the other side of puberty, Hannah and her pierced nose, brow and lip do make an impression.

On a different day and in a different mood, Darby and Alexander and Hannah and Jennie might all get along well. Darby can imagine Jennie coming over to Alexander and Hannah's low-rise apartment complex where Alexander could introduce her to the intricacies of *KillCraft WarMachine*, and then all four of them could cross the street to the Southgate Bayview Mews Mall and browse together through the used bookstore. In the food court, Jennie could tell Hannah all about Veterinary Dentistry, and Hannah could show Jennie the rows of aquaria at Chez Animaux. Darby knows none of what he imagines will occur, but the fantasy feels good.

"Why did Billy write that about my mom on the picture?" Jennie asks.

She doesn't direct the question right at Darby, but also, it isn't entirely rhetorical either, and she does wait for an answer. Darby reasons that since neither Alexander nor Hannah saw what was written on *Sunday in the Park with Georgette*, neither can give an answer, and while Alexander does know about the pornographic picture and could thus clarify some of Jennie's confusion, he doesn't know about the school nurse and her neckerchief, so his answer might just only confuse the matter. Hannah probably has no idea at all what Jennie is talking about.

"I have no idea at all what you're talking about," Hannah says.

Forced to talk, Darby does. To ensure everyone understands, he explains that Billy and Alexander played the same mean trick in the morning; he explains that the photographs were pornographic photographs, and he explains that Billy wrote what he did to upset Jennie based upon a misunderstanding about Jennie's mom. Once the explanation is out, no one says anything, but then Jennie chuckles.

"You thought my mom was cheating on my dad?" she asks. "With Monsieur Desjardins?"

"The vice-principal with your teacher?" Hannah asks. She looks from Darby to Alexander, tightening her mouth. She is suppressing a laugh like she did in the classroom.

"And you think you saw them doing that in the parking lot of the Capital Baptist Church?"

"It was First United," Alexander says. "But yeah?"

Hannah gives up on suppressing her laugh and allows herself a chuckle. "Well, well, well."

"Monsieur's car was there," Darby says. "And he was, you know. He seemed to be, you know."

"You know, smoochie-smoochie," Alexander says in help.

"No, that's the thing," Darby says. "I don't think it was your mom. I'm almost sure it was the nurse. Neckerchiefs and scarves look a lot alike."

Jennie's got her eyebrows raised all incredulous.

"You're not joking?" she says.

"No," Darby says.

"Smoochie-smoochie," Alexander says again. "Yeah."

Hannah kicks her brother with the side of her foot. "You're not helping." She kicks him again, but she's smiling as she does so.

Feeling grateful, Darby grins at Alexander. Grateful that Alexander's there to back up Darby's explanation to Jennie, grateful Alexander was in the classroom to calm him down.

"I am too helping," Alexander says and bumps back at his sister with a chuckle.

Again, Darby understands just how much he previously misunderstood.

"Nurse Rose?" Jennie says.

"Her name is Rose?" Alexander asks. "I didn't know that. Rose." He nods at the name.

"Billy Pace is mean," Jennie says.

"Yes," Darby agrees.

"Yeah," Alexander agrees.

"Kid's a little prick," Hannah says.

Jennie laughs again, and her laugh is a quick bark that startles. She looks at the door to the inner office to judge just how loud she was, but Hannah assures her no one heard. Everyone is quiet for a moment and Darby thinks maybe he could ask Alexander if he knew about the mean trick in the morning or the meaner trick in the afternoon, but such a question was probably better without Jennie and Hannah there, so Darby decides he'll ask later. Or maybe he won't ask at all. Maybe it's better to let a question like that go and just move forward toward a clean slate future.

"So you attacked the little prick for Jennie's sake?" Hannah asks.

Darby shrugs and looks again at the floor.

"Well, *for Jennie* isn't accurate," Hannah says. "Losing your temper and violence are, well, problematic. But your intentions were good."

"Yeah," Alexander says, "messed up but well-intentioned."

Darby feels Jennie lean into his side.

"Violence is never a good idea," she says, "and in the long run, it can only harm all parties involved. But thank you."

"I wonder where he got the dirty pictures?" Hannah asks.

Darby looks up to see Alexander shrugging. "Billy?" he says. "Who knows? Who knows with that guy."

"He is strange," Darby adds.

While Darby knows his words are closer to lies than sins of omission, he also knows that he's brought enough trouble upon himself today.

"We just can't know," says Alexander.

Across from Darby, Hannah comically wiggles her eyebrows, and she lets out a skeptical *hmmmm*. She's playing silly and giving off the impression of a cartoon detective who uses deductive reasoning to weigh the facts of a case, but when Jennie turns to her for explanation, Hannah only shrugs. Whatever she knows or suspects or doesn't know or suspect, she's decided to let the matter go.

"Not anything to worry about," Hannah says. "Except them." She hooks a thumb toward the door to the inner office and reminds Darby that his relief may well be temporary. He can only imagine how much or how little his dad is admitting to inside the inner office.

MONSIEUR SUBSTITUTE:

Mon Dieu, those graphic photographs of such an explicit nature.

VICE-PRINCIPAL PHELPS-CHRISTIANSON

Upsetting.

FATHER:

Yes, such content can be upsetting in many contexts, and in the context of a classroom, such material is certainly inappropriate.

VICE-PRINCIPAL PHELPS-CHRISTIANSON:

Those stickers in particular strike me as most mysterious. "The Frenchman." "Your mom." Whatever do you suppose the boy was getting at with such nonsense?

FATHER:

Well, young boys at this age.

MONSIEUR SUBSTITUTE:

Who can suppose and guess at what might be in their heads.

FATHER:

It can be a confusing time.

VICE-PRINCIPAL PHELPS-CHRISTIANSON:

Yes, confusing. But where might Billy have gotten such old magazines? To the best of my understanding, the periodicals have long been defunct and out of print. Confusing, indeed.

MONSIEUR SUBSTITUTE:

C'est vrai. Such things are mysteries, you know. We may never know.

FATHER:

Perhaps we just cannot know.

MONSIEUR SUBSTITUTE:

Que sera, sera.

Darby cannot imagine his dad will ever bring up the magazines with him either. The ones in Billy's desk will be confiscated and probably destroyed by the school custodian, and the ones in his dad's closet don't need to be discussed. Adults must commit sins of omission all the time, he realizes. Reaching in his pocket, Darby feels for the morning's presentation rubric, and he decides he'll show it to his mom and dad without any explanation or additional information.

From the foyer hallway, a couple with a toddler crowd in and look across the anteroom. They don't seem to recognize anyone but send tired smiles nonetheless. The couple, Darby realizes, are Billy's parents and his younger sister. The young girl puts her hands up while her father helps her remove her winter coat.

"Upsy daisy," he says. "There you go."

With the girl's coat off, the mother crouches down next to her. "Mittens go inside bunny hat and then bunny hat goes inside the coat sleeve," she says.

She's narrating her actions while tucking away her daughter's hats and mittens. Darby has seen parents execute such performances for their children before – a way of teaching but also a way of filling the air with calming conversation. Though he has no specific memory of such events, his parents must have done the same with him.

Billy's dad looks about the front office, and pointing towards the inner office door, murmurs that the others are probably waiting in there already. When Billy's mom nods, he asks her if she's all right, and she puts her arm on his and nods again. These sad people are not what Darby expected of Billy's parents, though he's not sure what he expected. He's not thought about them too much.

"Hello Mr. and Ms. Pace," Jennie says and points toward the inner office. "Yes, this is the place."

The look on their faces change at the sight of Jennie, and though the change lasts only a moment, it is enough to make Darby realize they've met before. Jennie knows their name, and they know hers. Once again, Darby has to remind himself that the students of the enriched program shared many years together before his arrival.

"We haven't seen you since the Holiday Concert Celebration in December," Ms. Pace says.

Hannah and Alexander smile in greeting at the Paces as they pass into the inner office, and the couple smiles back in acknowledgment, but none of the faces reveals familiarity or even recognition. What this means, Darby is unsure, but it probably means Billy has so seldom invited Alexander over to his house that Mr. and Ms. Pace don't at all remember Alexander. Or it means Alexander has never been invited over to Billy's house. In all the enriched program years they've been together? It hardly makes sense, but Darby thinks he's right, and he understands something he didn't understand before. Alexander is lonelier even than he is.

"We should all hang out at my place," Darby says.

The confused looks on his friends' faces tell Darby that he's spoken too quickly and excitedly and maybe his invitation came out as a non-sequitur without any preamble or context, so he repeats himself.

"We should all hang out at my place during March Break. My mom and I make jokes about where we're planning on going for the break, but really, we're just having one of those staycations. I'm probably going to be in trouble about today, but March Break isn't until next month. Alexander's been to my place before, but Jennie's never been, and we could all do activities together. Lego or Clue. Jigsaw puzzles?"

Because Hannah looks the most surprised of all the surprised faces and because she is eighteen, Darby understands that it might be odd for her to join them for March Break hangouts.

"You can come if you want," Darby says to Hannah, "If you don't have to work at the pet store or you don't have other previous obligations and stuff."

Hannah doesn't answer, but she nods as if she'll check her schedule and keep her fingers crossed.

"I've got Jenga too," he adds. "And Battleship, which is only for two players, but we could take turns."

The outer office door opens once again, and when Darby looks, he sees his mom coming in.

ON THE SAFETY OF THE BACKSEAT

After a child passes a tenth or eleventh birthday, conscientious parents will reflect upon and reconsider experiences that might have been beforehand prohibited. The child's right to roam and select from the young adult shelves of the Ottawa Public Library. The freedom to listen to CBC radio news stories of local, national, or international significance no matter how unpleasant or sensationalized the subject matter. The independence to travel the interconnected worldwide network unmonitored within the reasonable confines of parental controls and site safety filters. By recognizing and permitting a child's increasing responsibility in a considered and gradual manner, mothers and fathers can foster a child's growth and ease their dependents into independence with care.

Some regulations and limitations must remain rigid, however, and one such non-negotiable is the backseat of the car. Regardless of his responsible nature and no matter his trustworthy honesty, a boy of eleven should belt himself safely in the backseat – preferably on the driver's side of a vehicle behind his mother where he will stay most protected in the event of black ice slip-slide or a left-turn collision. The standard front-seat airbags in modern vehicles come with specific height and weight restrictions for a specific reason: once deployed, they will cushion and protect adult passengers, but the force of the inflation can harm young children. With shoulder belts provided for all passengers in modern vehicles, the superior protection provided in the backseat should be obvious to parents.

Riding home in the backseat after an unhappy Career Day, a boy might well contemplate other advantages beyond physical safety. If his thoughts dwell on unpleasant matters, for example, and his emotions turn unsteady, the backseat makes eye contact less likely. Following a trip to the front office of the boy's school for disciplinary matters and a two-week suspension, the mother's disappointment might be enough to choke up the boy's throat, and the backseat provides a healthy distance to soften further emotional damage. Weekend visitation to the boy's father might be temporarily or indefinitely postponed, and the weight of these consequences might well cause the boy to tear up. The backseat helps. Although the lump in his throat refuses to move or shrink, he can at least look out the car windows and distract himself with the sights and sounds of the late drive home – the passing lights of the highway that speed by and the news of the day that broadcasts from the car radio.

The sights, unfortunately, do little to lessen his sadness. The boy and his mother left school late, so beyond the barriers and soft shoulder of the night-time highway, he can only see snowbanks and snippets of scenery passing by. Lit by highway streetlamps, the dark sky unkindly reminds the boy of night-time drives in previous years on previous evenings. In Calgary, where he and his mother once lived in the same home with his father, the three of them for three years running attended early December performances of *the Nutcracker* at the Arts Common. They chose weekend shows and chose an adult restaurant with tablecloths for an early evening dinner before the ballet, and so by the time the show was good and ended and Clara had awoken from the Land of the Sweets on Christmas morning, the boy felt ready for a rest, and by the time he climbed into the backseat of his family car and belted himself in, his mind felt fuzzy with fatigue. Up in the front seat, his mother and father commented upon the orchestra's performance that year, and in the backseat, the boy could quietly eavesdrop. As the car turned onto Stoney Trail and merged into the middle lanes of the TransCanada Highway, he would give into exhaustion and let his body slump to the side. Belted in safely, the boy could lie nearly flat across the backseat, and from his reclined perspective, all he could see outside of the car windows was the night sky in winter. Occasionally, the overhead lights alongside the highway sped by, their brightness bent and blurred by the car windows, and the boy imagined the streetlights were gooseneck desk lamps for big friendly giants. Tired, his waking logic merged into dream logic, and with his parents' low voices murmuring on up front and the car growing warmer and warmer, the boy fell asleep in his winter coat.

The memory worsens the boy's sadness at the end of Career Day, and then in the front seat, CBC switches to the news. The lead international story speaks of trade negotiations between nations whose names the boy thinks he might maybe probably know but couldn't isolate on a globe or map of the world. The lead national story speaks of possible fluctuations in interest rates that the boy neither comprehends nor cares to comprehend, and then, the lead local story catches his attention.

The solemn CBC voice speaks of the suspected murder-suicide deaths of a Kanata family, and there have been developments in the ongoing investigation. As reported earlier, police suspected arson after learning that the father and husband of the family had recently lost his real estate license and filed for bankruptcy. Following the removal of the bodies from within the burnt-out home, the major crimes unit has conducted a forensics inspection of the garage where traces of accelerant were found, and they have made a significant breakthrough in the case.

From the backseat, the boy watches his mother's head tilt, and he wishes he could stop the news story. He wishes he could tune the radio far, far away from the local news of the day. Such news can only sadden his mother, but from the backseat, the radio controls sit beyond his reach. He is powerless to stop the news that will further diminish his mother's already diminished mood.

Together, the abrupt end of a family Nutcracker tradition and his inability to stop the news story feel overwhelming. Like the sudden death of a hardworking teacher, such matters are not only unjust, but incomprehensible, and connecting them to the sadness of his day, the boy feels the hard lump in his throat grow. Far too much feels unjust and incomprehensible, and – cause and effect – the boy feels his throat constrict and his pulse increase and he gasps softly, disrupting the quiet in the car.

"Breathe," the mother says.

At the sound of her voice, the boy looks up toward the rear-view mirror and makes eye contact, understanding that her place in the front seat does not mean she hasn't been watching over him in the backseat. In a calm, slow voice, she again tells him to breathe, which is the kind of instruction parents give to toddlers and preschoolers and should be off-putting, but it is not. The boy feels he should apologize, but he has apologized a half dozen times today, and his voice would only crack if he tried again, which wouldn't exactly help prove his maturity. Instead, he slows his hyperventilation, calming his breaths until he feels his pulse normalize.

"Breathe," she repeats.

Behind her soft voice, the solemn announcer continues to speak of the Kanata family of four, but the news is not the news that the boy expected. Upon inspection, the accelerant in the garage came from extra gasoline and oil stored by the family's snow blower, and the suspicious deaths have now been categorized as accidental deaths. The major crimes unit would like to thank the forensics team for its dedication and hard work and would like to remind the general public that all fuel for snow blowers must be stored only in the proper regulation gas cans.

The announcer shifts to an unrelated local story about increased funding for snow removal, and just like that, the boy realizes that he has worried more than he has needed to worry. He has a habit of doing so. His mom has told him as much any number of times, and even in the backseat of the silent car, he can imagine her voice reminding him that he needs to focus on the positive, which he does.

a. Milk is a positive.

Snug inside an environmentally friendly and reusable tote, a four-litre-three-bag sack of 2% milk rests on the valleyed floor behind the front passenger seat and the back passenger seat. Previously, the boy's mom has always bought the family's supply of milk in two-litre cartons, and he chooses to see this new development as heartening progress – not only because it means that his mom realizes he is a growing boy with calcium needs that will increase with further growth spurts in his fast-approaching adolescence, but also because it means that his mom has been paying attention all along. Few pleasures match breakfast cereal with milk first thing in the morning.

b. Family get-togethers are a positive.

In addition to the two-week suspension and the daily composition reflections that the boy received as disciplinary measures for his poor behaviour on Career Day, the vice-principal expressed concern and suggested that he might benefit from counselling where he might learn to express anger and frustration in a more productive manner. To this advice, the boy's mom looked at the boy's dad and looked sad and asked that although their own couples counselling in Calgary had not successfully salvaged their relationship, maybe they should try family counselling for the boy's sake? The boy's dad nodded, and his mom sniffled, and as much as the boy hated to see her sad, the fact that they'd tried marriage therapy was news to him and interesting. How had he not known this? When both parents turned to him, the boy understood that he too was supposed to nod in agreement, so he did because even though twice-weekly therapy sessions aren't exactly the same fun as outings like skating on the Rideau canal – something he's still not tried even though they've lived in Ottawa nearly all winter now – family counselling still counts as a get-together.

c. Ducks are a positive.

In a few weeks, all the winter snow will melt, and in a couple of months, the Ducks Unlimited mallards sponsored by Richmond East Elementary will show up in the courtyard. Eventually, love will bloom, and ducklings will appear, and the boy can easily imagine three or four fluffy and downy hatchlings taking their first unsteady steps. They'll stand at the shore of the courtyard's manufactured pond, unsure about the surface of the shallow water that unexpectedly ripples as they take their first steps in. With quick turns of their heads left and right, they will give one another looks of healthy skepticism, and they will pause before chancing the water. The bravest of them will launch their tiny torsos into the pond, wobbling on the water but staying afloat nonetheless. The ducks of Ducks Unlimited are something to look forward to for sure.

"So what do you want to do for March Break?" the mother asks as she switches off the car radio.

The question is a running joke between the mother and the son, but the question is also a parenting strategy not unlike the backseat. As with her conscious decision to permit her maturing son more freedoms, this strategy allows the mother to exert a degree of control over the uncontrollable. Although many childhood discomforts cannot be eliminated, they can be deflected by a running joke.

"A bus trip to the Yukon where we might witness the Northern Lights firsthand?" she asks from the front seat.

As children age and mature, parenting strategies change. While a son of seven or eight might not realize that his mother is distracting him with a running joke, a boy of eleven will most likely see through the well-intentioned ruse.

"A train ride to Peggy's Cove where we might try lobster rolls and take a tour on a fishing trawler?" she asks.

Conscious awareness of the strategy's mechanics doesn't mean that it won't work, however. Indeed, if parent and child both know and contribute to the running joke's absurdity, it can deflect discomfort even more effectively.

"A flight to Victoria where we could have a truly authentic replica of an Anglophile high tea?" she asks.

A trip to Iceland to see the Fjords at sunrise? Moscow and the former Soviet Union to have a snowball fight in Gorky Park? Denmark to traipse in wooden clogs from windmill to windmill and all the way to Billhund and the birthplace of the Lego brick? The mother has suggested all of these March Break trips to her son over the months since his father's departure, and he played along with every suggestion. In playing along, he could both at once and simultaneously accept and ignore unpleasant realities.

"Maybe I could just have friends over?" he asks from the backseat.

"We could do that." His mother nods as if planning for an important and elaborate social occasion. "We could do that. Alexander?"

"Yes. And maybe Jennie?"

"Jennie-not-Jennifer."

"Both?"

"Both it is," she says, and with a nod, they agree to put Career Day behind them.

ACKNOWLEDGEMENTS

An Unruly Little Animal evolved out of two stories that first appeared in *The Dalhousie Review*: "The Gifted Class" and "Before Our Worldwide Interconnected Networks." "The Gifted Class" subsequently appeared in the collection *Character Actor* (Signature Editions, 2008) and *Journey Prize Stories 20* (McClelland & Stewart, 2008). Short story versions of two chapters appeared in *The Walrus* as "The Arithmetic of Common Ground" and *Event Magazine* as "What Befalls Us Away from Home." I'm grateful to the editors who've given me their time and attention, to the 2017 Walrus / Writer's Adventure Camp fiction contest judges Zsuzsi Gartner, Yasuko Thanh, and Jessica Johnson, and to Neil Smith's kind words in the Journey Prize anthology.

Early drafts of much of the novel were written in the UBC MFA program and benefited from the advice of workshop professors Caroline Adderson, Charlotte Gill, and Annabel Lyon. A number of kind classmates encouraged me by not only providing insightful feedback, but also genuinely enjoying the material: Jennifer Amos, Stephany Aulenback, Georgina Beaty, Heather Debling, Mason Hanrahan, Matthew Lawson, Jill MacKenzie, Jeff Miller, Margaret Nowacyzk, Deborah Vail, and Karin Zuppiger. I got lucky with my thesis committee too. Reader Kevin Chong went through the novel closely and asked the right questions. Advisor Alix Ohlin generously walked me through the difference between novel-writing and story-writing, and her approach to teaching was an ideal balance of kindness and intelligence.

The Lego model described in Chapter 9 owes a debt to JK Brickworks, much of the presentation information in chapters 5 and 9 comes from Dave Scully's *Art of Oratory* class, and Nathaniel Steffler told me about the sound of yogurt cups that appears in chapter 1.

Later drafts of *An Unruly Little Animal* were supported by a Production and Creation Grant for Literary Artists from the City of Ottawa. Katherine Root and a work sabbatical allowed me the time to finish the novel. Editors Keith Henderson and Ken Radu gave this book and my last one a home at DC Books, and I'm indebted to them.

Thank you to Thomas Steffler and Julie Treadwell for their time and close reading talents, to Marco Campagna for many hours of good movie-book-music conversation, to Heidi Upson Ferris for a touching letter of recommendation, and to my writing community Laura Nicol for all her correspondence.

And of course, the book and I both owe a big thank you to Ke and Molly, Molly, Molly.

The author of three short fiction collections, Scott Randall has published widely in Canadian literary magazines and has been twice included in the *Journey Prize* anthology. His most recent collection, *And to Say Hello*, was published by DC Books and won the Ottawa Book Award for best fiction. He lives in Ottawa with his wife and daughter.